ZANE PRES

GUARDING
SECRETS

Dear Reader:

If you're looking for a read that will deliver you a glimpse of life behind prison walls that's full of drama, you will find that and more in Pat Tucker's *Guarding Secrets*.

DaQuan runs a gang inside the Jester unit of the Texas Department of Criminal Justice where contraband abounds, correctional officers are corrupt, and sex is plentiful. This leader is feared by all as he uses his power to make demands from his prison soldiers. And he's a ladies man among the female COs. But things heat up once his main lover, KenyaTaye Dunbar, is threatened by newcomer Charisma Jones. With this challenge, KenyaTaye is determined to exact revenge on the two, as in her eyes, no one is allowed to break her bond. She refuses not to be replaced.

Pat's novels *Daddy by Default* and *Party Girl* focus on legal issues surrounding paternity and Texas laws, and this time, she takes readers to new heights in the twists and turns in this lockdown drama.

As always, thanks for supporting myself and the Strebor Books family. We strive to bring you the most cutting-edge, out-of-the-box material on the market. You can find me on Facebook @AuthorZane or you can email me at zane@eroticanoir.com.

Blessings,

Zane

Publisher
Strebor Books
www.simonandschuster.com

ZANE PRESENTS

GUARDING SECRETS

PAT TUCKER

STREBOR BOOKS

NEW YORK LONDON TORONTO SYDNEY

Strebor Books
P.O. Box 6505
Largo, MD 20792
www.simonandschuster.com

ISBN 978-1-59309-682-3
ISBN 978-1-50111-951-4 (ebook)
LCCN 2016948697

First Strebor Books trade paperback edition November 2016

Cover design: www.mariondesigns.com
Cover photograph: © Keith Saunders/Keith Saunders Photos

10 9 8 7 6 5 4 3 2 1

Manufactured in the United States of America

For information regarding special discounts for bulk purchases,
please contact Simon & Schuster Special Sales at 1-866-506-1949

The Simon & Schuster Speakers Bureau can bring authors to your live event.
For more information or to book an event, contact the Simon & Schuster Speakers
Bureau at 1-866-248-3049 or visit our website at www.simonspeakers.com.

ACKNOWLEDGMENTS

I remain honored to be able to once again, give gratitude for all of the blessings bestowed upon me. I thank God for his continued favor... As always, unlimited appreciation goes to my patient and wonderful mother, Deborah Tucker Bodden; my life-long cheerleader, and the very best sister a girl could have, Denise Braxton; my patient and loving husband, Coach Wilson, thanks for your love, and support. I'm a handful, but Coach is in it for the long haul and he understands: the good stuff never goes on sale! I'd like to thank my handsome younger brother, Irvin Kelvin Seguro and Amber; the two best uncles in the world, Robert and Vaughn Belzonie...

Aunts, Regina, and Shelia..., my loving and supportive family in Belize, Aunt Elaine, Therese, my cousins, Patrick, Marsha, and Cassandra, and the rest of my cousins, nephews, nieces, and my entire supportive family including my older brother, Carlton Anthony Tucker, who hustles to sell my books to anyone who will listen and buy a copy! If you know me well, you know I'm a walking poster girl for my beloved Sorority, Sigma Gamma Rho Sorority, Inc., but my love goes even deeper for my Sorors, Miranda Moore, Nikki Brock, Karen Williams, Jeness Sherell, Gloria Shannon, Keywanne Hawkins, Desiree Clement, Yolanda Jones, and the rest of those exquisite ladies of Sigma Gamma Rho Sorority Inc. and especially all of my sisters of the Glamorous Gamma Phi Sigma

Chapter here in Houston, TX. I'm blessed to be surrounded by friends who accept me just the way I am. ReShonda Tate Billingsley— Thanks for your constant support, listening ear, and unwavering faith in my work. Victoria Christopher Murray, your kindness, giving heart, and willingness to help others are the truth! Special thanks to my agent, Sara, and a world of gratitude to my Strebor family, the dynamic duo Zane, and Charmaine, for having faith in my work. Special thanks to the publicity Queens led by Yona Deshommes at Strebor who help spread the word about my work.

Again, I saved the very best for last, _____ (your name goes there!) Yes, you, the reader! I'm so honored to have your support—I know you are overwhelmed by choices, and that's what makes your selection of my work such a humbling experience. I will never take your support for granted. There were so many bookclubs that picked up Daddy by Default, Football Widows, Party Girl, Daddy's Maybe, and A Social Affair, I wanted to honor some of you with a special shout-out: The bible of AFAM Lit: Johnnie Mosely and the rest of the wonderful men who make up Memphis' Renaissance Men's book club, Sisters are Reading Too (They have been with me from day 1!!)

Special thanks to Divas Read2-Happy Hour-Cush City-Girl-friends, Inc.-Drama Queens-Mugna Suma-First Wives-Brand Nu Day-Go On Girl, TX 1-As the Page turns-APOO, Urban Reviews, OOSA, Mahogany Expressions, Black Diamonds, BragAbout Books, Spirit of Sisterhood, and so many more, I appreciate you all! If I forgot anyone, and I'm sure I have, always, charge it to my head and not my heart. As always, please drop me a line at rekcutp@hotmail.com or sylkkep@yahoo.com I'd love to hear from you, and I answer all emails. Connect with me on Facebook, and follow me on Twitter @authorpattucker-I follow back! And I love taking pics...mostly selfies, so check me out on IG as well.

CHAPTER ONE
KENYA TAYE

I always said I'd rather slice my own wrists with a butter knife than give head. Yet here I was. On my knees, I struggled to stay focused. It was hard because my knees throbbed and my jaws hurt. But that ache was nothing compared to the intense pain I felt in my heart. Still I worked.

I wanted him to feel good.

When he finally exploded, I exhaled, and fell back onto my butt. I used the back of my hand to wipe my mouth.

"Daaaymn, ma! That was good. You the best, ma." He groaned, and sounded spent.

For a long time afterward, all you could hear was us breathing loudly and heavily in the small, dark, area. That was the only sound until I mustered up the courage to say what I had practiced in my mind.

It wasn't easy for me because I loved DaQuan Cooper like I loved my right arm. But DaQuan only loved himself—and money.

"You know what, DaQuan; you a good-for-nothing liar and a low-down cheat, a straight-cold heartbreaker." My chest tightened, but I sucked in some air, drew my eyebrows together and blurted out the rest of the words I'd been dying to say. "I don't even understand why I let you do the things you do to me."

When I glanced up into his shifty eyes, he didn't seem the least bit pressed by my words. He looked like he was still lost in bliss, but his pleasure was just that, his alone. He didn't give a damn about whether or not I was satisfied.

A few tears gushed from my eyes and I felt even worse. I quickly wiped them away. I cringed inside and wanted to crumble right there on the floor. He had gotten his, was completely satisfied, but I still felt empty.

"Aww, c'mon, ma; you don't mean none of that."

He touched my chin and lifted my head. Those intense eyes locked onto mine and I felt completely trapped, stuck like I was attached with super-strength Krazy Glue. I stared into his eyes.

Was there a slight trace of something in those eyes? I wanted desperately to see some love there, but deep down, I knew there wasn't.

My brain was confused; even though I was mad, the way he looked at me still made me feel warm all over. There was something intense and electrifying about our connection. The thrill of it all made my stomach churn.

His cool and calm demeanor was just the right amount of swagger that drove me bananas. All of a sudden, my anger seemed like it was about to melt. Now, all those things I'd said, felt stupid and pointless.

He was everything! In all my twenty-eight years, I ain't never loved a man the way I loved DaQuan.

I shook the traitorous thoughts from my head.

Stay focused! I silently coached myself.

Enough was enough! It wasn't gonna work this time. His intense eyes that pulled me in, his touch that made me happy. I was sick and tired of him and his bullshit. I'd risked everything for him. Everything, and he couldn't care less.

"My family and friends all tell me I should leave you alone. This thing has gone way too far." My voice was shakier than I wanted, but those words had to be said.

He didn't say nothing. Instead, he swung his leg over my head and got up from the makeshift bed. He grabbed an old rag, wiped at his crotch, then tugged on one side of his underwear and pant leg. He balanced himself on one foot, stepped into his clothes and pulled them up.

DaQuan moved away from me, but his essence was still on the tip of my tongue.

The air in the room was thick. It was a mixture of sex, tension, and cleaning products. But it was like I was the only one who noticed or even cared.

"I 'ont know why you let them thirsty bitches get in yo head like that. They 'ont know nothing about us and how we carry it, ma."

He had turned his broad back to me, and I was annoyed.

"DaQuan—"

He adjusted his clothes and moved toward the door, like he didn't hear me call his name. I sat frozen, on the floor, unable to move. I needed a moment to get my shit together.

There was no way I could go back out there with nothing solid from him. I needed to hear him tell me he loved me. I had practiced those words for weeks. I thought about if they were too strong, or if they'd be enough to get a response, but I never considered there would be nothing.

I expected so much more from him.

Suddenly, tears poured from my eyes like a busted faucet. It was like I had lost all ability to control my emotions. And he still couldn't care less; he didn't give a damn. The bottom line was, to him, I was just another one of his workers, plain and simple. He walked out of the closet and left me alone with my tears.

Hours later, I sat inside the guards' booth and thought about ways to get things back on point with me and DaQuan. My mood was foul because he wouldn't act the way I wanted him to act. There was no doubt that he ran the place and could do whatever he wanted, but I needed him to make it clear that I was his number one. Damn the rest of 'em. In a prison, possession was everything.

My mind was so deep in thought, I nearly missed Edwards and Bishop when they bounced into the booth.

"Hey, what's wrong?" Correctional Officer Diane Edwards asked.

We all wore the standard issue uniform; black pants, white shirts, with a belt and steel-toed boots. But Edwards always flipped her collar. She starched it so that it would stand up all day.

She had a gum-bearing smile that was too big for her small face. Despite her slim and lanky frame, as a correctional officer, she had no problems with respect from the inmates.

Quiet Jane Bishop, on the other hand, was thick and considered mean unless she liked you. The three of us rounded out DaQuan's A-team, with two other officers, Richard Swanson and Billy Franklin. The females held it down during the day and the guys acted as our backup. He had another crew that worked the night shift.

"Nothing. I'm cool. Just been feeling kinda sick lately," I said.

"Oh?" Edwards' eyebrows went up.

I playfully swatted in her direction as if to knock what she implied into a lie.

"Don't start that mess, with me, D," I said.

She pursed her lips and raised both eyebrows.

"Whaaaat? I ain't sayin' nothing!" Edwards said.

Bishop stepped closer. "Hey, let's go check out the newbies. They're wrapping up their last session before they get their assignments."

I swirled my chair around. "Do we get anybody this go-round?"

"Yeah, I think so. I wanna say two," Bishop said.

"Let's go mean-mug 'em real quick," Edwards said. "It'll help you feel better."

DaQuan had left me in a sour mood, but the last thing I wanted to do was alert my girls to trouble between us, so I shook it off. Maybe checking out our new underlings would help me feel better. If nothing else, it would take my mind away from my complicated situation with DaQuan.

"Where they at? And who's teaching the class?" I asked.

"C.O. Owens got it this time. C'mon, let's roll," Edwards said.

I followed them to the part of the building with the classrooms, and we slid inside just as the group was getting up for a fifteen-minute break.

"I need some water; let's go into the break room."

Edwards and Bishop followed me into the break room where a few of the new hires hung out.

New correctional officers always brought new and interesting twists to the job. I hoped we'd get some team players this time around.

CHAPTER TWO
CHARISMA JONES

"Cha-ris-mah? Umph, where'd you get a name like that?"

The question broke my concentrated train of thought and pulled my focus away from the dreary gray walls inside the windowless room. The room smelled dank like mold had grown somewhere close by, and the constant hum from the appliances irritated me. My eyes quickly grazed over the woman who had asked. I didn't try to hide my irritation.

It was a common question, so I was used to people asking. Still, I allowed my cold gaze to travel up her thin body, stopped at her name tag that read *Bishop*, and continued up to her handsome face.

Why was she so perplexed by my God-given name in the first place? Why couldn't people ever mind their own damn business?

I wasn't trying to make new friends. My circle was small for a reason and I wasn't about to change that just because I was new to the job.

"My daddy named me after this chick he loved."

"Oh, yo mama?" she asked.

"No. His chick on the side."

Bishop's eyes grew wide, and her mouth fell open.

I gulped down the remainder of my water from the paper cup, crumbled the cup, and tossed it into the wastepaper basket. I shrugged, then turned to leave. Her expression was still frozen with her mouth agape.

By the time I'd made my way back to my seat, I was more than ready for the break to be over. This was not a social gathering and I wasn't under the false impression that it was. I was there because I desperately needed the job, and that was the best I could do for the time being.

From the corner of my eye, I saw Bishop and another correctional officer as they strolled by, whispered to each other, and another woman. They all turned and looked at me.

I rolled my eyes as I fell onto the chair and hoped the fifteen-minute break was the last for the day. I was in the final part of a mandatory training class for my new position at the Texas Department of Criminal Justice's Jester Unit, a prison of about 300 inmates, and I was already tired of what I was certain would be an uninspiring, dead-end job.

But what choice did I have? It was all I could get and I'd been lucky to get it.

A hot wave of humiliation washed over me every time I thought about the fact that I even had to accept this position.

We needed to wrap up training and get on with the job. This is not what my life was supposed to be. I had actually gone to college, for Christ's sake! When the instructor finally moved to the front of the room, I was relieved. We needed to wrap this up.

Sweat made his white uniform shirt look more like the color pink as it stuck to his skin. Every few seconds, he swiped his hand through his greasy, dirty-blond hair and sweat ran down the sides of his head. C.O. Owens looked down at a piece of paper on his desk, then began.

"This is the start of your career in law enforcement. You are not here to make friends; you are here to help keep an eye on people who could not obey the law. They are the bad guys."

Beefy fingers went through his hair again.

"There's a very thin line between being the guard and the animals being guarded. If you break the law, you will be brought up on charges, and you will turn into the animals being guarded."

Owens walked to the edge of his desk, pivoted, then walked back again. I could've sworn some sweat went airborne when he turned. But that might have been my imagination because I was bored. I adjusted myself in the chair and struggled to focus.

"Please, if you forget everything else I tell you, do not forget you are not here to make friends. This is the jungle."

The more he moved and talked, the more sweat poured from his hairline and down over his face.

"In here, it is a them against us mentality. You already know, misery ain't happy unless it's got some company, and these inmates will try each and every day to drag you down with them. They're lonely and they want company."

He paused, exhaled and looked around the room, then asked, "Does anyone have any questions?" He stopped at the desk again, looked at a notepad, then back out at the group. When no one raised a hand, he looked back at his paper and continued.

I sighed hard.

"You are not here to socialize or fraternize with inmates. If you're looking for a date, this ain't the place. You want to mingle with these guys, or hook up these guys, or go into business with these guys, get ready to go to jail. It is illegal for you to carry on a relationship, any kind of relationship, with an inmate confined to the Texas Department of Criminal Justice."

Once again, he paused like we needed time to digest what he'd said.

"You've been warned. Especially you women," he said, then snickered. He pulled at his uniform shirt. "This uniform is a target; they will be out to get you. You will hear endless sob stories. They will compliment you, flirt with you. They will say, and do, whatever they can to get you to break the rules because their lives are miserable, and they have nothing but time on their hands."

He walked again.

"If he's so handsome, and so incredibly irresistible, and you must have him because your pathetic lives just don't lead you to anyone in the free world, wait until the sorry bastard is done serving his sentence!"

He snapped his fingers. Once again, he looked around, then asked, "Do any of you have any questions?"

When no one said a word, he looked down at his paper again. "Well, since none of you have questions, you know the rules. You've been warned. There are a couple of lists near the door. Check them for your name and number; that's gonna tell you your assigned department. Some of y'all already met some of your new coworkers. Be on time, learn the ropes, follow the chain of command, do what you're supposed to do, and you'll be fine."

He looked around the room again. "Welcome to the Texas Department of Criminal Justice."

That day, I had no clue that his warning would one day haunt me during my time at TDCJ.

CHAPTER THREE
ON THE JOB—KENYA TAYE

"Oh, hell no! They don't pay me enough to deal with that kind of foolishness," C.O. Jones said as we discussed cleaning up after prisoners. Jones tossed the clipboard onto a nearby desk and stormed out of the guards' booth.

All eyes were glued to her and her antics. I had called a quick meeting before the next shift change and she acted like she had better things to do. Nobody wanted to think about having to clean up an inmate's feces, urine, or sperm, but the way she walked out during the meeting wouldn't change anything. What did she expect when she took a job in a prison? Inmates threw all kinds of crap.

"Good damn riddance," I said, and rolled my eyes as she left.

"What's wrong with her?" Edwards asked.

I shrugged. "What's right with her?"

Nearly three grueling weeks had passed since the new people had joined us on the job. And in that short amount of time, I already knew which ones would be team players and which ones we should send back marked *rejects*. Correctional Officer Charisma Jones had a serious attitude problem and I hated that she was on our shift.

Her entire disposition was cold; she was mean, standoffish, and kept to herself except on the few occasions when she talked with C.O. Tiny Scott. But C.O. Scott was a loner too, so it wasn't a complete shock that they jelled.

Jones' dramatic exit made things easier for me; after that, the meeting went smoothly. Besides, my mind was overrun with enough as it was.

The most pressing of all my issues was the fact that I hadn't been back in the closet with DaQuan in what felt like forever. Time away from him made me feel agitated and irritable.

Although we hadn't spent much intimate time together, business was still being handled. So that meant I still talked to him nightly on the phone, and reports flowed in as usual.

All of that flooded my mind as I sat inside the guards' booth when R.J., one of DaQuan's soldiers, came to fetch me. He was thin with a muscular body and he was cool. As a trustee, he wore all white.

"Yo, Dunbar, Bossman needs to holla at you," he said.

There were two other correctional officers in the booth, so it wouldn't be a problem for me to leave. Both of them were on the team, which meant I'd be covered for as long as I needed.

"I'll be there in a sec," I told R.J. I barely turned to look at him.

Nothing kept me from going right away, but I wanted to go when I felt like it. I was still uncomfortable over the fact that DaQuan never responded to the things I said to him.

I needed to set up some rules with our relationship and I wanted the talk to lead to better communication between us. But instead, he had been impossible and made things complicated.

It wasn't like I was gonna make him wait too long, but I wasn't about to snap to, just because he summoned me, either.

Several minutes later, when I felt good and sort of ready, I got up and strolled into the day-room area. The room was loud and completely abuzz with lots of activity and chatter. Inmates watched TV, and played cards, and some stood near the wall in groups of three and four.

Sometimes it was hard to tell we were in a prison. I glanced around the room and took in the action that played out in each section. When inmates were on their best behavior, it made our jobs easy. My eyes focused on the two correctional officers who stood post nearby.

That bitch Jones looked in DaQuan's and his soldiers' direction every few minutes. I had no idea what she thought, or whether she was just being nosey, but I didn't like it. I didn't like any of the attention she threw his way.

All the other female C.O.s on our shift knew he was off-limits, and as far as I knew, they respected the fact that I kicked it with him—all except Jones.

The other day, I'd noticed she waited until DaQuan finished talking to someone, then stepped to him like they were out on the streets. I wanted to flush my ears when I heard him call her by her first name.

That was a complete violation and he could've been written up for that. They were far too chummy with one another, and I didn't appreciate that shit. Because she looked funny and was ugly, I wasn't too worried about her.

I wasn't sure what she was up to. Later, as she walked toward the locker room, I stopped her and tried to give her some friendly advice.

"Hey, Jones. I'm not sure if you're aware, but inmates are supposed to refer to you by title and last name only. You don't want to get too comfortable with these guys. Otherwise, they'll think you're a mark, label you weak, and try to take advantage; just some friendly advice." I even ended with a fake smile.

I nearly fell down when the bitch sucked her teeth, looked at me, allowed her eyes to start at my feet, roll up to my face, then said, "You should let me worry about my own label and handle yours. Besides, when I want friendly advice, I go to my friends."

She pivoted and sauntered away.

Dumbfounded was the only word that could describe how I felt as I stood there and tried to process what she had just said. I couldn't remember a time I had come so close to reaching out and slapping the piss out of a coworker. Ever since that exchange, I'd kept a watchful eye on Jones.

From where I stood, it looked like she wanted to get DaQuan's attention. I was furious, but I decided not to act out on my anger. I'd let the bitch hang herself. At the rate she moved, I wouldn't even need to provide the rope.

When the guys moved away from DaQuan, I strolled over and greeted him the proper way.

"Inmate, I heard you were looking for me."

You never knew who tried to ear-hustle on a conversation. So I scanned the area around us, to be sure no one was being nosey.

DaQuan's eyes shifted as he spoke. "R.J. says ya ain't done payroll yet; what's up?" The frown on his face made me want to take him into my arms and erase whatever it was that was *really* bothering him. Maybe he missed our intimate time too.

"Oh, nothing. I was waiting for the right time to pass the envelopes out."

"Listen. We don't play with nobody's money. They got bills and need they shit just like ya need yours. If ya can't handle payroll, let me know and I can get someone else to take care of it."

He spoke to me so matter-of-factly. There was no softness in his tone, and no affection in his eyes. He was in straight business mode. I was crushed by the way he had handled me.

"Babe, do you wanna talk about it?" I asked once he finished his threat.

His face fell into a deeper frown.

"There's nothing to talk about. Don't play with people's paper. It's that simple, ma."

"DaQuan, I heard you. But now, I'm talking about us. We

haven't been in the closet in weeks now." I lowered my voice to a whisper. It was a move I hoped would signal to him that I didn't want to fight anymore.

"I'm here to discuss business. Anything else, we can talk about that shit later." He did a half shrug.

I swallowed back the tears that wanted to push forward and out.

"Is everything okay over here, Officer Dunbar?"

I whipped my head around just as C.O. Jones approached. Was she that fucking stupid? When I didn't answer, because I couldn't find my voice, she spoke again.

"Inmate, is everything okay?" she asked DaQuan.

What the hell was happening? Had I underestimated her?

CHAPTER FOUR
CHARISMA JONES

I watched him and his boys from across the room. I was nothing if I wasn't patient. When their meeting ended, I sashayed up to him and immediately got lost in his sexy, dark eyes. His thick lips looked so inviting. Everything about DaQuan turned me on. It felt good when Dunbar's radio went off and she left us alone.

"Hey, Charisma, you know you wearing the hell outta that uniform, right?"

His words made me feel all warm and good inside. Who didn't like a man who greeted you with a compliment?

"Umph, thanks. But you always say that." I grinned. When he flirted with me, it made everything right. "Besides, I'll bet you tell all the C.O.s that," I said, and blushed despite myself.

"Aw, man! I'm hurt." He feigned insult. "So ya really think I say the same thing to Swanson?" he asked. He scrunched up his handsome face.

Could his smile be any sexier?

I laughed. "No, silly! Swanson's a man, but I'll bet you probably tell Edwards, Bishop, Scott, and the other female C.O.s the same thing." I intentionally left Dunbar's name off my list. He didn't seem to mind.

He shook his head. All the while, his eyes did a slow roll up my legs, lingered at my hips, then traveled up to my breasts, where my nipples suddenly got all hard. He looked at me like I was wearing a sexy wrap dress instead of the standard issued slacks and white shirt.

I couldn't explain it, but there was nothing slimy about the way his greedy eyes threatened to devour me. As a woman, you wanted DaQuan Cooper to notice you. And when he noticed you in a sexual way, that made it even better. There was definitely something between us.

Even when he frowned, he was handsome. His features were real strong, almost chiseled.

"Who ya been talking to, Charisma?"

I loved the way he said my name. Inmates were supposed to address us by our last name, after our title, of course. But when we were alone, I didn't care what DaQuan called me. When he called me by my first name, it helped me forget where we were.

"Whatever, Bossman," I joked. I used the nickname his soldiers called him to let him know I was aware of the power he carried.

His right eyebrow twitched a little. His white shirt and white pants were always clean, pressed, and starched. He stayed groomed, freshly shaved, with his hair lined up nicely.

DaQuan was also a beast about his workout. His arms, abs, and thighs were all cut up and added to his sexiness. I already knew, if we was out on the streets, there was no way in hell a man like *him* would take a second look at *me*.

But we wasn't on the streets; we was inside the Jester State Prison Farm. And although the circumstances weren't ideal, I loved being the center of DaQuan's affection, real or imagined.

Sure, I had heard all about his reputation, but that wasn't none of my business. All I knew was, he looked good, he ran the yard, the building, and everything else.

"So what's good, baby girl?"

He sounded so sexy, and I liked the way he licked his lips when he knew I was looking.

"I got a lead on some Xanax and Percocet," I said.

Instantly, something happened. The air between us got thick. His jawbone tightened and his features hardened right before my eyes.

Silence hung between us for a long while before he spoke.

"Is that right?"

His lack of excitement confused me at first. I expected him to be hyped considering his workers had been trying to get me on the smuggling team for the past two weeks. I felt special that they wanted me. And I thought it was because DaQuan had told them I was cool and could handle it.

"Yeah. It's legit too," I said.

My feelings were crushed. I wanted to make him proud. I wanted to prove to him that I could be on the team. I had been off for two days and had dreamed of the moment I'd get the chance to deliver my news directly to DaQuan in person.

I thought he'd scoop me up in his strong arms and kiss me passionately to show his appreciation. Instead, his lackluster reaction left me dejected.

Maybe he didn't think I was good enough to join his team. I thought he liked me. I was so confused.

DaQuan's eyes held mine, but it became obvious he wasn't about to discuss any business with me.

"So what's up with ya?" he asked. He cocked his head slightly.

I was perplexed, and felt the heat of disappointment as it traveled through my entire body. All of a sudden, I was nervous about being in his presence. Everybody knew DaQuan was the boss. Maybe that was all part of the game. Maybe there was a different chain of command with his team too.

He tapped the empty spot on the bench. "Here, why don't ya cop a seat?"

He didn't ask, and I understood that. I glanced at the other inmates who moved around in the large room. If anyone paid attention to DaQuan and me, they weren't obvious about it.

I eased onto the bench and felt his eyes cover me even more. It was so good to have his attention all to myself, but I was saddened by the fact that I had failed in my attempt to get closer to him. If only I could prove that I'd be a valuable asset to the business, I knew we'd be great together.

"Yo, ya need to get with R.J. about that business. But I wanted to ask about your ol' man. Did y'all ever work that out?"

I glanced down and felt odd about the way I had told him all my business. We'd talk for hours on end, and I felt like he really cared about me and the drama my baby's daddy had put me through.

"It's okay, baby girl. Ya ain't gotta feel no kinda way about talking to me. It's all good. I just wanna make sure ol' boy know what he's got in ya."

"Yeah, he was still trippin', but I went on and took your advice," I admitted. "I'm done with him and his drama."

"See, that's what's up. That tells me, ya not only pretty, but ya smart too," he said. "That's what's up."

Whoa! Earth just slipped from its axis. People usually never called me *pretty*; actually, no one *ever* had. Words like that were usually reserved for my cousin, Lena. His compliment made me blush.

"Don't think I didn't notice yo hair too. I like that color on ya. Most women with your complexion not bold enough to rock that shade of red, but ya owning that, ma."

I grinned so hard, my cheeks started to ache. DaQuan was dangerously handsome. He dripped power, and in a place like this, that was a good look. He wore it so well, thoughts of him made my panties wet.

"Well, listen, I need to get back to my post, but I'll holla at you later on," I said.

His eyes held me and I wanted to melt right there and give him anything he wanted.

As I got up, he didn't say anything. He nodded slightly and kept his gaze glued to me. Our connection was *fyah*. It might have been lust, but I felt it and it felt good. I wanted him, and as I moved away, I decided I'd do whatever I needed to get him.

When I made it back to the guard's post and stepped inside, I felt odd. Suddenly, it got quiet and everyone looked at me like I had just disrupted a secret conversation.

That usually meant that I had been the subject of their gossip. The thought didn't really bother me, because they barely knew anything about me, and I wanted to keep it that way. It was only my eighth week on the job and I needed to get past my three-month probation period with no problems. I needed the job more than I needed the drama, so I checked my temper.

"Hey, y'all, what's up?" I spoke, even though I didn't want to.

No one said anything, but C.O. Dunbar shot me an icy look that was meant to kill. If I wasn't sure about that glance of death, the minute I looked in her direction again, she boldly rolled her eyes at me. The roll was so hard, it looked like her eyes might pop square out of her head.

I held a straight face, but on the inside, I was on fire. There was no need to let them know they had gotten to me, so I tossed them one final glance before I turned and walked back out of the booth.

There was no doubt. I had received KenyaTaye's message, and even though she didn't utter a word, I still heard it loud and crystal clear.

CHAPTER FIVE
KENYA TAYE

I was so sick of being fed up. I walked out into the searing Houston sun and found the building where I was supposed to meet another correctional officer.

We wanted to be away from curious minds and tongues that wagged. She worked a different shift, but we agreed to finally meet and talk face-to-face. I had a severe case of the jitters that I couldn't shake. My heart raced with each step I took.

Before now, we'd only heard about each other through rumors and coworker gossip. There'd been a couple of nasty phone calls too, but for the most part, it was the work chatter that kept the drama going.

It made me sick that people stayed in my business, but I told myself that was the price you had to pay when you kicked it with a Boss. And DaQuan was definitely a Boss.

I walked out to the far end of the yard and waited. The wait was the worst. I thought about the catfights, rumors, and some of the nasty words we'd exchanged.

After about fifteen minutes, I looked around again and really considered leaving. It was hot, my skin felt sticky, and I wasn't in the best mood. Besides, I should've known she'd be a no-show. Some people just lived to keep drama going. I turned to leave and had taken a few steps when I heard her.

"You Dunbar?" a voice asked.

I turned and faced a woman I would never have suspected

would be in the same situation as me. She was fair-skinned, about five feet three inches, curvy, with dark eyes and unruly, curly hair. I noticed one of those eyes looked a little slow, but otherwise, she looked okay. Envy began to flood my veins because I had hoped more would be wrong with her. Under different circumstances, we might've actually been friends.

With the brick fortress as the backdrop and only a few feet of barbed-wire fence between us, she eyed me up and down before she spoke again.

"Yeah, that's me."

"Umph. So, did he tell you we was having a boy this time?" She placed a hand on her stomach. "Did you know about our other kids?" She huffed in disgust.

Actually being in her presence and seeing her for the first time was more awkward than I'd imagined. I swallowed the dry lump in my throat. She didn't look pregnant to me, but I knew she was because people had already talked about it nonstop.

"We having one too," I said bitterly. "So what?" My tone was as stiff as an upper lip.

She had an innocent face, but the tattoo on her wrist that spelled DaQuan's name in perfect cursive reminded me of the one on the back of my neck. I knew she intentionally had come without a watch because she wanted me to see it. I wondered who else carried his mark. For a quick second, I thought about how many times she had probably had these types of meetings.

"He takes care of me and my other kids," I said. I wasn't sure why I felt the need to tell her that, but something made me want her to know I meant more to him than she probably thought.

"So you're gonna keep it then?"

Rage tore through every cell in my body, but I looked at her with a straight face and told myself to ignore the question. For me, nothing had changed. I knew whom I was dealing with when I got involved with DaQuan, so very few things about him surprised me.

"You keeping yours?" I shot back, with an eyebrow raised.

Her face clouded over, and she said, "Of course!"

"Then I guess there's nothing left to talk about."

The whole time she stood there, I boldly scanned her up and down, but told myself I needed to retract my claws; doing anything to her still wouldn't change a damn thing.

She was free to have child number three for DaQuan if that was what she wanted to do. I couldn't do nothing to stop DaQuan from screwing C.O.s no more than he could stop me from being me; it was who he was. It pissed me off and made my heart crumble, but what could I do?

"Well, you and your friends should cut down on all the dirty little whispers. I had him first." She could barely mask her disdain, but I didn't care.

Deep down, I knew she was right. She did have him first. She had two other kids and one growing in her belly to prove it, but obviously she hadn't done something right, because despite all of that, he still came to me.

The life that grew inside my own stomach was evidence enough that I didn't need to tell her that. It was obvious that after years with her, he wanted something different. Me and him had been kicking it for almost two years.

"We're all grown. I don't tell grown people what to do," I said.

She seemed taken aback, but still nodded slightly.

"Well, I need to get back in; my shift starts in fifteen," I said.

It didn't matter if she had something else to say, I was done with her and the conversation, so I turned and made my long trek back into the building.

The minute I stepped back into the crisp, cold, air-conditioned building, Bishop and Edwards were waiting for me. I prayed the tears in my eyes wouldn't fall.

It was all I could do to face C.O. Clarkson without having a complete meltdown. And now that I'd made it through the face-to-face with DaQuan's baby mama, I didn't want my girls to think the meeting had reduced me to a puddle of tears.

"What did she say?" Edwards asked, as they approached.

"Yeah. You tell her you pregnant too?" Bishop asked in a whisper.

It wasn't common knowledge that I was with child, so I appreciated that she tried to keep her voice down on that part. I confirmed it after my period was a week-and-a-half late, but that was only two weeks earlier.

"I'll bet that made her want to upchuck," Bishop added. "What'd she say?"

I didn't want to talk about it, but I knew I couldn't avoid the conversation. We were like the Three Musketeers and they'd been on the journey with me since day one. They worked for DaQuan too, but I still didn't want to talk about it.

It was stupid that me and Clarkson were pregnant at the same time by the same damn inmate.

"KenyaTaye, don't start acting all brand-new now," Edwards said. I knew she definitely sensed my hesitation and for sure, she wouldn't give me a pass.

"She's right. What that bitch say; why you trying to hold out now?" Bishop chimed in. Bishop didn't usually say much, and I wished this was one of her quiet times.

"It's not like that. But this whole situation is so foul. He ain't shit!" I said, disgusted over the position he'd put me in.

Edwards stopped walking. She looked at me and said, "Do he take care of you and those kids that's not even his? What you pushing out in that parking lot? And what you carrying around on your shoulders?"

I sighed.

"Look, I know DaQuan got dog-like characteristics, but real talk, he's holding it down better than a lot of these other dudes who are out on the streets." Edwards shook her head. "I don't know what 'ol girl told you out there, but if I was you, I wouldn't let my man go without a fight."

"She's right," Bishop said.

I knew they were both right. As we walked to our side of the building, I replayed the meeting between C.O. Clarkson and me. I left out the parts where I compared myself to her, wondered what he saw in her, and wondered whether he treated her the same way he treated me when we were alone.

"She's having his third baby! Wow!" Edwards said.

"And she's not the least bit fazed by me. She stood there just as calmly as ever and didn't even bat her lazy eye when I told her I was pregnant too."

"Damn! DaQuan ain't no joke!"

We turned our heads at the same time, and much to my horror, two male correctional officers fist-bumped each other.

"What that make? Three? Four?" the male officers joked to each other.

Alarm settled into my nervous system. Nobody was supposed to know about me being pregnant. But what could I do? Sooner or later, everyone would know anyway. It was already widely known among the male C.O.s that I was DaQuan's girl. His name inked across the back of my neck had a little to do with that, but it was known more because of the way he marked his territory.

We waited for our coworkers to pass before we spoke again.

Edwards looked at me with empathy in her eyes. "If you know like I know, you'd better tell DaQuan about this baby before they do!"

She was right. I should've told him the last time we were together, but I had other things on my mind. Ever since I'd found out I was pregnant, my emotions had been all over the place.

The last time, when we were in our private place, all I could think about was letting him know how much he'd hurt me. He had two kids on the way, by two different women, and he was locked up!

My life was a hot funky mess!

But I laughed when Bishop said, "Whoa, hold up, his baby mama; the trick got a lazy eye?"

CHAPTER SIX
CHARISMA

"Yo, you ain't gotta slip it in your coochie or nothing like that, but what I'm saying is, you gotta get creative. The more you think about it, the better the ideas you'll come up with."

I looked at R.J. like he was crazy. The thought of sliding a cell phone up in my twat to sneak it into a prison was too much for me. I wanted in on some of the cash flow, but I didn't want to do anything too stupid. And that sounded real stupid.

"How do the other females do it now?" I asked. "I mean, besides up in their coochies?"

"They sneak baggies in their weaves, in their shoes, their underwear; man, you just gotta get creative. Or," he looked at my lips, "maybe you not cut out to be a mule; you could do other thangs." He sucked his teeth and grinned.

The way he stared at my lips made me feel dirty. R.J. was a trustee, which meant he had a job in the mail room and had more freedom than the average inmate.

Basically, he and a few others had the freedom to roam the facility as they pleased. We were near one of the back doors.

"So how am I supposed to make extra money if I don't join the team?"

"There are other ways." The gleam in his eyes told me I probably didn't want to know what those other ways were.

"Like what?" I asked anyway.

"Inmates pay a hundred-fifty dollars for blowjobs. Have your name added to the wall, and you could start making paper real fast. Yo, I'm jus' sayin', you got nice lips," he said and laughed.

"Inmates pay one-hundred and fifty dollars? Where they get that kind of money?" I was stunned.

The fact that female C.O.s were tricking didn't surprise me as much as the fact that the inmates actually were able to pay. How could they afford that kind of money?

R.J. looked all around. "Baby, there's paper flowing all over this place. You'd be surprised." He winked.

"I think I'll stick to the other kind of contraband," I said.

His shifty eyes held some disappointment. But I didn't need a man; I needed extra money.

"Your choice; it's up to you." He shrugged.

"So it seems like pills would be the easiest. I think I'll stick with that. What's the best thing to get?"

"Well, you said you had a lead on something already. Whachu' got?"

"Percocet and Xanex."

My cousin Lance worked at one of those old people's homes and he couldn't wait to offload some pills. I knew he'd be a good connect.

"Ooh. That's the good shit. Yeah; those will go for at least thirty bucks a pill."

My eyes grew wide and I nearly lost my train of thought.

"Whhaaat?" I lowered my voice.

R.J. laughed. "Damn, what's up, baby? You don't know nothing, huh?"

As I talked to R.J., my mind did some fast math. I couldn't believe a pill that might cost ten dollars on the streets went for three times that amount behind bars. My mind was completely made up; I'd leave the cell phones and the weed for the other chicks who didn't mind stuff up in their vaginas.

My side hustle would be smuggling pills.

"Yo, you straight?" R.J. asked.

"Oh, yeah. Thanks. I'm good."

"Okay, well, practice that, yo. Then step to me when you think you got something."

Thoughts ran through my mind as R.J. walked away. I knew for sure that if I was able to pull off a successful job, that would get DaQuan's attention.

There was nothing I wanted more than to get his attention. For the rest of my shift, all I thought about were ways that I could sneak pills into the prison.

When other female correctional officers entered my space, I studied them from head to toe.

Edwards was tall and kind of lanky, but shaped oddly. She also wore her uniform really tight. I seriously doubted she'd be able to smuggle anything in those pants, but I couldn't be sure.

"What the hell you looking at?"

I didn't realize I had stared at her so hard until she spun around and barked at me.

"Jones, you got issues with me?" Edwards asked as her head swiveled like a bobble-head doll.

Before she could say anything else, I got up and walked out. I wasn't about to start any shit. On my way out, I thought about how Kenya-Taye must've smuggled all kinds of stuff all up in her nasty pussy!

As I imagined her hitching up a leg and jamming things into her twat, all I could do was laugh to myself.

Then, I hoped something would get stuck up in there and she'd have to explain to the ER doctor why a cell phone, a bag of weed, and some Xanex pills were stuck up in her coochie.

Thoughts of her in that situation dominated my mind as I rounded a corner and ran smack into DaQuan.

"Oh—"

"Aey, watch where ya going, ma," he said jokingly.

"Uh, Bossman, I'm sorry, my head was—"

"Yo, ma, no worries. But ya bet not let me catch you slipping around the way," he said, and winked.

His touch sparked something in me. I liked everything about DaQuan. We were already friends and talked quite a bit, but being so close to him made my heart flutter.

"Everything okay over there, C.O.?!" someone yelled.

"Yes. It's good." I waved my coworker off.

DaQuan turned his head and tossed a dirty look in the officer's direction.

"Don't worry about that. He's just doing his job," I said. "Besides, what are you doing walking around here alone, like you own the place?"

DaQuan stuck his chest out. "Yo, you betta ask somebody; I run shit around here." His eyes were filled with heat. "When problems break out, they call me before they call the warden. Ma, ask somebody!"

I shivered with excitement, because I knew he told the truth.

Our eyes locked, and my heart thudded. I wanted him.

Then all of a sudden, he strutted around me, boldly slapped my ass, and moved down the hall. His swagger was irresistible. The look he tossed over his shoulder made me want to give it to him right there.

CHAPTER SEVEN
KENYA TAYE

My mind was overrun with getting back into the closet with DaQuan. How could he stay away from me for so long and not even miss me? It drove me crazy at work and at home.

I tortured myself because I constantly replayed our last time together in my mind. If only I hadn't gone off on him all at once like that.

A constant battle brewed in my mind. While I was happy I had gotten it all off my chest at first, the more I thought about it, the more I wished I had just kept my mouth shut.

As I contemplated my next move, a C.O. whose name I couldn't remember bum-rushed the booth.

"Hey, Dunbar, I got something for R.J. and I can't find him," she said. Her voice was shaky and she was very fidgety. Blankets of sweat covered her face and she trembled as she stood with her hands in her pocket.

"What's your name again?"

"Erin, er, I mean, C.O. Sheppard."

I knew exactly who she was, but she looked a hot mess. I wanted to tell her she needed to go somewhere and get cleaned up.

"You got a direct line to DaQuan, right?" she asked. This time her voice was lower than before.

"I need to see somebody. I got this cell phone, actually two of 'em, so you want 'em or what?"

My eyes lit up. I couldn't believe she put the business out in the streets like that. She knew how we operated, but yet she acted like her life depended on finding R.J. or DaQuan.

"Are you okay?"

"I just need to offload this contraband. Now if you don't want it, I don't know what to do with it, but I don't feel comfortable walking around with it on me."

She looked around the area.

It was hard to tell if that's what her nervousness was really about. It seemed like she was hooked on that shit, but I had problems of my own. I needed her gone so I could focus on what was important to me.

"Go to the mail room. R.J. is usually hanging around over there."

She scurried off without saying anything else.

I needed to talk to DaQuan about how he brought people into the business. If he didn't watch it, he'd fuck it up for us all.

Maybe that was the line I needed to use to get to him. He cared about his business and his paper. Maybe my approach had been all wrong.

Hours later, I was still vexed as I sat at the guard's station and looked through paperwork. My eyes took in the words and letters on the paper, but my mind was elsewhere and everybody knew it. So they gave me space; there weren't too many questions or requests, which was cool with me.

Images of my last time with DaQuan flashed through my mind—his selfishness, and how cold he behaved when I poured my feelings out to him.

In the weeks since our last hook-up, I thought about all the things I should've said and done.

He needed to act like I meant something more to him than just another mule. I was tired of the lopsided relationship with him. But obviously, that had been the wrong approach.

I realized if I had talked to him about how I thought he might be putting the business at risk, versus talking about my feelings, maybe he would've been more apt to listen.

A few of my coworkers stood off in the other corner of the booth and talked. Thank God they didn't try to interrupt me or my thoughts. All was quiet for a change; no drama on the cell-block meant I had nothing but time.

There was time to think, and pick apart everything that had gone wrong with DaQuan and me and how I could fix it.

I worked so hard at me and him because I didn't want to end up all alone like my mother, Mary. I had already crapped out twice, so the third time, with DaQuan, had to be my charm. It just had to be, no matter what it cost.

I wondered if C.O. Sheppard had found R.J., then decided that was her problem, not mine. I was about to return to the paperwork when something pulled me in.

Out of the corner of my eye, I saw the monitors flash images of different parts of the facility like a slideshow, and nothing was out of the norm, at first.

But suddenly, one image in particular caught my attention. At the sight of it, I felt my body stiffen, my mouth dry. I blinked, and forced myself to focus on all of the monitors.

It took a few minutes for the image to come back around in the rotation, but when it did, it was vividly clear.

"This bitch don' lost her ever-loving mind!"

"Who?" C.O. Edwards asked. She and two other C.O.s rushed to my side. "Whassup?" Edwards asked as we all focused on the screen.

When the image popped back onto the screen, a collective gasp floated up from us all.

"Is that who we think that is?" C. O. Bishop said more than asked.

"Yeah, that's her ass!" Edwards confirmed.

There it was, right on the screen, right in front of the camera for all eyes to see.

CHAPTER EIGHT
CHARISMA

Three weeks after I had done what DaQuan had told me and connected with R.J., I felt I was ready. My time with DaQuan had been limited. We still talked a little at work, but mostly we talked when he called late at night.

He and I never discussed my training with R.J. But it had been going really good.

After I studied my reflection, I fussed with my hair in the mirror. My weave was loose enough for me to slide my fingers up underneath the stocking cap. I adjusted the packets underneath and studied my image in the mirror. Everything looked normal. But I was scared.

My heart thumped so loud in my ears, it felt like I couldn't think straight.

I needed to look for anything that stuck out as odd. I had taken before-and-after pictures with my cell phone and studied those too. I made several adjustments until the after pictures looked as close to the before pictures as possible.

I studied my reflection even more. You couldn't tell. I mean, you could a little bit, but you'd have to stand there and stare at me really hard for a long time. I snapped two more pictures once I adjusted the packets and secured them again.

My cousin Lena could be a real bitch, but when I needed her, she would come through, especially if she thought there might be something in it for her. Our relationship had always been one mixed with love and hate. She usually loved to hate anything that was right with me, and loved to make sure she told me. As I dialed her number, I prayed she'd be in a good mood.

"I was just gonna call you. Why you send me these pictures of your head?"

"Hey, Lena," I greeted her cheerfully.

"Hey!" Her response was flat. "Now what are you up to?"

"I just wanna know how it looks," I lied.

"It looks like you need to get in the shop and get your shit tightened up; that's what it looks like."

"Okay, but can I rock this for another week, til I get paid?"

She chuckled. "Personally, I wouldn't, but you could probably get away with that."

Lena thought she was better than somebody just because people always told her she was pretty. It exhausted me that I had to play the Robin to her Batman all our lives. They'd look at her lovingly, and shower her with compliments about her beauty; then, they'd look at me and say I looked smart. Like really? Who does that to two kids?

We had grown up together by default. We'd lived with her mom, my aunt, and our grandmother. My mother was unstable for a long time. When she'd finally found religion, she wanted a do-over. But of course, no one gets to do it over. It worked out for me that by the time she was ready to be a mother, I was going through a hard time with my own kids.

"So, it doesn't look funny or anything?" I asked Lena over the phone.

"Nah, it just looks like you need to get your hair done."

As we talked, I looked at my reflection in the mirror again. If it was grossly poufy or looked too bad, she'd be quick to tell me, for sure.

"You sure I could get away with this for another week or so?"

"Since when you care so much about the way you look?" I could hear the irritation in her voice, and knew it was only seconds before she'd start going off.

"Okay, I'll take that as a yes."

"Hold up a sec. Wait, I know you didn't meet a new man, did you?" That was the first time she sounded excited since we'd been on the phone.

Thoughts of DaQuan popped into my mind. "Bye, Lena!"

"Now hold on a second. Who is he? Where you meet him at?"

"Thanks for weighing in on my hair," I said.

Confident that all was good, I wrapped up the call with Lena and finished putting on my uniform. Once dressed, and ready to go, I went back to the mirror for one final glance.

I twisted and turned, as I tried to look at my hair from every angle. I scrutinized every aspect of my appearance. Once I was convinced that I looked okay, and my hair could pass the test, I left for work.

During the two dry runs, I had already done, I was more nervous about whether I looked suspicious.

"You straight!" R.J. would tell me.

"Are you sure?"

"Yeah, shorty, you straight. Trust me; we do this on the regular. I wouldn't let ya go out like that if your shit wasn't tight!"

I understood him, but I was still nervous.

"Besides, just focus on who's doing the pat downs. If it ain't nobody friendly, you might have to wait until they change shifts or something."

I practiced being and acting normal. Although correctional officers had to be screened, our screening process wasn't extensive, so I felt confident that I'd be able to make it through security with no problems. Usually we were patted down by a coworker, and most of them were in on what was going on. Both of my dry runs went well, but I wasn't dirty during those, either.

My moment of truth came faster than I wanted, but I had practiced and worked with my hair so I needed to go through with it and get it over with.

I calmed my breathing as much as I could and tried to make sure my hands didn't shake. The breathing exercises I had practiced came in handy. As I walked in and saw the sheer chaos that was going on, it didn't bother me one bit.

People were all over the place. The entrance was busier than usual and I wasn't sure whether I should abort. I wasn't nervous, but the line was simply too long. Just when I was about to turn back and go to the car, one of the security officers called out to me.

"Jones, you ain't gotta wait. Don't you have to punch that clock?" he asked.

He waved me up to the front of the thick line and allowed me to walk through ahead of the person who was next. I swallowed dry and hard.

"Your bag goes here," the other guard said. "Now, just walk through. Keep your shoes on."

I followed his instructions and slid through the metal detector with no problems. No one even tried to pat me down. I was so relieved I wanted to jump for joy on the other side. My heart raced a million miles a minute. Just when I thought I had pulled off my very first job, something happened and I almost peed myself. Someone called my name again.

"Yo, Jones!"

The smile melted from my face and I stopped cold.

Damn!

CHAPTER NINE
KENYA TAYE

I kept an eye on the clock and waited anxiously for my nightly phone call. He was only ten minutes late, but my mind raced with all kind of thoughts about why he'd be late.

Was he talking to that bitch Clarkson?

Was that bitch Jones trying to throw it at him?

Was he with someone else?

Being involved with a man behind bars wasn't supposed to be stressful. *He* was supposed to be close to the perfect man. There was never a reason to question his whereabouts, because where else would he be? He'd call daily, because he needed the connection to the outside world, and theoretically, it wasn't like he'd be able to cheat on me, or so I thought.

DaQuan had debunked every single one of those myths about being with a man who was behind bars. He had brought so much stress into my life, at times, I wondered whether he was worth it.

Still no phone call.

Now if I'd been late to take his call, he would've been ready to bust out of prison to hunt me down. I waited patiently because I was sure he'd act like it was no big deal anyway.

As I waited, I thought back to the disaster that unfolded when I told him about the baby—our baby.

We had just walked into our spot when he immediately turned and started to take down his pants.

I motioned to stop him. "Hold on a second, baby. I need to tell you something."

"Really?" His eyebrows inched up slightly.

"Yeah. I need to. I mean, I don't want you to hear it from anybody else."

"What? Ya getting transferred or something?" His face held a frown, and he watched me numbly.

"Nah, it's nothing like that."

DaQuan tugged at his pants again. He really pissed me off because he acted like that couldn't wait until I'd said what I needed to say.

"Look, if ya not shipping out, anything else can wait. I need some head," he finally said.

"DaQuan, this is important. We need to talk about this."

"Okay, then spit it out! Shit! Ya know we don't have a lot of time. We could talk on the damn phone. I don't come in here to talk," he felt compelled to point out.

"I know. I know," I said. My nerves were bad and his reaction hadn't helped.

"Well, c'mon with it then."

The mood had changed. I should have waited until we were finished because now he seemed agitated with me. That was no good way to deliver the kind of news I had.

When he snapped his fingers a few times to hurry me along, I couldn't get mad. I knew I had tried to stall.

"DaQuan, I don't know how to tell you this, but I'm pregnant," I blurted out, before I lost my nerve again.

Blank stare.

The room fell into an awkward silence. I had forgotten how to breathe. It felt like forever before he said something, and when he finally opened his mouth, I wished he hadn't.

"Say what?"

He frowned.

"I am pregnant," I repeated.

Both his eyebrows danced up on his forehead and his expression seemed stuck between bewilderment and confusion.

"Wait a minute-" He held his hands up in surrender, and took a few steps back.

Before he finished the thought or the sentence, I cut him off.

"It's yours. I'm sure of it," I sputtered in confusion.

"Wait, that's not what I was gonna say. Hell, it better be mine."

In that split-second, I was so happy I didn't know what to do. But my joy didn't last long because he cocked his head to the side and asked, "But on the real, ya being pregnant, is that a DaQuan problem or a KenyaTaye problem?"

When the phone rang, it pulled me back to the present. His call was nearly thirty minutes late, but I didn't dare complain.

"Heey, Daddy!"

I silently begged God to soften my tongue because I wanted to let his ass have it. But I knew we needed to finish the conversation about the baby and what I didn't need was his attitude or his slick tongue.

"Aey," he grunted.

It was obvious that time had done nothing to change his mind about the baby news I had delivered earlier.

"Listen, DaQuan, I understand you probably stressed out 'cuz you locked up, okay, but I am too."

At times I felt like he forgot I was essentially doing time right along with him. I didn't date. I worked, came home, waited for his call, and coordinated shipments. He needed to understand it wasn't just about his damn life. My shit was all twisted too.

"You locked up and I'm fucking pregnant again. Like really,

who the fuck does that? Only my dumb ass do shit like that, for real. I can accept that I fucked up. I know I did, but I did that shit cuz I wanted to. I don't regret it."

He just held the phone.

"DaQuan, I don't know what you want me to say. I know you probably scared and shit," I said.

That was when he found his voice again.

"Scared?" He chuckled. "Baby, I'm a man! What the hell I'ma be scared of? Scared?" He huffed.

That single word triggered more of a response from him than earlier when he asked whether my pregnancy was his problem or mine. What I needed him to say was that he had me and we'd be good no matter what.

There I was on my third kid, and although I knew DaQuan would handle his, I was still more than a little mad at myself. Not even two weeks ago, I was fed up and frustrated with him over his lack of affection for me. Now the only thing that had changed was the fact that I was knocked up.

He still behaved like I was just another one of his workers.

"DaQuan, say something. I need you to talk to me, tell me what you're thinking."

"I ain't thinking shit. I'ma let ya handle this. Ain't nothing changed. Ya know I got ya, so what's what?"

"But that's my issue, DaQuan. The fact that nothing's changed is an issue for me. A few weeks ago, I tried to tell you how I was feeling and you didn't even blink an eye."

"KenyaTaye, what ya expect me to say? Ya sit up and call me a liar and a cheat and a bunch of other shit. What ya expect me to say?"

"I expect you to try and do better. We're in this together," I said.

"Aey, do me a solid."

His entire tone softened and I felt a little hopeful. I released a breath that had been trapped deep down in my chest during the whole time we'd been on the phone.

"Anything," I said with conviction.

"Cool, go outside real quick."

I got up and walked out of my front door.

"Okay, what's up? Somebody coming by?" I expected someone to pass through with a shipment or something.

"Nah, nothing like that. I need ya to look in the driveway and tell me what you see."

I was so fucking mad at DaQuan.

"Wait! I don't hear you. KenyaTaye, is that pearl-colored 2012 BMW 3 series Coupe still parked out there?"

I stormed back into the house, highly pissed. I slammed the door so hard it rattled a few pictures on the wall. My mother rushed out of her room. I waved her away, and pointed to the phone. She knew I was on my daily call. So she shrugged, looked around and went back to her room.

"Oh, can't talk right now, huh? Well, that's cool. But dig this. When I met ya ass, ya and yo kids was riding the bus. Hell, ya was living in the damn projects with yo mama! Them two broke-ass baby daddies ya got ain't done shit for ya or they kids!"

I was so glad we were on the phone and not in each other's presence. He continued.

"Don't come talking no shit to me about trying and doing better! From where I'm sitting, yo ass is doing better because I'm making it happen. So the next time ya got some shit ya wanna unload on me, make sure it's related to my damn money, or my business. Otherwise, ya keep that shit to yo damn self!"

I was stunned silent, which was probably okay because soon thereafter, the call ended.

He had hung up on me.

CHAPTER TEN
CHARISMA

I thought back to that moment at work when I just knew I had been busted. The adrenaline that flooded my veins made me nervous. Frozen in place, I pulled in a rugged breath and slowly turned my head after they'd called my name.

"Yo, Jones!"

When I looked over my shoulder, C.O. Franklin said, "You forgot your bag!" He dangled it in the air for me to see. He frowned and gave me a look that said he thought I was absentminded.

"Oh, shoot! Thank you," I said.

I quickly grabbed it and ran off to remove the plastic bags of pills from my weave.

Yes! I had done it.

I'd smuggled in my first load of contraband, and I couldn't wait to see DaQuan's reaction once R.J. told him I had done it. I slipped into the bathroom and waited for two people to leave.

The moment the door closed, I checked the bottom to make sure the stalls were empty. Once I finished, I looked at my reflection in the mirror and started to remove the plastic bags from my weave.

It didn't take long to remove my bags. Once I finished, I went to make the drop. If I had it my way, I'd deal directly with R.J., but there were times when I had to go to Dunbar instead.

Unfortunately for me, R.J. was nowhere to be found. I didn't want to take the chance and hold on to the pills for longer than necessary, so I went and found Dunbar.

Her face twisted at the sight of me. If I didn't need money the way I did, I wouldn't be bothered with her.

"Dunbar," I said as I stepped to her.

She looked at me, but didn't respond.

"I have some stuff."

When she acted like she didn't want it, I was tempted to go find R.J.

"We need to go to the bathroom?" she asked.

I glanced around in both directions.

When I slid the plastic bags to her, Dunbar took them and eased them somewhere under the desk.

There was no way I wanted to hang around for fake small talk with her, so I turned and left.

She didn't say anything to me and I didn't utter another word.

As I walked away, I thought about all I'd been told about Dunbar. For a sergeant, she seemed pretty dumb to me, and her stupidity told me that anybody could advance at that job.

My shift had finally ended and I couldn't wait to leave the prison. The smell of the place followed me home and seemed to seep into my skin.

My cell rang when I got into the car. I prayed it was a call back about the job I'd done for DaQuan and the pay I desperately needed, but it wasn't. It was my pathetic baby daddy, sorry-ass Corey McCray.

"What do you want?" I asked.

"Yo! I'ma have to get that money to you next week," Corey said. I rolled my eyes as I listened to his lies. I could never ever count on his trifling behind, and I knew that.

"The cable is off. I ain't got no food. And I'm short on the rent. When I let you hold that money, you said you'd have it back early, Corey."

"Look, I know what I said, but something came up. I'ma make it up to you."

Corey must've thought I was a fool. If I waited on him, I'd be hungry and homeless.

"Whatever, Corey." I rolled my eyes, even though he couldn't see me.

"For real," he insisted.

The rest of his promises fell on deaf ears. I didn't have time to wait around for him and his lame promises. I needed more money than what I made at that pathetic job. My neighbor's cousin, Tiny, had told me the prison was hiring at the Carl Vance Unit. She said if they hired her, she knew for sure they'd hire me, so I applied and they called me in for an interview.

I had only been working there for a month-and-a-half, but I was so far behind on all my bills, everything had piled high.

"So, I'ma come through later so I can talk to you and explain everything," he said.

"Don't bother, Corey. I don't wanna see you unless you got my money."

I meant it too. He didn't know what I had to do to make ends meet and I was sick of depending on somebody who only cared about himself.

Corey was the reason I'd sent our kids to stay with my mom in Georgia. I could barely take care of me, much less the kids too. And even though they wasn't with me in Houston, I still had to send money to help take care of them. Corey knew that too.

Corey would learn soon enough, I didn't have time to sit and wait on him or anybody else. I needed to make things happen on my own and that was exactly what I was about to do. As soon as that call came through from DaQuan, I felt different. I knew with him my life would surely change. I just had no way of knowing exactly how drastic of a change it would be.

CHAPTER ELEVEN
KENYA TAYE

When I walked into the guards' booth, Jones sat there like her shit didn't stink. I wanted to slap the taste buds from her mouth. Instantly, a nickname for her popped into my mind: B.U.R.T. It completely described her. Jones was *Built Up Real Terrible*.

Jones and C.O. Scott talked to each other and all but ignored me. I couldn't stand neither of those bitches. But Jones had another thing coming if she thought I was about to let her slide into my place.

I was already dealing with one female behind DaQuan and I'd be damned if I'd get in line behind another.

Since I didn't know C.O. Scott was a team-member, I didn't wanna put the business out there in front of her. I was frustrated because they took too damn long with their pointless small talk.

"So, was there an incident report on that?" Scott asked.

"Yes. There was. I didn't witness what happened, but when she came in, she asked Franklin to sign off on it."

I didn't want to pull rank, but they had about five more minutes to wrap up the nonsense that they were discussing.

Neither of them budged when I walked in, which was fine with me. That didn't bother me one bit. Their mind-numbing conversation was what did.

"Okay, the report is signed and filed. Look, I need to holla at Jones for a few," I said.

They both turned around in their chairs, and looked surprised to see me. Scott frowned, but an expression barely registered on Jones's face. She only turned down her lower lip, or maybe that was what she always looked like.

She made me so sick.

She'd better be glad I'd found out she worked for my man, because when I saw that she had gotten next to him on that monitor, I didn't know what was going down. Like I said before, I was not about to jump behind another chick for DaQuan.

"Oh, we're almost done," Jones had the audacity to say.

"I ain't trying to pull rank, but—"

Scott got up from her seat. "No worries, Charisma, I need to go make some rounds anyway." She tossed me a nasty look as she slid by me and out of the booth.

As she walked outside, she stared me down, but I didn't care. I had seniority over both of them, as sergeant, and I could make this pissy-ass job even worse for both of them.

"So you on the team now?" I asked Jones.

"What team?"

Her attitude sucked ass. Give a hood-rat a Gucci bag and she acted like she was suddenly too good.

"Don't play."

She frowned. There was really no point; it was clear to me that she and I would never get along. I really wished DaQuan respected me more and talked to me before he recruited. Why did we need her ass in the first place? Our team already held it down.

There was so much about Jones's ass that I didn't like. I wasn't completely convinced that she wasn't trying to push up on DaQuan, and now I had to work with her ass.

"I don't know what the hell you're talking about," she hissed.

Did it look to her like I had time to sit and hold her hands? I rolled my eyes, looked around and pulled a small envelope from my bra. I put it on the table and slid it across to her.

When the bitch looked down at it, then back up at me, I wanted to spit in her face. She'd better be glad it was only Edwards and Bishop who walked in while she sat there and tried to act all bourgeois.

Edwards looked down at the envelope, then at me. I didn't even get a chance to tell them that DaQuan had recruited her.

"Hell, I'll take it if she don't want it," C.O. Edwards said.

Slowly, the tramp Jones reached for the envelope and stuffed it into her breast pocket.

"You should go put that in your locker," Bishop said.

The chick had a serious problem and I needed to discuss her with DaQuan. Her attitude was shit and I didn't see how we was expected to work with her ass.

I had no idea if she was going to take the advice she was given, but if her simple ass got us busted, she'd be in a world of trouble.

Jones got up and walked out of the booth. She didn't say a word to Edwards, Bishop, or me.

"You're welcome," Bishop said to her back as she left.

"When did she join the team?" Edwards asked.

I shook my head. "Girl, men are so fucking simple!"

"So that's what they've been cozying up and chit-chatting with each other about?"

I nodded. "Guess so. Don't ask me, 'cause he don't tell me shit!"

"So he just up and added her to the team without even talking to you?" Bishop asked.

DaQuan had no idea what his actions and careless moves did to me and my image as the team leader. It was so hard to reason with his simple behind. But this move with Jones was the worst. He'd made me look bad in front of the people who worked for us. It also made it look like I didn't know what was going on.

"So, you know what she bring in?" Edwards asked.

"I think pills, because she got like two hundred-fifty dollars."

"You should've skimmed some off the top. I mean, if you gotta deal with that shitty attitude, you oughta get a percentage off the top," Edwards said. She popped her collar.

We all laughed at that.

I couldn't admit to them that DaQuan and I were on shaky ground. He still hadn't said anything to me in person, and since the other day when he'd hung up, all calls were business-related only.

When I thought about all that I risked for him, it really made me feel like a fool. Not only did I help with the smuggling operation, but I carried his fucking child, and he had the nerve to treat me like trash.

DaQuan was already behind bars, but if I got caught, that was my future down the drain too. What about my kids? What about our kid?

"Hey, Dunbar, what's up? Lately you've been zoning out, like you're deep in thought, you're lost. What gives?" Edwards asked.

I felt like I was seconds away from breaking down and dissolving into a puddle of tears. Everything took a serious toll on me. I knew it was the baby that made my emotions ape-shit crazy, but just because I knew it, that didn't change how I felt.

"It's all good; just a lot on my mind."

Edwards gave me a long side-eye, but she didn't press the issue. "Well, if you need to talk, just let me know."

"Thanks, girl."

She looked at Bishop and said, "Can you come watch the door? I wanna go to the closet and fuck R.J."

They got up and left and I thought about the last time I'd had sex with DaQuan. Before I told him I was pregnant, he'd been on a serious blow job kick. I wasn't sure what was up with him, but we hadn't actually done it, like intercourse, in nearly a month. All of our trips to the closet had involved me on my knees.

My heart suddenly dropped to the bottom of my feet. Horror crept up on me at the thought. Was he still fucking Clarkson? He had to be. Nothing else made sense. If he wasn't fucking me, he had to be fucking her, still.

I got up to go look for him. We kept it low-keyed while I was on the job, but I needed to get to the bottom of our relationship.

CHAPTER TWELVE
CHARISMA

The $250 I got for the pills came just in time. I needed that money, and more, so I knew I'd do it again and again.

Now that the weave had worked, I decided to focus on the shoes as another way to carry pills. I noticed most of the female C.O.s on the team wore either work boots or those old granny shoes with the hard toes. I bought a good pair of boots, then took my time and peeled them apart.

I was able to get two bags of pills in each boot. The key to that was, I had to be careful not to crush the pills. So I used sole inserts, and put a piece of plywood between the soles and the bags.

R.J. would literally inspect each pill to make sure they weren't cracked or crushed. They didn't play when it came to the money.

Dressed, satisfied with my image, and filled with courage, I left the house and headed to the Jester unit. On my way to the prison, I thought about how I looked forward to getting an envelope more than payday.

I parked, took a deep breath and pumped myself up to smuggle in another shipment of prescription pills. It was more of a challenge for me, because unlike the other female C.O.s, I wasn't trying to put anything anywhere in my body. If I couldn't fit the pills in my weave or in my shoes, I'd have to stop my side hustle.

As I walked up to the entrance, I paid extra attention to what was going on. It seemed like a typical day. Security officers chatted with one another, as they processed people through the metal detectors.

"Ma'am, we need you to go through again," a security officer said to a woman three people in front of me.

Franklin walked by and looked in my direction. He whispered something to the security officer and they both looked at me.

"Jones, you don't have to wait," the officer said.

I hesitated.

"Yo, Jones," Franklin called out.

His loud voice made me snap into action. I wasted little time as I rushed out of line, and in front of the woman who had trouble getting through.

"Just holla when you coming in. Ain't no point in wasting time standing in line," Franklin told me after I coasted through security and made it safely to the other side.

"Okay, I'll remember that."

He walked with me almost halfway to the restroom. Then he turned off and went down the hall. I hated that he tried to act like we were good friends. I didn't want friends at work. His constant attempts left me curious about Franklin's intelligence level. Everything about me said I wasn't the social type, but he still tried. The only reason I was at the job was because it was the only one I could get. I needed money, not friends.

Once I opened the bathroom door, nothing could've prepared me for what I heard.

It was Edwards's voice.

"We need to get it out," she sobbed.

She sounded like she was under duress. I froze where I stood and strained to listen.

"So, what you want me to do?" That was Dunbar.

I quickly looked down at the bottom of the stalls. Edwards was on the ground with her legs cocked open. I saw Dunbar's boots as she stood near Edwards. They were in the last stall. It was bigger because it was for the disabled.

What the fuck was going on? I eased closer to the stall.

"You sure it's still in there?" Dunbar asked.

"Look. I'm gonna need you to try and fish it out." Edwards's voice was whining. She sounded like she was on the verge of tears.

"Oh, hell naw! You expect me to dig all up in your coochie?"

That was Dunbar. If the shit wasn't real, I would've doubled over in laughter. In my dreams it was always Dunbar who got something lodged up inside her pussy. And she was surrounded by doctors and medical personnel who couldn't understand why any sane person would willingly shove items inside their body.

"I can't do it. Lemme go find R.J. or something, 'cause I'm not gonna be able to do that."

"Are you serious right now? We know we not gay. It's like going to the doctor. Why you trippin'?" Edwards asked.

"There's just something so wrong about me sticking my hand up in another woman's twat. I just can't do it! I'm sorry."

"Dunbar, why you being a bitch right now?"

"Me? Who told you to try and bring in so much stuff? How'd you even walk with all of that stuck up inside of you?"

Edwards started to sob. "It feels like a condom lodged up in there. God! I want it oooout!"

"I'ma go get R.J."

"What? You can't leave me like this! What if you can't find him? Noooo, just try to get it out, please."

"Girl. I can't!"

"Dunbar, you have to. Here, let me try to spread my legs as wide as I can."

"No! Don't! I've already seen too much. I just need to go get R.J. I can *not* be a part of this. We need to stop before somebody comes up in here."

"I don't care! I just want it out."

"Edwards. I know you panicking and shit right now. But hear

me out. You can't afford to have just anybody walk up in here on this. There would be way too much explaining to do. Now, I'm telling you. We need to get R.J. Just let me go!"

Edwards sniffled a few times.

"Actually. We probably need to have you go to the closet. Y'all should do it in there. That way, once he gets it out, he can help you feel better."

Finally, Edwards faintly said, "Okay."

There was silence for a bit. I forgot all about the shipment I needed to get out of my hair and shoes. When I heard the door swing open, it was too late for me to even pretend like I hadn't been ear-hustling.

Dunbar looked at me.

"What the fuck you doing in here?" Her teeth gritted when she asked.

I frowned.

"Bitch, I ain't here to play with nobody's coochie, that's for sure!" I shot back.

The horror on her face was priceless, as I walked out of the bathroom.

CHAPTER THIRTEEN
KENYA TAYE

We took too many risks for DaQuan. He didn't appreciate half of the work we did to get the contraband into the prison and although he paid us well, most times I felt like the rewards didn't match the risks.

I wondered how much Jones's nosey ass heard before she hightailed it out of the bathroom. I hated her with a passion. Edwards's situation was enough to deal with.

When I walked out and realized it was Jones there instead of Bishop, I was pissed. I had distinctly told Bishop to guard the damn door and not let a single person in. What the hell was she thinking? And where the hell had she vanished to?

"Somebody's out there?" Edwards had asked.

She had gotten up off the ground and was putting her damn clothes back on. I knew she must've wondered the same thing as me. How the hell did Bishop allow anyone in, and of all people, Jones's ass. I didn't want to get Edwards worked up, so I let her get dressed before I told her who it was.

Edwards looked worn out as she opened the door and walked out of the stall. Even her collar was laid flat. I felt for her, but I couldn't bring myself to dig up in another woman's twat. I just couldn't do it. If she felt like we weren't good because of that, she'd have to deal with it on her own.

"I need to wash my hands and try to pull myself together," she said as she leaned over the sink to look at her reflection in the mirror.

"This is too damn much. I don't know what happened."

"Yeah, well, I'm gonna go find R.J. and tell him what's up."

"Okay, cool, but who was in here earlier?"

I stopped and turned to her. "It was Jones."

"What? How'd she get in?" Her eyes bugged.

Suddenly, Edwards's eyes looked around the room frantically. When her face twisted like she was about to break down again, I braced myself for the worst.

"What the hell Bishop let her in here for? That's fucked up. So she knows?"

I didn't have the heart to tell her that I wasn't sure, so I said, "I don't know what happened to Bishop; she was gone. And I don't think Jones heard too much of anything. Actually, as I walked out of the stall, it looked like she had just walked in," I lied.

Instant relief flooded Edwards's features. She dried her hands and exhaled. "This shit is just fucked up."

She was right about that, but there was nothing we could do about it. I left the bathroom and went in search of R.J. He was the only one who would be able to help with her situation.

As I walked up on the booth, I saw Bishop and Scott. I wanted to go straight ballistic on Bishop, but I knew it would cause problems if I did it in front of Scott.

I needed to find R.J., but I also needed to figure out what those two were doing.

"Yeah, he can't keep gassing C.O.s and not get an infraction for that," Scott said.

"Listen, I'm not the sergeant in charge; you gotta talk to Kenya Taye, I mean Dunbar, about that."

"Talk to Dunbar about what?" I asked as I approached them. When Bishop turned, her expression looked like she'd seen a ghost.

"Oh, we were talking about an incident. I heard it over the radio and that's why I had to leave the bathroom."

Scott's head whipped in her direction. I could've slapped Bishop's simple behind.

"Why would you be in the bathroom?" Scott asked. Confusion was plastered across her face.

"Why do you go to the bathroom?" I asked.

Bishop and Scott chuckled at that.

"Of course," Scott said. "But the way Bishop said it, it made it sound like y'all had a meeting in the ladies' room or something, that's all."

I tossed Bishop a knowing look. She needed to use her head more than she'd been doing. It made no sense that she slipped up in front of anybody like it was no big deal.

"Well, I finished the report. It's over there," Scott said. I glanced in the "out" tray's direction, but I didn't say anything. She took the hint, and finally left.

The minute we were alone, I turned to Bishop and let her have it.

"When you left your post, you left us all exposed! Guess who was lurking around in the damn bathroom because you left?"

"It's not like I chose to leave. What was I supposed to do? We was all in the bathroom. The radio went off. I had to go!"

"You could've said something. Instead, you take off and just leave. Next thing we know, Jones's nosey ass is up in there with us."

Bishop's eyes got big.

"Did she hear what was going on?"

"I'm sure she did. How could she not have heard? I was trying to help Edwards. I couldn't do that and keep an eye on the damn door. Hell, I didn't even know I needed to. Damn, Bishop, you had one job!"

Bishop threw her hands up, like she had a reason to be frustrated.

"What did you expect me to do? Did you really want me stuck to the bathroom when shit fell apart over the radio? I did what I thought was right. I made an executive decision."

It took everything in me not to slap her ass.

It was a good thing I didn't because I turned and Sheppard was right there.

"What's wrong?" she asked. She acted like we were all friends.

We both looked at her.

"What makes you think something is wrong?" I wanted to add, "And if it was, why would you think we'd discuss it with you?" She worked my nerves like it was a second job.

"Looks to me like y'all fighting. I hope it's not over nothing I brought in. My shit is legit. I don't play none of that knockoff mess."

That comment confirmed for me that Sheppard was an idiot.

"What's up, Sheppard? What do you need?"

"Oh, I wanted to talk to you about something." Her eyes darted to Bishop like she didn't want to talk in front of her.

Bishop didn't budge.

Again, I wanted to slap her. If she had been that diligent at the damn bathroom door, we wouldn't have had a problem with Jones.

"Bishop, can you give us a minute?"

"What am I supposed to do?" she asked. She had the nerve to act like she was irritated.

"Oh, you can go look for R.J. I need to talk to him."

It seemed like recognition finally registered in her features; she nodded and left.

Once we were alone, Sheppard moved closer. "Hey listen, I really need to make more paper. So I'm trying to figure out, do y'all know what y'all need beforehand or you just take what we bring in?"

"Why?"

"I may have a connect on some cell phones, but I don't wanna go outta my way if y'all can't move 'em. I don't know for sure yet, but if this thing works out, I'm talking at least one or two brand-new cell phones a week."

She had my full attention.

"Brand-new? How can you guarantee that? And can you guarantee that?"

"I ain't saying shit else until I know for sure that there's a deal on the table."

I understood her point, but I didn't need her to know that.

"Maybe I need to be talking to the boss man instead of you."

It made me sick how all the females wanted to get next to DaQuan.

CHAPTER FOURTEEN
Charisma

When I saw Bishop and a couple of DaQuan's men outside the closet, I figured R.J. must've helped Edwards with her situation. It was still funny, even though I would've paid money for it to happen to KenyaTaye instead of Edwards.

I passed by the guards' booth and saw Franklin and Dunbar. If they hadn't seen me, I would've kept walking. But my eyes connected with Franklin, so I turned to go inside.

"Say, Jones, you straight?" Franklin turned and asked.

"Yeah. Good looking out earlier."

Dunbar didn't say a word. That was fine with me. There was no need for us to make small talk or act like we could stand each other when we couldn't.

I was about to take a seat when it dawned on me, I was still loaded.

"If y'all got it under control in here, I'm about to go make some rounds."

"Oh yeah, you straight," Franklin said.

Again, Dunbar didn't speak. To think she was the damn sergeant on duty, but she ignored me unless she couldn't avoid it.

The thought of going back into the bathroom made me uneasy. Even though I was sure R.J. and Edwards were in the closet, thoughts of what happened to her earlier stayed on my mind. I couldn't erase the sound, sight, or smell of them in that bathroom.

Once inside the bathroom, I checked to make sure it was empty. Relieved that I was alone, I went into the stall and felt around my weave to get the plastic bags out. I had four. Once that was done, I sat on the toilet and removed my boots. I carefully removed the packages from each shoe and inspected the bags.

The last thing I needed was for R.J. to find broken pills. He'd try to dock my pay, and I couldn't have that.

I took the packets and slipped them into my pockets. Once I was confident that it didn't look too obvious, I went back to the booth.

This time, Edwards was with Dunbar. The second I walked in, they stopped talking. That was just fine with me because I wasn't interested in their pussy-diving conversation anyway.

With the two of them in the booth, that meant I could go deal directly with R.J. and that's what I preferred.

"S'up, Charisma?" R.J. said, the moment I approached.

"I got something for you." I winked at him.

"That's what's up, ma! That's what's up!"

His enthusiasm made me feel like I could pull anything off. I wished I could deal only with him and not Dunbar's mean and ignorant ass.

"C'mon around here so we can do this real quick."

I followed R.J. to one of the areas outside of the cameras' range. I pulled the packets out of both pockets and discreetly handed them over to him.

"Ya did real good this time, ma. That's like double what ya did last week. Oh, boss man's gonna be real happy when I let him know."

And that right there was what made it worth it for me. I was sure R.J. was just talking, but I knew he reported everything to DaQuan.

DaQuan paid well in cash and other things too. Thanks to my cousin Lance, I was able to keep a steady flow of pills coming into Jester. In the short time I had been on the team, I had already solidified myself as the go-to C.O. for pills.

Once I unloaded my contraband, I left the secluded area ahead of R.J. just in case someone paid attention to us. It felt good to unload the pills. The last thing I wanted was to have pills on me as I walked around the prison. It was hard to get the contraband inside, and even harder, or downright dangerous to hold on to it once it was inside.

With one eye on the clock, I made a couple of rounds, then prepared to end my workday. It dawned on me that outside of work, I really didn't have much of a life. But after all I had been through, that was fine.

The money I got for the pills would help me get out of some debt and be able to live better.

I rounded the corner, and walked right into a melee. A group of inmates was kicking and stomping someone on the ground. I froze. I couldn't even tell who was down there, and I looked around for backup, but there was none. I didn't know what to do. Nothing from training popped into my head. I was frozen.

After a few seconds, I fumbled to get to my radio.

All of a sudden, DaQuan walked up on the scene and everything changed.

"Yo! What the fuck is y'all doing?"

At the mere sound of his voice, the inmates stopped what they were doing and the person on the ground quickly scurried away.

"What the fuck was y'all thinking? I don't remember telling nobody to handle that kind of bi'niz. This ain't gonna do nothing but make things hard around here. Y'all know the rules; ya don't touch nobody unless it's cleared." Their eyes fell to the floor.

He had reduced big, grown men to children.

"Dude tried to steal my Green Dot card," someone said.

"So ya'll jump him because of *that*? Why didn't ya go through the proper channels? Y'all trippin'!"

Since he had the situation covered, there was nothing for me to do but stand and watch as he handled it. After it was all over, a couple of male correctional officers rushed to the area. They were late and out of breath.

"What's going on here, Jones?"

I wasn't sure what to say.

"The situation is over," DaQuan said.

I thought I saw relief flash across the C.O.s' faces. If it wasn't on theirs, I knew for certain it was on mine. When I saw the group as they beat that inmate, I couldn't help. It reminded me of a pit bull on a piece of raw steak.

That's not a situation any female wants to handle. There was little I could do. When a mob was angry, it's liable to turn on anybody. I wasn't ready for the hazards of the job.

The C.O.s looked around and said, "You okay, Jones?"

"Yeah, she straight," DaQuan answered.

The way he moved in and took complete control of the situation made me feel like he could handle anything. Words couldn't describe the intense attraction I felt for him at that moment. His power was incredible.

"DaQuan, you gon' handle this or what?" one of the C.O.s asked.

"Yeah, lemme see what was really going on and I'll take care of it."

"Okay, now, you better handle it because if we do—"

"C'mon, man! Go on with that bullshit! I just told ya I'ma take care of it. I don't need to hear all the extras. I got this."

DaQuan pushed himself between my two coworkers and walked away.

"Look, man, we don't want to make him mad. He's the reason our jobs are easier around here," one of the C.O.s said.

"How's that, man?"

"You must not have worked in a prison before. Man, fights break out over the simplest shit; somebody always trying to punk somebody else. Not in here. DaQuan keeps it calm and for whatever reason, they listen to him, so it's all good." The C.O. shrugged.

I had heard about DaQuan's power before, but in that moment, I came to understand the real power he had over the Jester unit, and I liked it.

CHAPTER FIFTEEN
KENYA TAYE

As I strode around the cell block, everything was quiet and in order. I approached the TV room and saw him surrounded by his soldiers.

He was in the middle of a meeting, but I didn't care. I wasn't going to interrupt, but I got close enough to hear what he was talking about. I was careful not to let him see me.

"If it ain't 'bout the money, then it ain't my business. In here, pussy is our connection to that paper, and that paper is the business." DaQuan looked around at the workers, then continued. "When I came back to jail, I'm like, shit, I'm not going to stop making my money. Ya feel me? I seen what the fuck was going on, asked a few people what was up and who was who, and what was what. I am just about my money. Ya hear me? I got to get it."

A few heads nodded.

"Money and pussy!"

He turned to the Minister of Finance, Ryan Jacob, better known as R.J., and said, "You up, playboy."

Jacob fixed the glasses on the bridge of his nose and cleared his throat. "Okay, so peep this. We only pulled in sixteen G's last month. Ten of that alone came from pills. The rest is a combination of weed and meth." I wasn't surprised to learn that profits were down. DaQuan had been sloppy.

"What about the strips?" DaQuan asked.

R.J.'s forehead wrinkled as he looked down at the paper he was reading from. Sixteen thousand was a slow month. We took a hit on the north side when we lost a man over there. That meant sales would be down until we could fill the void, and I knew DaQuan was still trying to figure out how to recoup.

But when the business suffered, we all suffered. It was all about money and how to make more money. That's why I didn't understand how he took the risks he took. Why put Jones on the team when she hadn't even passed her probation period on the job yet? Why have Sheppard on the team when she was clearly strung out?

How come he couldn't stick to the system? Our system had worked for years. Trusted correctional officers smuggled pills, phones, and drugs into the prison.

The working men consisted of trustees, those inmates with jobs at the facility. They pushed Suboxone Strips, Xanax, and Percocet. It was simple enough because they had free reign of the prison and its grounds through their jobs as kitchen helpers, janitors, or mail room workers.

In addition to the pills, and depending on who came through, we got weed, meth, and some crack too. But lately, pills sold like free hotcakes.

Some of the chicks that wasn't on the team also sold ass or blowjobs. Before DaQuan and I got serious, I used to sell blowjobs too. It was a way to make fast cash. I wasn't proud of it, but it was what I did. That was before me and DaQuan started kicking it.

A lot of money floated through the system, and the way DaQuan had it set up, everybody was on the payroll, basically. Most of the inmates used Green Dot cards. Those were like preloaded credit cards, and they worked better than cash. Inmates would get their relatives and friends to put money on their cards. Inmates used them to buy everything from liquor to ass. But cash still found its way behind bars.

"Oh, yeah. That's right, I see it now. Ten is from the pills and the strips. My bad," R.J. said.

"Okay, so how'd we do on taxes?" DaQuan asked.

"Real small amount; wasn't even worth its own column on the report."

Taxes were like gravy. DaQuan charged ten percent to other inmates who sold anything outside of our crew. That was a rule that had to be enforced. One time an inmate lucked up on some tobacco. He had to get DaQuan's permission before he sold any of it. He held it for nearly two weeks. After the inmate agreed to the tax, dude sold out in less than two hours.

DaQuan made it clear; he couldn't have anyone selling willy-nilly. He insisted that if others thought they could sell without paying the tax, eventually that would cut into our profits and DaQuan couldn't have that.

At first, I thought a tax was too risky and would cause problems, but he knew what he was doing. My baby was smart as hell.

"Hmm. That's not cool." DaQuan turned to Larry Reed, aka Lucky, the Minister at Arms. "So ol' boy ain't paid yet?"

They were talking about Colt Anderson, a new dude who had transferred in a few months ago. He thought he was above the law and probably thought he could get away with not paying. If he knew like I knew, he'd better get in line because he didn't want DaQuan to have to show him he meant business.

"Nah, not a dime," Lucky said.

DaQuan's face became stoic. I could nearly see the wheels that spun in his head as he made a decision. A few seconds later, he looked at Larry and said, "Make the message clear after breakfast tomorrow morning."

"Bet that," Lucky said.

That meant Colt would soon be headed to the infirmary. He wouldn't be dead, but by the time they were finished with him, he'd wish he was.

The minister of education, Darius Patterson, or Don Juan, nodded slightly when DaQuan looked at him.

"Three soldiers are working their C.O.s. They should be flipped by next week. Oh, and we got two new ones on the yard, and I got a good feeling about both of 'em."

Don Juan's job was to teach the working men, soldiers, and everybody else how to do business DaQuan's way. The key to our success was the females who helped move product. Everybody had a job to do and that kept the business successful.

"Oh yeah? Why's that?"

"You ain't seen 'em yet?" Don Juan's eyes got wide.

A couple of the guys laughed. One pressed his lips together, blew air into his jaws and spread his arms wide, to show how big one of the women was. They all started to crack up with laughter—everybody but DaQuan.

That bastard liked all shapes and sizes.

"Hear what I'm telling ya, playboy. Just because a female big, that don't mean she got low self-esteem. Them confident broads ain't nothing but trouble, and we don't need trouble. I don't care what size she is; stay away from them confident broads. They too hard to flip."

I wasn't sure what he meant by that, or how one could tell such a thing, but I continued to listen.

"Okay, boss man, I feel you," Don Juan said.

They were in the corner near the kitchen where they met once a week. The C.O.s pretty much knew what was up, so we made sure everybody stayed away so DaQuan could conduct business.

"Pay attention to the target. I don't care who's new. Let's not lose focus on those we been working on. Remember we only interested in the ones who are loners." He was in his zone. That shit was sexy to watch.

"Send mixed signals; be tough. But chill too. One day drop a bunch of compliments, but two days later, act like ya don't even know her. We need her to be unhappy. Ya gotta handle it right. If ya get straight to the point too soon, ya risk resistance that's impossible to get through."

He used his hand to count down his points. "This is a proven system. Start out as a friend, then slowly work yo way toward hitting it. Once ya lull her into feeling secure, that's when ya strike. Even better, try to get at her through a third party."

At first it felt good to watch him in action. But the more I listened, the more the things he said started to make me sick. Is that what he did to me? Was I a guinea pig?

"Damn, Boss, you a master at this shit," Lucky said.

The other inmates looked up to DaQuan and hung on every word that flowed from his mouth.

"It ain't brain surgery. Follow my lead and we straight. When y'all try to do this shit yo way, that's when ya fuck things up, believe that."

A few heads nodded. He looked at R.J. and said, "Tell Dunbar to pay e'erbody by the end of the day. Anybody else got anything?"

"Nah. I think we straight," Lucky said.

"Okay then, cool. Let's go get that paper!" DaQuan said.

I watched as everybody got up from the table and walked away.

"Yo, Lucky, fall back for a sec."

Larry told R.J. he'd catch up to him later; then he walked over to DaQuan.

"Whassup, boss man?"

"Tell Jones I need to see her in the closet this afternoon."

"I'm on it," Lucky said, then left.

Did he just say he wanted to meet *that* bitch in the closet?

That cut deep. I cringed inside, and my ears began to burn. What the hell was he thinking? And what did that mean for us?

My heart took a nosedive, and my legs threatened to give out.

CHAPTER SIXTEEN
CHARISMA

I was in paradise right here on Earth, inside a prison of all places. Ripples of pleasure flooded through my body in what felt like time-released waves. I used the back of my hand to wipe sweat from my forehead. I buckled at the sensation, arched my back, released a cry, and wiggled against his movement.

"Take it," he said.

My heart rate fluttered. I wanted it, all of it.

"Oh yes, daddy, yes!"

"I knew you wanted this dick!"

The sound of his voice, slow and passionate, only fueled my mission. I was gonna get it all.

He groaned as I pulled him closer and deeper and deeper. I was completely caught up in the rapture and couldn't think of a single thing that could compare to the sheer bliss I was experiencing. He was the best I'd ever had, an attentive and giving lover.

I pulled in a deep, rugged breath, closed my eyes and released that strong guttural groan that had been trapped in my throat. I rotated my hips, and ground down on him in slow motion.

"Ooooohhhh, weeeee." I slapped the sides of his head in an attempt to grab ahold and keep him in place.

DaQuan clamped his hands down on my hips, and pulled me into him. We'd been holed up inside the small makeshift bedroom, and I rode him like I wasn't sure when I'd have another chance. I had to try and make the best of the ride.

"Jesus, daddy! You hittin' my spot. You hittin' my spot! Right there, baby," I cried, and shuddered as waves of pleasure flooded my central nervous system. I was in paradise.

"You like that, ma?" he breathed before he smothered his face into my breasts.

"Oooh, yèeesss!"

DaQuan pulled back, caught one of my nipples between his lips, and suckled it. He worked his hips and I noticed his eyes fluttering. His mouth was agape, and he looked like he was in a world all his own. I just hung on for the ride.

"Good . . . real good," he groaned incoherently as he palmed my breast, squeezing it so hard I winced from the pain, then smiled at the surge of pleasure I was now experiencing.

Women like me didn't have that kind of mind-blowing sex. I couldn't wrap my mind around everything that had just happened. I had already cum once. The way he was working it, I was on my way to number two.

He was intense, with long, powerful strokes. When I felt his body jerk, I knew success was within my reach.

"I'm coming, Charisma! I'm coming, baby; hold on!"

DaQuan exploded with such force and power, I swore I felt his fluids in me. I beamed with pride.

I had fucked DaQuan!

Our sweat intertwined and mixed into one.

"Whew!"

He was satisfied and I was happy.

We cuddled a little, shared some sweet pillow talk; then he got up. He put his clothes back on, and started to move toward the door. My legs felt too weak to hold me up, so I wasn't in a hurry to move. Besides, the wonderful aftershocks still flowed through my body.

"Yo, just to be on the safe side, let me go out first. I don't want nobody all in our business," he said.

Alarm settled into my system and grabbed my heart. Getting caught never crossed my mind. And why would it? DaQuan was in charge. Why did he care if someone saw us?

"Hey, don't trip. Ya cool. I just don't want those nosey hens all in our shit! Trust me; that's how a good thing gets all fucked up."

Just that fast, relief washed over me. I thought he was scared, but he was just looking out for me. I felt so incredibly proud to be his. It was still so hard to believe that I had managed to pull a Boss.

DaQuan came back to the bed and stooped down. "Ya straight, right?"

The look in his eyes told me he really cared.

"Yeah. I'm good, daddy."

"Ya know I like when ya call me that shit, right?" He grinned. "Ya got some bomb-ass pussy!"

Never in my life would I normally call a man "daddy," but I had heard it in one of my favorite rap songs and thought, why the hell not? Whoever would've guessed I'd be able to get a man worthy of such deference? Being with DaQuan made me feel like I could do anything, regardless of whether I could.

DaQuan pecked my lips, then walked out of the small room. I looked around and wondered how long I needed to stay in there before I could ease out, undetected.

He was right. Dunbar, Edwards, and Bishop already hated my guts. If they found out I was kicking it with DaQuan, I could only imagine how much more shade they'd throw in my direction. No, I needed to keep our secret for as long as possible.

Later, as I walked into the locker room, I heard those hens before I saw them. Anytime I looked at them, I thought about DaQuan when he referred to them as hens. He was so on point; they stayed loud and gossipy.

"Girl, I literally just laid my ass on the couch because I was so weak from laughing," KenyaTaye said. She was overly animated as she told her story. It was obvious she lived to be extra. Females like her were nothing but trouble.

I ignored them. I wanted to be invisible for as long as possible.

The other two correctional officers howled with laughter. So far, I had not been impressed by any of the people I'd come in contact with at work except DaQuan and R.J.

"KenyaTaye! KenyaTaye! Girl, stop!" Edwards yelled.

I eased by the trio and made my way to my locker. I continued to ignore the story being told and reminded myself that the best way to be successful on any new job was to keep to oneself.

KenyaTaye and her girls were obnoxious and behaved as if they ran the place. Not that I wanted to be acknowledged, but the trio acted like I hadn't even entered their space. Their little middle-school, mean-girl treatment worked just fine for me. I didn't need them all in my business anyway.

This was no popularity contest and I was determined not to make it one. I'd come to work, do the shitty job, and collect the paycheck.

In the time I'd been working, I had picked up on quite a bit. I was certain most of that had come because I was quiet and kept to myself. Of what I'd gathered, what stayed on my mind most, was all that was wrong with the new job.

The most problematic was the large number of women who worked in my assigned unit. Experience had taught me that wherever there were lots of women, there was bound to be ten times that amount of drama. And drama was the last thing I needed.

I grabbed my jacket and purse from the locker and turned

to leave. I had made it only a few steps past the pack when someone spoke.

"'Scuse me," Edwards said.

If I wanted to ignore them and keep it moving, the next words forced me to stop.

"Aey, you. Jones!"

It was obvious they were talking to me.

I stopped and turned.

"That bag, is that a real Gucci?"

My expression twisted as I followed their eyes down to the clear bamboo shopper tote I carried. DaQuan had sent it to the house for me.

"Of course my bag is real."

I didn't try to remove the sarcasm from my tone. I did notice when one of the women nudged Dunbar.

"That's what's up," Dunbar said, but she acted like it hurt her mouth to say so. I wanted to tell her she could keep her flat compliment to her damn self. I didn't need it. I got all the compliments I needed from DaQuan, and as long as he liked it, I was good.

The other women nodded approvingly and I turned and left.

I didn't have to look over my shoulder to know that the women's eyes were still glued to me. And I already knew the first stone had been cast, so I braced myself for the drama that was bound to begin.

CHAPTER SEVENTEEN
KENYA TAYE

"Aey, Dunbar, I got two bags of weed and two brand-new cell phones." C.O. Sheppard pounded a fist into her palm to emphasize her words. "And this time I want top dollar for my shit 'cause these ain't no cheap burners, either."

She was so loud. I glanced around and was relieved that the cubicles were empty. The inmates were in the rec room.

As Sheppard ran down the contraband she had smuggled in, all I could think was, why did DaQuan insist on padding our workforce with so many ratchet females? Sheppard was crazy. I had no idea how she even got hired for the legit job, much less for some illegal shit.

But at least this time Sheppard didn't shake or tremble like she was going through withdrawal. My eyes darted around the area again. One of us needed to make sure nobody was ear-hustling nearby.

The truth was, no one needed to eavesdrop as loud as she talked. Sheppard carried on like we were talking about sale items at Macy's instead of *contraband*, illegal contraband.

"Okay, I'll keep that in mind," I said.

I lowered my voice to help her realize how loud she was being, and bring hers down, but that didn't work.

"So that means I'm getting mo' money, right?"

I wanted her gone!

"You need to let me know, 'cause if y'all don't want to pay top dollar for the phones, I could…"

When I looked at her, her voice trailed off like she had just realized the threat before it left her lips. My eyebrow was still elevated. I knew she wasn't trying to threaten to sell DaQuan's stuff to someone else. That was as close to a death wish as possible.

"So, you gon' ask DaQuan and get back to me later?"

She leaned in then and asked, "Oh, who all is working with us? I need to know who to look for at the door. I could bring a lot more stuff in if I knew who to look for."

That was the smartest thing I had ever heard her say. And she had a good point.

I nodded. "Yeah, Sheppard, I'ma get with him, and lemme talk to him about letting you know the others on the team."

"Well, I know about Edwards and Bishop, but what about the new C.O.s?"

She couldn't take a hint.

"Lemme get back at you," I snapped.

Sheppard shuffled back a few steps.

"Oh, okay then. It's all good. I can wait."

The minute Sheppard turned the corner and left, I eased back into the guard's station and picked up some paperwork. My mind stayed on the problems DaQuan and I had.

It dawned on me that I was too valuable to him and his company. Who else would put it all on the line like I did? I held it down and dealt with all kinds of things that kept the business running smoothly. He needed to do right by me. I didn't smuggle as much stuff in anymore, but I handled the books and kept track of inventory.

As hard as I worked, he needed to check in with me before he added crazy chicks to our team. He shouldn't have accepted Sheppard or Jones.

Thoughts of the misfits made me think about Jones. It took two days for me to stop thinking about the sight of that Gucci bag she carried out of the locker room. Who did she think she was, and how could she even afford a brand-new Gucci bag like that?

"She must be boosting or knows somebody who is."

"Who you talking to?"

I turned around at the sound of Edwards's voice.

"Oh, girl, I'm just sitting here thinking about this business."

With her stiff collar upright, Edwards gave me the side-eye like she didn't believe me.

"That's what we call it now, *thinking*? Okay, well, think on, as long as you don't go answering yourself."

"Girl, actually I was thinking about that bag ol' girl was carrying."

"It was everything!" Edwards's eyes got wide like she was overcome with excitement.

The bag was nice, but it wasn't all Edwards made it out to be.

Bishop rushed into the booth. She was out of breath and breathing hard. She placed a hand over her chest, and held the other out to get our attention.

"DaQuan is holding a dinner party."

"Come again."

My heart threatened to burst right up out of my chest.

"What you talking about a dinner party?" Edwards sounded just as confused. "He got the kitchen to fix something, or what?"

We looked at each other. I got up from my chair and made my way to the door. Bishop had finally caught her breath.

"C'mon; I need y'all to see this for yourself! Oooh, wee, he's something fierce!" Bishop said. Her voice was giddy, and she could hardly stand still.

"Wait, the booth; we can't just leave," Edwards said.

"Girl, it's been quiet all day. We not gonna be gone that long; let's go!" I said.

As we rushed down the hallway, C.O. Scott hurried toward us from the opposite direction.

"We got a situation on the C-block. Man the radio in the booth," I said as we passed her. "I'll be back in ten."

Scott looked confused, but she didn't question me.

We heard the party before we saw it. And even when I saw it, I couldn't believe what I saw. Off to the back of the kitchen area near the opened pantry, DaQuan and five of his soldiers were at a table. The table was covered with cloth.

Music played; they ate, drank and talked.

"Yo, ya'll comin' through or y'all just gonna watch?"

Two C.O.s stood by. One exchanged a knowing glance with me and I walked closer to the table. Bishop and Edwards were close by.

"Is that catfish?" Bishop asked.

The scent of fresh fried fish grew stronger the closer we got to the table. There was shrimp, and po'boys too.

"I eat tilapia," DaQuan said.

He looked good in his white tee and white pants. My desire for him was just as strong as ever and I hated myself for it.

"Damn, y'all having a feast, huh?" Bishop swung a leg over and sat on the bench next to R.J.

"Yo mouth watering, ma?" DaQuan brought a glass to his lips.

I was waiting for DaQuan to say something to me. But he didn't. Instead he only talked around me and to my girls.

"Vodka?" Bishop asked. Her eyes got wide.

"Only top of the line for my soldiers!" DaQuan stuck his chest out. "Yeah, we' celebratin' a record month."

I bit down on my lip because what I wanted to tell him was, that record month wouldn't have been possible without me. So while he tried to act all brand-new with me, he needed to recognize that I had made all of that shit possible, including his five-star dinner.

"Bishop, Edwards, y'all chillin' over here?"

The question was just about ignored because both of them had taken a seat and were stuffing their mouths. I was mad, but what could I say?

DaQuan didn't even look my way. He made me so sick, but there was nothing I could do. If I messed with his money, that would be like messing with my life. He had made it clear that everything came second to his money, and obviously, that included me.

CHAPTER EIGHTEEN
CHARISMA

Something had been in the air from the moment I pulled in a deep rugged breath and strolled past security and into the gates that led to the main building.

I wasn't about to brag or anything, but it was so easy to smuggle in the pills, I couldn't remember why I hesitated in the beginning. On this trip alone, I had eighty stashed in my weave, and another 120 divided between the soles of each shoe. Security was so lax, sometimes I'd convince myself that what I was doing wasn't really a big deal.

Complete silence greeted me the moment I entered the building, a signal that it would be a good and easy day. The cubicles were empty, which meant the inmates were at lunch.

Even though they were gone, their scent lingered behind. But my senses were close to becoming immune to that.

Quiet time in that area was precious; outside of my co-workers gathered at the guards' station, the place was vacant. I wasn't one for hanging with the crowd, so once I put my stuff away, I decided to go walk the halls.

When there was no trouble to be found, I tried to busy myself with anything that kept me occupied. It didn't matter if I was counting the square tiles on the floor. I just wanted to be away from Dunbar, Edwards, and Bishop. C.O. Scott, who had helped me get the job, kept her distance too. Since she was on another shift, it was easier for her to do. But I felt like her distance was more about their childish behavior than the illegal behavior.

By the time I rounded the corner near one of the back classrooms, I heard the commotion before I saw the inmates. There went my easy day.

"Dawg, you ain't paid, so you ain't got no turn!" R.J. said to another inmate. R.J.'s arm was extended away from his body and high above a shorter inmate's head. The cell phone he clutched seemed to be the issue.

The shorter inmate looked like he couldn't understand what was being said.

"But my folks don' paid in full, playboy!" a different inmate said.

"Granger, I got you, dawg. But you not the only one scheduled to use the phone. Lemme handle this situation and you gon' get your time, dawg."

"It's gotta be some kinda mistake; my moms said she paid, R.J."

"Well, she didn't. I gots the list right here. Granger, D-Bob, Bubba, and Tyler are all paid in full."

R.J. held out a piece of paper and showed the shorter inmate.

"Gon', man. Check it for yo'self; then you bes' check ya folks 'cause somebody gassin' you up."

The inmate snatched the form and started to inspect it himself, as R.J. handed the phone to Granger.

Granger turned back. "I got thirty minutes and I want all my time, R.J. Don't be tryna short me over this bad misunderstanding that went down. I wants my full thirty!"

"Dawg, ain't nobody tryna short you! Ya need to make yo call and stop bumpin' yo gums, before I snatch yo spot and let Tyler jump the line!"

R.J. spotted me and a quick flash of alarm washed over his features. It softened when our eyes connected.

He turned back to the group. "I'll be back here in thirty. Tyler, meet me here; then at six-thirty, it's D-Bob. Bubba, you up at seven."

"What about me? Can I hold it after Bubba?" the inmate left off the list asked.

"Dawg! Yo bill is outstanding. I can't keep extending credit and letting you make free calls like that. We ain't runnin' no damn charity over here! Get yo folks to pay the bill and ya get in the game. Until then, I can't do nothin' fo ya, man."

For a second, I thought I might have to intervene. The shorter inmate looked like he might be ready to pounce, and I'd have no choice but to send him to solitary if he took a swing at R.J.

Something must've clicked in his head. Even though there was a scowl on his face and at least one fist clenched, he turned and walked away.

R.J. left the other inmates and approached me. "Whassup, ma?"

I motioned my head in the direction he just left. "What was that all about?"

"Oh, that ain't nothin' but a pay phone situation."

My eyebrows knitted in confusion. "A pay phone?"

"Yeah, ma. Can't everybody afford a celly up in here. If ya ain't got two grand, ya gotta pay to make yo calls."

"You can't be serious."

The fact that inmates paid two thousand dollars for a cell phone stunned me. How the hell did they get that kind of money? I started to think about all the cell phones that were smuggled in and that made the numbers real to me.

R.J. shook his head, like I was a challenge for him to understand.

"Look, ma. Everything got a price tag up in this bitch. The shit ya take for granted is valuable in here. Ya name it and I can sell it, for top dollar."

I thought about other things I could sell to make money. The pills were good, but seeing R.J. rent out a cell phone made me wonder what else inmates might be willing to pay for.

"Ya got anything for me?"

"Oh, yeah. I got about two hundred this time."

His eyes lit up. "Damn, ma. You just a lil' pill factory these days, huh? That's what's up! That's what's up, fa sho!"

I stepped off to a corner where I thought a camera wouldn't be able to spot me. There, I tugged at my weave, and removed the plastic bags. I stepped out of one shoe, removed the sole and took the little plastic bags out.

Once I had everything, I motioned for R.J. to come closer. He glanced around like he needed to check the coast and moved in.

"Damn, ya a beast with these pills, ma. That's what's up."

The excitement in his voice made me feel even better about my new talent. It was so easy and I knew for sure he'd tell DaQuan all about the progress I had made. I didn't smuggle pills daily, but at least three or four days a week, I brought in the pills my cousin Lance got from the old folks' home. Lance, Lena's brother, was so glad to get the extra money, he even offered to recruit some of his coworkers. But I felt like another supplier would complicate things, and I didn't want that.

His constant supply made me a real game changer. And since Lena couldn't hardly stand her own brother, I didn't have to worry about her being in my business. Or at least that's what I thought.

Lance's hook-up really helped me out. Every time I did something to help the business, I thought about DaQuan and how pleased he would be. Thoughts of making him happy made me want to work harder.

It seemed nearly impossible because of where we were, but I rarely saw him. As the leader of the caged empire, he was busy and had to spread his time around.

"Where is he right now?"

R.J. looked up from the packets of pills. I could tell I had thrown his count off.

"Uh, who? DaQuan? He probably handling some bitniz; ya know how he gets down."

I didn't really know, but I nodded anyway. I swallowed a dry lump and told myself I'd get another turn in the closet soon enough. Unfortunately for me, I had no control over when that would be. Kicking it with a boss meant I just needed to be ready when he called and be patient when he didn't.

CHAPTER NINETEEN
KENYA TAYE

My body crumbled into one million tiny pieces as Jones peeked into the booth, slipped in, then took off. I wanted to follow her simple behind, but I couldn't.

My heart felt like it was beating in my throat.

Was she going to meet with DaQuan?

Maybe she spent her time trying to track him down in hopes that he'd pull her into the damn closet. I needed her gone!

The way he treated her, and the way she tried to act like she was better than everybody else made me hate her more. I needed to do something to knock her ass back down.

Edwards and I exchanged knowing glances the moment she walked out. It burned me up that I couldn't stop her. One of the other guards who was not on our team for the umpteenth time talked about an incident that had broken out overnight.

I wanted him to shut up, but I couldn't say so. The radio buzzed to life and a fuzzy voice crackled through. I snatched it up quickly and spoke into it.

"Come again? C.O. Dunbar here."

"Delivery to the east rear," the voice said.

"Roger that. C.O.s Dunbar and Edwards are headed that way now."

Bishop shot me a dirty look, but there was nothing I could do. We couldn't all leave to go meet the delivery truck. She'd have to suck it up and continue to listen to C.O. Watson hear himself talk. Everyone had a job to do, and that was hers.

Edwards jumped up from the chair so fast, I thought it would tumble to the floor. As we rounded the corner away from the booth, she said, "Thank you! That damn Watson can talk!"

"Girl, I know. I was like, why we gotta be trapped listening to this madness?"

We made our way to the back of the main building and opened a side door. Three other C.O.s stood by, but one, C.O. Franklin, winked at me. I nudged Edwards who walked over to the other two C.O.s. Her job was to keep them distracted, so that I could handle the business.

I rushed to the driver's side and the driver rolled his window down. He was a regular.

"Look between the sacks of flour, near the back behind the passenger side. You need to hurry 'cause they just called for the K-9 unit."

A trustee met me near the back of the truck. Two others pulled the back door up.

"Let me get in there," I said.

One of the trustees extended a hand and helped me hop up onto the truck. The air inside was hot and my skin felt instantly sticky. I pulled a small flashlight from my breast pocket and headed toward the section where the driver told me I'd find the flour.

My adrenaline was on speed as I made my way around in the dark. The little light helped, but not much. It didn't take long for sweat to run down the sides of my head and down my back.

It was a tight fit between stacks of crates, but I spotted the ones that held flour. Pulling in my stomach, I eased between two narrow rows and slid my hands into a crate. I felt along the sides and touched the ridges of a freezer bag.

My heart nearly stopped.

I knew I was racing against a clock, because the K-9 unit would be there in less than fifteen minutes. I needed to work fast.

I put the flashlight between my lips and tilted my head so I could get a better look at the stacks of flour. I tugged and pulled out two large freezer bags. I slid my hand down the sides of the remaining sacks and felt the flap of another bag.

Quickly, I rushed back to the door and flung the plastic bags down to the trustee. He tossed them into the wheelbarrow, turned over a large can of soil and placed some other stuff on top of the bags until they were hidden.

The other trustee helped me as I hopped off the back of the truck. He quickly lowered the door and I made my way back to the driver.

"Got everything?" he asked.

"Three freezer bags?"

"Yup." He nodded and motioned straight ahead. "Perfect timing; here comes the cavalry."

I turned in time to see another officer as he led the K-9 officer in our direction. I released a breath I didn't realize I'd been holding when they rushed to the passenger side of the truck and greeted the other C.O.s.

My relief was even greater when the dog led his handler toward the back.

"How much longer?" I asked, as I approached the C.O.s who still stood off to the side.

"What'd you go back there for?" one of them asked.

My heart took a nosedive.

"Dude! She had to pull a couple of trustees for the unload," Franklin quickly answered.

"Oh. Okay."

I was glad Franklin answered because I was at a loss. I didn't expect to be questioned. I thought everyone was on the team. That was yet another slip on DaQuan's part.

How he gonna have a delivery come in and not secure the perimeter? That could've been all of our asses!

Edwards glanced at me and slowly shook her head. I knew she must've read my mind.

The mental list of issues I needed to discuss with DaQuan seemed to grow every day. How hard was it to make sure team members greeted delivery trucks?

Once the truck was unloaded, Edwards and I made our way back into the building.

"Lawd ha' mercy! What was that shit back there?"

"Hell if I know. If he ain't part of the team, why was he even out there?" I asked.

"I think I remember him from weekend nights. He looks familiar, but I just knew he was down with us."

"See, this the type of shit that makes me hot about DaQuan. I get that he's got this successful business and all, but you can't be slipping like that. We're the ones on the fucking front line."

"Yeah, and how much longer you gonna be able to hop on and off those trucks?"

When I turned to her, she motioned with her hand in front of her stomach.

"Well, we still got lots of time before I start showing. I'm not worried about that as much as I'm worried about the fact that he keeps making these simple mistakes. How you gonna have an outsider meet the truck? Makes no damn sense," I said.

"Just talk to him about it."

If only she knew. It seemed like these days just talking to DaQuan had become more and more of a challenge. And something told me it was the fault of nobody but that damn Jones. She probably whispered softly in his ear with all kinds of self-destructive information. I needed to handle that situation before we all suffered.

CHAPTER TWENTY
CHARISMA

"What's going on?"

My question didn't need a verbal answer because of what played out right before my eyes.

I had walked into sheer chaos.

Clothes, bedding, and other stuff were piled up all over the walkways. Inmates stood quietly outside their cubicles, as C.O.s turned over mattresses, and rummaged through their personal belongings.

"Damn, Franklin, you ain't gotta break my shit like that!"

Chatter and curse words rose from different sections of the large room. My chest felt like a vise-grip squeezed my heart.

"This ain't right!"

I eased next to the other C.O.s and mumbled again. "What the hell?"

"Somebody don' snitched," Edwards said.

Her tone told me she was irritated by what appeared to be an unannounced shakedown. But I didn't like the way she looked at me. I thought we were supposed to be notified when shakedowns were gonna happen.

Luckily for me, I wasn't loaded with a shipment today, but the scene still caused alarm. I needed to remind myself not to appear too nervous. I didn't need anybody to point a finger at me. After all, I had just walked in on this.

When I looked up and saw Dunbar with one of the teams of three, conducting the shakedown, I nearly busted out with laughter.

Instantly, relief washed over me because I knew it was only for show if *she* was part of it.

As I watched the show, the irony was too much. Dunbar was personally responsible for 99% of the contraband smuggled into the prison, but she led the pack, walking around conducting a shakedown?

Dunbar was so full of shit.

I stood back and took it all in. And that trick knew how to put on a show too.

"Inmate, if I find anything, any type of contraband, that's your ass, and you goin' straight to the hole! Do I make myself clear?" she shouted at the inmate who stood outside the next cubicle.

Kenya Taye ransacked that space like a tornado doing damage on a small wood-frame house. She ripped pictures from the walls, tossed and shook clothes, flipped mattresses, and talked shit the whole time she searched.

"We ain't gonna be putting up with none of this shit on my watch!"

The other C.O.s who were with her, didn't say a word, and they barely moved. Her antics were enough for all of them.

I wanted to go and bust her out for fronting like she was really doing something, but I knew better. Doing that would put DaQuan in the middle of the drama and I didn't want that.

Nearly three hours after the so-called shakedown, the assistant warden, Preston Richards, stood in front of a table that was loaded with cell phones, makeshift shanks, and a variety of tobacco products. I was personally relieved that I didn't see any pills.

"This is a serious, serious, problem."

His raspy voice made my brain immediately try to calculate whether he smoked three or four packs a day. As he spoke, Richards took deep breaths between each word. His labored breathing made me think he might keel over right in front of us. But he didn't.

Dunbar had the audacity to stand next to a clean C.O. near the table as Richards spoke. Richards's wide body nearly blocked them and the contraband until he started to pace.

"We need to get a handle on this situation. Heads are going to bounce all around this prison if we can't control the flow of contraband. This is a prison, not a frat house! Do your jobs or you'll lose your jobs!"

Richards pointed a chubby finger in our direction.

"This is a damn embarrassment to the uniform!" Spittle gathered at the corners of his mouth.

He let that linger in the air for a few minutes, while he caught his breath.

We all stood silent. It was so quiet all we heard was Richards's loud breathing.

Suddenly, Richards nodded, and Dunbar and the other C.O. rushed to the table with two large trash bags. They scooped the items into the bags, tied them, then placed the bags on top of the table.

"Now. We're going to get the inmates caught stashing this shit, but I'm going to get to the bottom of this situation."

His pie-shaped face was red and blanketed with sweat.

The threat was real to me. No one else seemed pressed by what he had said, but I didn't want to lose my job and I damn sure didn't want to go to jail.

It took a while for things to calm down after the shakedown. Some people mumbled about how DaQuan hadn't spread any warning. Apparently, he usually got information about shakedowns and warned inmates to stash their phones and other contraband.

Hours later, inmates organized and rearranged their items back into their cubicles. And things slowly returned to normal.

As I strolled around a few areas, I watched as they fixed their beds, picture frames, and other personal things that survived the shakedown.

When I stumbled across DaQuan, he had just wrapped up a meeting with some of his workers. I stepped back a few feet to give him privacy.

But while I stepped off, someone else had the nerve to bump me as she passed and made her way toward the group of inmates. It was Dunbar. I watched as she got close to them. I was too far away to hear what she said. But the expression on DaQuan's face said quite a bit.

The excitement I felt at the sight of her being mad at him made me smile on the inside.

Dunbar gestured, one hand on her hip, weight shifted to one side, and her neck twisted. I wanted to laugh. She was so extra, her foolish antics were pure entertainment.

DaQuan nodded a few times, but he didn't make eye contact with her much. It felt good to see her get all worked up. After I watched from a distance for a while, I strolled in their direction just to fuck with her.

Her back was to me as I approached, so by the time I spoke, she couldn't do anything but stare at me with a look of bewilderment on her face.

"DaQuan, you need something?"

I sweetened my voice as much as I could; I knew it would burn Dunbar up.

She whirled around so fast, I thought her head might roll right off her neck. She huffed.

"We are having a private conversation," she snarled.

My eyes locked onto DaQuan's. When he smiled at me, I pretended like Dunbar wasn't even there.

"Aey, you find out anything else about what we talked about?" he asked.

I knew for sure she didn't miss the way his tone dipped and softened when he spoke to me and all but ignored her.

"No, not yet, but I'm still working on it," I said.

Dunbar whipped her head back to DaQuan.

"What you got her doing for you?" Dunbar asked. Her voice was whiny and completely out of place.

DaQuan ignored her again.

"Lemme know when you got that; okay, ma."

Dunbar turned to me and proceeded to stare me down. I wanted her to know that she didn't scare me one bit. I stared right back and all but dared her to make a move.

"I sure will," I said. Honey all but dripped from each word.

"Jones!" Scott interrupted. "Girl, I've been searching all over for you." She stopped and looked between Dunbar and me.

"Hey, inmate, what's up?" Scott finally said.

That was when I pulled my gaze away from Dunbar. In that moment, I knew the beef between us wasn't about to be squashed anytime soon.

CHAPTER TWENTY-ONE
KENYA TAYE

Sleep was the last thing on my mind when it should've been the first. It was 2:30 in the morning and all I could do was think about the way DaQuan allowed that trick Jones to dis me. I couldn't sleep for thinking about ways I could get her ass caught up. I wanted her gone and I meant, laid up on her deathbed somewhere. Her being fired wasn't good enough for me.

Two thoughts stayed on my mind: if it wasn't about the fact that DaQuan and I hadn't been back in the closet, it was ways that I could kill Jones.

I knew for sure he was getting ass elsewhere because he hadn't gotten any from me in way too long. And DaQuan only loved money more than he loved sex.

I wanted to hate him so badly, but it was hard. As if I needed something else to worry about, I remembered the last confrontation I'd had with him.

"So, you screwing her too now, DaQuan?"

The face he'd made was all the answer I needed.

I had sucked my teeth.

"What the hell is up with you? You gotta screw everything that moves in here? I mean, damn. Your baby mama is pregnant again; I'm knocked up. What you trying to do? Leave your mark on us all?"

"Aey, this ain't the time or place for this, ma."

He'd spoke so calmly, like none of my issues concerned him. It drove me bananas. He refused to be bothered by me or anything I said.

"DaQuan, if you think I'm about to sit here and let you keep making a fool outta me, you got another *think* coming. I ain't for the bullshit."

"Look, ya knew this job was dirty when ya signed up. Why ya trippin' now?"

He had made a face.

My eyes had got wide. No he didn't!

"What?"

"Aey, I ain't stutter. It's not like ya didn't know I had kids by ol' girl. Ya didn't care then, so why ya tryna trip now? Let's jus make this paper."

I had put my hands on my hips and struggled not to go upside his friggin' head. Did he think he could just play me like that? Didn't he realize I held the key to the success of business? One move from me and his entire empire could unravel like it never even existed.

Before I could say anything else, I'd heard the trick's voice.

Jones needed her ass whipped. There was no doubt about it. She wouldn't be happy until I got in that ass. This was the second time she had walked up on me and my man, like she had been invited.

She only did that shit because he never checked her about it. That was the kind of stuff I tried to talk to him about. If he allowed her to blatantly disrespect me, how would I be able to run the business the way I needed to?

The smell of bacon pulled me out of a deep sleep. I couldn't remember when I had finally fallen off to sleep, but I knew I was up too early for a Saturday morning.

Weekends off were rare, and it felt good to know I didn't have to go in and deal with DaQuan or Jones. My brain needed the time away, especially if I was going to come up with a way to make her ass pay.

My bedroom door flew open and my kids came bursting into the room. I may not have been ready, but they didn't care.

"Mama, Grands made breakfast!"

"Yeah. She said get up and come eat!" my eight-year-old son said.

The food smelled really good. By the time I had cleaned up, changed clothes, and made my way to the kitchen, my mom and the kids were almost done eating.

"Took you long enough," my mom said.

"Good morning to you, too."

The kids giggled.

"I need some money. You got any cash?" my mom asked.

"Yeah. How much?"

"Well, I need to buy some clothes for these kids. They outgrowing everything, and summer's right around the corner. And the vacuum cleaner is broke again. I think about three hundred dollars will do."

As I ate and drank orange juice, I struggled to keep my mind off DaQuan. "I'll get the money for you in a little bit."

My mother got up from the table and started to clean up.

When I finished, I put my plate on the counter and walked back to my bedroom. I closed the door, then went into my secret stash. I counted out twenty twenty-dollar bills. I didn't mind giving my moms a little extra because she took good care of the kids and the house.

Because she handled everything from getting the kids back and forth to school, and afterschool care, to cooking and cleaning, I was able to focus on bringing money into the house.

Since my world seemed to revolve around DaQuan and the business, I was happy to have her help. As I walked out of the room, she passed on the way to hers.

"Here, Mom." I extended the cash to her.

She looked down, and took the money from my hand. "Thanks. You want me to take the kids shopping with me so you can have some time alone?"

"Oooh. That would be really good."

Money well-spent.

I turned and went back into my bedroom.

By noon, I had been home alone for nearly three hours and I liked it. So much of my time was still spent on Jones and DaQuan, but it felt good to be alone.

When the phone rang, I didn't need to see caller ID to know it would be him. DaQuan had his own cell phone, so he called from jail whenever he wanted. Most of our nightly calls, however, were made from the jail phones.

"Aey, you hear what happened to Hernandez?"

My heart sank because he didn't even say hello. Lately when we talked, he'd jump right into business mode. Then he'd rush me off the phone like there was nothing else to discuss between us.

"DaQuan, I didn't, but there's something else I wanna talk to you about."

"Whassup?"

"Since it's obvious you wanna be with Jones, we really need to talk about this baby and what's gonna happen between us."

Silence.

"You obviously don't wanna be with me anymore, so I think we should talk about how things are gonna be different going forward."

"Man! What happened to ya?" His question confused me. "Ya used to be so cool and shit. Now all ya do is nag about this and that. If I want someone nagging me all the damn time, I woulda stayed married."

Married? I never knew he was married.

"If you kept your dick in your pants, I wouldn't have changed.

You're right. I did know the job was dirty, but I didn't think you'd be so quick to screw anything that came your way. Look at Jones. What do you see in her? I just know I can't go on like this."

"I feel ya, ma."

I was floored. That was his response? That was all he had to say?

"But peep this. I know ya like driving around in that Beamer, and I bet ya like yo bills being paid, and I know fo sho, ya like your bank account being fat, right?"

Had he just threatened me?

"Do what'chu gotta do, but dig this. If I ain't kicking it with ya, then, I ain't takin' care of ya or ya kids. I gotta respect what ya say ya can't do. Real talk; ain't got no choice but to respect that."

As he talked, I felt the life slip from my body. I couldn't understand how it was so easy for him to erase me from his life. We'd been together for more than two years. Then some nasty-looking, fat chick, with a tired-ass weave came along and he threw "us" away.

Despite what I'd said, I couldn't lose DaQuan. He was right. My life didn't start until we started kicking it. He was the reason I lived comfortably, drove a luxury car, and always kept money.

I had no choice. I had to do what I had to do because there was no way I'd take cabs everywhere and move back to the projects.

CHAPTER TWENTY-TWO
CHARISMA

"Something ain't right is all I'm saying."

Corey fixed his stare on me, like that was supposed to make me tell him all my business. I wanted to tell him those days were long gone. He no longer had any kind of power over me.

I rolled my eyes as my worthless baby daddy stood in my kitchen and told me he thought we were in the struggle together.

Since I was done with the struggle, I wanted to be done with him. But the challenge to rid my life of him would be more difficult than I could handle.

"When you going to see your kids?" I asked.

Usually asking him to help, feed, or provide any type of support for the kids he helped make was enough for him to scatter away like a roach hit by a bright light.

"So you not gonna tell a brotha what's what?"

Corey ignored my question, asked one of his own, then leaned against the kitchen sink, which meant he planned to stay a while.

"Corey, I told you. I work lots of overtime on the job. It's just that simple. I work hard and I'm able to buy a few nice things. I don't get why you tripping."

My hustle was what supported his kids, because he sure didn't. I sent money every two weeks, better than clockwork.

Corey studied my face and I struggled to look as normal as possible. Business was beyond good. After the last shakedown, the inmates seemed hungrier for pills than before. Many lost valuables and either couldn't buy them back right away or they just wanted to get high to forget about it all. Either way, the pills flew like free money in the hood.

As Corey talked, I eyed the clock on the microwave. I needed him gone because Lance was coming over to talk about expanding the business, and I didn't want Corey anywhere near the mix.

In order to try and keep the suspicion down with him, I didn't bother him about any money and I only asked about the kids because he used that lie to get into my house in the first place. He'd say his cell couldn't make long distance calls and there was no landline where he was staying.

"I'ma let you know when I'm ready to go see the kids. That ain't what we talking about right now."

His eyes shifted all over my body. I knew he wanted to find anything that might give him a clue about what was going on and where my money was coming from, but my lips would remain zipped.

"Okay, Corey. It's no biggie, but I got an appointment I need to keep, so that's why I was asking."

"So now you got *appointments* and shit?"

Nobody but a loser like Corey would find issues with someone because they had appointments.

I wondered what I had seen in his ass in the first place. Everything that had gone wrong in my life was closely connected to Corey McCray. I trusted him, believed we'd one day be married and trying to carve out a life for our kids, but that didn't happen.

"What you say you do over there at that prison again?"

This time, his features were intense, with a frown.

"I didn't, Corey. Listen, I really need to get ready to go."

I tried to appeal to him as gingerly as I could. Any sudden demands, insults or harsh words would take us into a verbal battle that was bound to drag on for hours. I didn't have that kind of time to waste on him.

"I don't like all this top secret shit about you now, Charisma. Something is going on and I ain't gonna be able to protect you once you get yourself caught up."

It was a serious struggle to hold in the laughter as I told myself I'd be better off if I turned to my man behind bars for protection rather than Corey's useless ass. But I couldn't say that to him. It would've opened up a discussion that I'd regret for sure.

"Corey. I need to get ready to go."

He eyed me like he might've missed something in the few hours he'd already spent checking me out.

"Where you say you going again?" His eyebrows bunched together like they were being pulled by a string.

This time, I moved behind him and tried to ease him toward the front door as he tried to figure out what was up with me. I got a little excited when he finally moved. But he only took a few steps, then did a quick maneuver and circled right back to where he was before. As he leaned back up against the counter, I was tempted to walk out and leave him standing there, but I knew that wouldn't work.

The more I wanted him to leave, the more he was intent on staying.

Nearly an hour after I needed him gone, Corey was still at my place. He struggled to dig up trouble.

"Who you fucking these days?"

I closed my eyes and shook my head. A feeling of dread overtook me. We had been on-and-off again over the years, but I'd meant it recently when I'd told him it was over.

"Lemme find out some other dude is doin' all this for you."

I exhaled through my nose and tried not to be as mad. I paused, looked away, then back at him.

"Corey, we not together anymore. Why are you standing here tripping for no reason?"

He got up in my face and started huffing.

"So you tryna tell me you seeing some other dude? Is that what this is all about? Is he on his way over here? Why you hell-bent on tryna make me bounce?"

Corey's breath smelled like warm shit. He was tacky. My stomach churned when I thought back to how much I had once loved him and how I had thrown my entire life away because I chased behind him.

The knock at the door pulled our attention away from all the heat in the kitchen. I had never seen him move as fast as he did when he tried to beat me to the door.

Suddenly, it dawned on me. Why even bother? I let him rush to the door. He yanked it open and stood there.

"Ah. Yo, Lance, man. Whassup? What'chu doin here?" Corey finally retreated a bit. He and Lance didn't get along.

Lance looked past Corey and straight at me.

"Whassup, Cuz? Everything all right in here?" Before I answered, Lance boldly eyed Corey up and down.

"Yeah. Corey was just leaving."

Corey looked at me, then turned back to Lance. "Charisma, I'ma holla at you later about the kids." Corey eyed Lance again, then gnawed at the corner of his lip. "That's what's up, Lance." He nodded, then walked through the open front door.

"Don't tell me you back with that cat," Lance said.

"Nah, it's nothing like that. But he is my kids' father, remember?"

"Who could forget that damn loser!"

Lance closed the door and we moved into the kitchen.

"Oh, wait. I got something for you."

I left and rushed to my bedroom to grab the envelope that held Lance's cash. Back at the table with Lance, he took the envelope and put it in his pocket. He leaned over the table, with bright eyes, a huge smile, and said, "Viagra and Valium."

"Viagra? In a prison?"

"What, Cuz? Don't front like y'all don't be getting it on with them horny-ass inmates. I know you read that damn blog. What's that shit called?" He snapped his fingers a few times.

I sat stunned. "What blog?"

"Some dude writes it from behind bars!"

I frowned and waited for him to jog his memory. I knew nothing about any inmate who wrote a blog. He had to be mistaken. Wouldn't we all know about an inmate who wrote a blog? And wasn't that illegal?

"Damn, what's dude's blog called again?" Lance's bony fingers were still snapping.

"*From the Inside!*" Lance yelled.

"What?"

"That's the name of dude's blog, *From the Inside*."

"Oh, okay. Well, I don't know about that, but I can tell you now, I ain't trying to sneak no damn Viagra into the prison where I work. If they can't get it up or keep it up, they probably just need to wait until they get out to get that looked at. I'll talk to my boss about the Valium, and let you know for sure."

"Okay, cool. But you should ask him about the Viagra too, 'cause I can get that. Here, you wanna check out what I brought?"

"No. All I want to know is how many," I said as I took the sandwich bag from him that continued several smaller plastic bags.

"Three hundred this time."

"Okay, cool." I got up from the chair and he did too.

Lance patted his pocket as he walked toward the front door. I stood in the doorway as he left, and he turned back to me. "Don't sleep on *From the Inside*. Dude be talking about all the drama behind bars."

I laughed at the thought and was about to close my door when Corey jumped from the bushes. Damn! I thought he was gone!

CHAPTER TWENTY-THREE
KENYA TAYE

I didn't need their help to pull the plan off, but it would be easier if I had it. That's what I thought about as I went over the details and tried to explain it to my girls. I didn't tell them everything, just the information I thought they needed to know.

Their eyes were glued to me, but their expressions registered confusion. I wasn't sure why my brilliant plan didn't seem so brilliant to them.

"So, I already pretty much know how she moves around. She smuggles in like two to three times a week. It would be simple, really. Besides, y'all know Richards is still on a rampage so he'd gladly take any tip he gets and run with it."

For a long while, we sat there. I stared at them and they stared between me and each other.

It wasn't like I expected a standing ovation or anything like that, but the way they sat there and stared at me blankly as if I'd just finished speaking Spanish left me a little bothered.

What the heck was the problem?

After a few more minutes when neither one had said anything, I made a move to jumpstart the conversation.

"Soooo, y'all ain't got nothing to say? No opinion, or comment about what I just told y'all?"

Bishop and Edwards exchanged awkward glances. Neither had any questions when I'd unveiled my plan, but I expected them to say something. I couldn't even read their reactions.

"Well, I dunno how to put it," Edwards began.

"Just say it!" I was eager to hear what they thought.

"Here's what I don't get." She leaned in, but her voice was still loud. "So, you plan to try and get her busted. I totally get that part. But what I don't get is, do you really think she's gonna go down alone and not rat out the rest of us?"

Bishop leaned back in the chair and Edwards did too. They looked at me like I had lost my mind. In a way, I felt like I had, but it was clear they didn't really understand that.

I couldn't sleep, could barely eat, and most of my thoughts were taken up by DaQuan and Jones. I needed to do something drastic and I needed to do it quickly.

"Dunbar, she ain't gonna take this fall alone," Edwards said.

"I'm with her on this one," Bishop said. "I know you don't like ol' girl, but what's tripping me out is, you trying to tell us you willing to risk it *all* just because she's messing with your man?"

The only thing missing from Bishop's audacious statement was the shake of her head as if I was so pathetic she couldn't fathom my thinking.

Edwards tried to give her the side-eye, but Bishop wouldn't look in her direction.

"Seriously, Dunbar, why you mad at her anyway, when you should be mad at him? Females trip me out when they do that," Edwards snapped back.

Her question made sense. But she didn't need to know that I was mad at him too. The problem was DaQuan was already behind bars, so what more could I do to hurt or punish him?

"Why don't you try talking to her? I don't see why we all gotta be dragged into this if the beef is between the two of you," Edwards said.

"Sshh!" I looked around the break room area.

The space was small; it was for the C.O.s and staff only. But we never knew who was nearby and we certainly didn't know if someone was right outside the door.

When Bishop spoke this time, her voice was lower. But she still said the same kind of stuff.

"It's not like she messes with anybody else. I mean, I don't care for her because she walks around here like she's the Queen or something, but other than that, she ain't never done nothing to me."

"But what about what she's done to me?" I asked.

For so long, I thought the three of us were a team. I thought if someone messed with one, it was like they'd mess with us all.

Edwards leaned in again.

"I feel like you really need to think this one through some more. I get that you don't like her, but it don't make sense to blow our entire operation over some locked-up dick, is all I'm saying."

Those words stabbed me like a thousand sharp knives. I thought Bishop and Edwards were my girls. There was no way in hell I would've come to them if I thought for a minute that they'd act the way they acted. It was clear. I was alone.

"What are you gonna do, go around and fight every female DaQuan fucks?" Bishop asked.

Her matter-of-fact tone really rubbed me wrong.

The look I tossed her way could've killed. She had gone too far. My blood boiled because they acted like the disrespect Jones showed me was no big deal.

I didn't say anything, but I wondered if she would've felt the same way if Jones had pushed up on R.J. instead of DaQuan.

For a little while, we sat and no one said anything else. I felt uneasy now that they told me how they really felt, but I didn't want them to know that.

"You know what, y'all are right. I'm tripping. I need to just chill and keep making this money. It's enough to go around, and even more to be made since the last shakedown. Sometimes, I let my emotions get all worked up and it drives me crazy."

"Yeah, that's that baby messing with your hormones. You know how it is when you pregnant," Edwards said.

"Yeah, what they call it, pregnancy brain?" Bishop added.

We all giggled a little at the thought that DaQuan's seed had suddenly made me absentminded.

But while we laughed, I couldn't help but contemplate which one of them I would have to sacrifice in order to get rid of Jones.

CHAPTER TWENTY-FOUR
CHARISMA

Everything about Lena had always been pretty. That had been drilled into my head from the time I was able to understand. When we were kids, people never passed up the chance to point out how pretty she was.

Oftentimes, they'd overlook me, and shower her with compliments about her beauty.

But even the prettiest girls had ugly ways. Nothing brought ugly out of my cousin more than when she felt jealous of me. And there were quite a few of those occasions.

The look on her face as we stood outside of my apartment and I showed her how the convertible top on my new BMW glided up and down with ease, was one of the ugliest I had ever seen.

Her arms were crossed at her chest and she had sucked her teeth as if a piece of chicken was lodged deep in them.

"I don't understand."

Even her tone was sour, to match the expression on her face.

"It's really simple, Lena. All I have to do is press this button and it—"

"I'm not talking about the stupid car!" She cut me off. "I'm talking about this new man of yours. How come he's such a secret? Where did you all meet and how come I can't meet him?"

I sighed and looked at her.

"Lena, why can't you just be happy for me for a change? I mean, really."

She eyed the car like she was mad at me and *it*. Her lips were pursed to the side, and she pushed air out through her nostrils. I knew it was hard for her, but I obviously didn't realize just how hard it had been.

"What if this guy is a drug dealer or something like that?"

She scrunched up her pretty little nose when she said that.

I wanted to tell her that *I* was the drug dealer, and not my man, but I knew that would crack her pretty little face even more and I didn't want to kill the poor girl.

"He's not. He's just real private. And like he said, if we start letting people get all in our business, that's when the drama creeps in."

Lena rolled her eyes at me. She moved closer to the car.

When my cell phone rang, I had to get it, because it was about business.

"Hey, Lance; what's up, Cuz?"

Lena was completely lost in the car. She fiddled with some of the features on the dashboard, and ran her fingers across the upholstery. I stepped off to the side so I could talk to her brother for a few minutes.

"Yes, I got your money, and no, like I told you, we're gonna pass on those."

"Y'all don't even want the Valium?"

"Yeah, we want those, but not the others."

"Okay, that's straight. Hey, did you ever check out that blog I told you about?"

"It's on my list of things to do; just haven't had the chance yet."

"Okay, well, I'll roll through later tonight, and I'll bring another shipment."

Once I ended the call with Lance, I moved back to Lena. By now, she had reclined in my leather bucket seats, and she looked comfortable.

"This car has everything!"

Her voice had lost some of the sour tone from earlier and she didn't act like she was mad at the car anymore.

"Yeah. I really like it."

As she got out of the car, she turned to me. "Oh, what is Lance calling you about? He's such a loser."

I rolled my eyes at her comment about Lance.

"You do know he's my cousin too, right?"

She snickered. "Well, first it's this new secret, billionaire boyfriend; now you're chatting up with my loser of a brother. It's like I don't even know you anymore, Charisma Jones!"

We laughed at that.

Lena was so off that she had no issues with the fact that she had all but alienated herself from the entire family. I wonder how that worked out for them. Lena always received the best of the best of everything before me, or even Lance. And once we were all grown, she barely talked to her own mother, despised her brother, and usually only spoke to me if I spoke first.

Later, back inside my apartment, I felt like Lena had channeled some Corey-type hate as she gazed around the place.

"Nice new furniture too. Something is definitely going on with you." She looked at me. "Did you hit the lotto?"

"No, silly. Do you want something to drink or are you gonna keep trying to get all up in my business?"

Lena sat down on the sofa and glided her hands over the supple leather. "Yup, this is definitely top of the line."

When the phone rang again and it was DaQuan, I nearly panicked. Then I realized she had no idea he was calling from prison. I grinned as I answered the phone.

"Hey, baby, I was just talking about you."

Lena's head whipped in my direction. Her eyes grew wide, and she frowned at the same time.

"Hey, ma. What's good?" DaQuan asked.

"Nothing much. I was just showing my cousin the new car you bought me."

"Oh, so ya boy Lance is there?"

"No. It's my girl cousin, Lance's sister," I said. "Remember I told you I was spending some family time today?"

"Oh, yeah; okay, bet that. Well, look, I need to talk to ya about something, but it can wait. How long is yo cousin gonna be there?"

"I'm not sure, but I can go in the other room if you want."

I knew for sure Lena's ears were all perked up as they strained to listen to my conversation. I was certain she wished she had bionic powers to hear DaQuan too.

"Nah, it's not urgent. I'll call back in a few hours. Say, why don't ya take her shopping and buy her a new bag or something; get one for ya'self too. I ain't mean to interrupt."

It was more than over the top, but I didn't care. I squealed so loud and screamed, "Thanks, babe! Wait till I tell her."

Lena's eyes were the size of saucers. By the time I ended the call, she was damn near in my lap.

"What? What happened? Was that your secret boyfriend? What did he say? What's the matter? What's wrong?"

The urgency of her voice and movement told me she was anxious for something to go wrong. I saw the desperation in her eyes.

"Girl, is everything okay?"

Worry lines made their way to her forehead.

"Oh, yeah, he told me to take you to the mall and buy us both a new designer bag. He felt bad because he forgot I told him we were hanging today."

"OHMYGOD!!" Lena's mouth dropped and her eyes stretched wide. She began to tremble.

I thought she was going to hyperventilate right where she stood.

"H-h-he said buy *me* a bag? Like what? Michael Kors or something?" Her petite hands trembled as they covered her mouth. Her entire body shook too.

"Michael Kors? Girl, please, that's not how he rolls. We 'bout to go hit up Gucci!"

My cousin shivered so badly I had to guide her back to her seat. Her limbs shook uncontrollably.

"Lena! Lena! Girl, you okay? You want some water or something?"

Unable to speak, she nodded.

I rushed, grabbed a glass and poured her some ice-cold water. She quickly gulped it down and exhaled.

"Okay, so are you trying to tell me that your new, top-secret man called and told *you* that because he interrupted our family time, you should go to the mall and buy yourself a fucking Gucci bag?"

"No," I said calmly, and shook my head.

"Girl, I was about to say. Don't play like that."

She placed a delicate hand over her chest, I guessed to calm her heart, and that was when I gave it to her.

"No, I said, my new, top-secret man just called and because he interrupted our family time, he told me to take *you* to the mall and buy us *both* fucking Gucci bags!"

She bolted from the chair, screamed, and danced around. I watched as she flung her arms and kicked her legs like she had caught a bad case of the Holy Ghost.

Even with all of her over-the-top antics, for the first time in our lives, I finally felt prettier than my pretty cousin Lena.

CHAPTER TWENTY-FIVE
KENYA TAYE

The other day when I drove past the apartments, I kept going because I knew there was nothing there for me to see. But on my way to work, I decided to take the scenic route, and boy was I glad I did.

My timing was perfect because not only did I see the trick and another chick standing outside, but the two of them were hovering over a new BMW.

I nearly pulled right over and told that trick what I really thought about her. As I drove on toward work, I wondered how Jones's face would've looked if I had stopped, and told her friend just what she must've done to get that damn car.

There was no way in hell DaQuan would buy her a new car unless she was now his woman. Oh, he took care of his for sure, and I knew that as a fact. The sight of Jones as she showed off her new car pissed me off more than words could say.

"So he's taking care of that bitch too! He bought her a fucking convertible?"

Hot tears burned the corners of my eyes, but I fought and stopped them from falling. I refused to shed a tear over his ass.

I smacked my steering wheel so hard, my palm throbbed. Both those bitches made me sick—*him* for treating her like she was something special, and *her* for screwing with a man she knew was already taken. Forget that I had done the same thing to Clarkson.

Clarkson and I didn't work on the same damn shift. The fact

that we were on the same team should have been an automatic deal-breaker for Jones, but she didn't give a damn; she still fucked DaQuan.

I turned on Highway 90 in Sugar Land, and made a right on Harlem Road. About a block away from the prison, I made a U-turn and drove in the opposite direction. I wasn't in the mood to be bothered with that foolishness today.

Initially, I didn't have a plan for my sudden day off, but a while later, I pulled up in front of my house, grabbed my cell phone and called the job.

"Hey, this is C.O. KenyaTaye Dunbar. I'm sick. I can't come in today."

I blurted out my message, and before the supervisor could say anything, I ended the call. I knew that would put them in a bind; we were always dealing with staff shortages, but I couldn't bring myself to go in there.

What would I say to DaQuan? "Hey, I see you bought her the same damn car you got me, but hers is a drop-top?" Or, "I wonder what she did to get such a nice new car?"

By the time I passed back by Charisma's apartment, the fancy new car was gone. That meant the trick was out joyriding and flossing in a car *my* man bought for *her*. He made me want to throw up.

It didn't take long for my phone to start ringing. The first call I ignored was from the bastard himself. About twenty minutes later, I ignored a call from Edwards. A few minutes after that, I sent Bishop's call to voicemail.

"Get the damn message. I don't feel like talking to anybody right now." I slid the power off and put the phone down.

My mother jumped when I walked back into the house.

"Chile, I thought you was at work."

Everything about my mother was plain. She had few friends,

and she lived to take care of me and my kids. I appreciated having her help, but I wondered if I was destined to turn into her one day.

"Mom, how come you don't have a man?"

Her eyebrows twisted as she looked at me.

"Who said I don't have one?"

I laughed.

"Mary Dunbar. Puhleease! I am your only child. I think I know everything there is to know about you. If you had a man, trust, I would know that too."

"Maybe I'm just a real private person who don't want to put people all up in my business."

She struggled to get that out with a straight face. I rolled my eyes at that answer.

I unbuttoned my uniform shirt, removed my belt, and stepped out of the boots. I was not about to think about those damn people or that damn job for the rest of the day.

"Why don't you go change? It's obvious you ain't goin' in today."

My mother was right.

"I'll fix us some lunch," she said.

"Nah. Let's go out. Let me change and we can go drop the kids at camp and spend the day out, having lunch, and shopping."

"You don't have to tell me again," she said. She took off the half apron, tossed it to the counter top, and darted to her room.

Why not spend some of DaQuan's money? Since he was so damn generous, I figured I'd like to have him treat my mother and me to a nice day of shopping and maybe even a spa trip.

We changed, got the kids together and dropped them off at the expensive aftercare program I had enrolled them in. They loved it and so did I.

Once we were back in the car, I asked my mother why things never worked out with her and my father.

"KenyaTaye, I've told you that story a million times."

She made a dismissive motion with her hand.

"No, you told me he wasn't ready for another kid. You said he married someone else, but he didn't tell you at first. And of course they all blame us for the breakup, but I never understood why things didn't work out in the beginning with the two of you."

"He was married when I met him. We were only together that one time."

"What?"

I nearly drove off the road. I knew the story of their relationship, but I thought he had chosen another woman over my mother. I thought he'd chosen the woman who had his kids first over her. I had no clue my mother had screwed a man who was unavailable.

"Sometimes men don't know what they want. He was in town on business. We met and hit it off. I had never done anything like that before. He was so nice, said all the right things, and next thing you know, I woke up in an empty hotel bed."

My heart broke as I listened to the story. She told it, like it was nothing. And even though it was nearly thirty years ago, I could tell she might have wanted to give that impression, but it wasn't true.

"So he was gone when you got up?"

"Yeah. He left. I figured he had an early flight. So, I told myself I could check a one-night-stand off my list, and I did. Well, six weeks later, I walked in to clean a room that had been trashed. The smell of vomit was in the air and it made me throw up all over the place."

"That was me, huh?"

"Yes, ma'am. It sure was."

We stopped at a light. I thought about some of the things my mother told me. I didn't know I was the product of a one-night stand, and I damn sure didn't know my father was married at the time. Could that have contributed to me being okay with unavailable men?

"How did he find out about me?"

At first, my mother didn't answer. She gazed out of the window until the awkward silence made me think she might not have heard the question.

"Well…" She sighed hard. "I went to his house about four months after you were born. I was tired of living in that little podunk town, and thought Houston would be a good place to start over."

She said that with a completely straight face.

"Wait. You did what?"

I was stunned.

"I didn't stutter."

Visions of my meeting with DaQuan's baby mama popped through my mind. I shook the thoughts from my head. I was not about to beat myself up over him anymore. What was done couldn't be changed.

As my mother told me the full sad story, I felt even more like I was destined to end up alone.

When we finally pulled up to Pappadeaux, I was relieved. The story depressed me even more and I needed alcohol.

The restaurant wasn't crowded, so we were seated quickly. As we looked over the menus, I thought about the similarities between my mother's life and mine.

I pulled the menu down.

"How come you never said anything about me being involved with DaQuan?"

She eased her menu onto the table and made eye contact.

"How could I? Look at what I did. Besides, KenyaTaye, that man may be down now, but from what I could see over the years, he's taken better care of you from behind bars than any other man you've ever been with who is free."

I hated when people told me that. It felt like they were saying I should lay down and take whatever he dished just because he spent money on me.

But what many of them didn't understand was that I helped DaQuan make that money, so it was just as much mine as it was his. And as far as I was concerned, if he thought he could spend our hard-earned money on all of his other women, I needed to stop the cash flow and teach his ass a lesson.

CHAPTER TWENTY-SIX
CHARISMA

Days after I took Lena to the mall and bought our new designer bags, she had been calling nonstop. She usually only called like that when she needed something from me.

"Charisma, my friends at work can't stop talking about our new bags. Tell your secret new boyfriend thanks for me."

She sent her *thanks* all day after we had left the mall, later that night, and the next day. She insisted she needed to meet my secret new boyfriend because no one had ever been so generous and especially not someone she'd never met.

She pointed out that men always showered her with gifts, and that she was accustomed to the finer things that men gave her, but it was the fact that my man had never even laid eyes on her and yet he had been so generous.

I didn't mind the gratitude because for years, she could hardly find anything nice to say to me, but the constant calls pinched my last nerve. I knew my cousin, and I knew she wasn't *that grateful. I also knew she was up to something.*

"Charisma, you never told me your secret new boyfriend's name."

"Charisma, does your secret new boyfriend have any friends?"

"Charisma how did you meet your secret new boyfriend?"

"Charisma, where does your secret new boyfriend hang out?"

A part of me wished I'd never said anything about him in the first place. I was in the break room when C.O. Scott walked in.

"Hey, Tiny, what's up?"

"Nothing much; filling in for somebody who called in sick."

"Hey, lemme ask you something." She turned away from the sink and looked at me. "Do you know anything about some blog *From the Inside*?"

"Yeah, we try not to give it too much attention. I mean, it's hard enough watching these guys while we in here. If they're gonna start making us watch them in cyberspace too, somebody's gonna have to give me a raise."

We laughed at her comment and I thought about being paid to police inmates on the Internet.

"I feel you there, but who does the blog and have you ever seen it?"

C.O. Scott looked surprised.

"Of course! We all have. Actually, I try to check it out every few months or so. It's this inmate Nelson Barnes, older dude. He mostly writes about his case and how he's innocent. But I think once a month or so, he'll feature an inmate and put a call out for pen pals to connect on Facebook."

My eyes grew. This was all news to me. Inmates were able to connect to people using social media?

"I don't know why you're so surprised; computers are everywhere these days. You should check out his blog. It's nothing to get all hyped about, but some people read it all the time." The radio buzzed and Tiny picked up the call.

"Hey, I'll catch you later; stay alert!" she said before she dashed out the door.

After she left, I thought about women who would hook up with an inmate on social media. Just when I considered how crazy they might be to do that, I remembered I wasn't too far removed. Alone with my thoughts, I went back to how far I had come after I was crazy enough to follow Corey to Baylor University.

He was a football star in high school and we were sweethearts whose story was supposed to end with a happily-ever-after. My good grades allowed me to go to any school I wanted on full academic scholarship, and I chose Baylor, because that was where Corey got a football scholarship.

It was going to be perfect. He'd be the star quarterback and I was going to be a head-nurse. We arrived on Baylor's campus and I loved it there.

At first, things were close to perfect. I was away from Lena; he was away from his family; and we were together. My mother didn't raise me, but later we connected. Corey's home life was just as unstable as mine. For us, being away was probably best for us at that time.

Trouble came when I got pregnant. I was sick with nervousness because nothing in our plans included a baby. And the campus was so religious; I was scared we'd get kicked out for breaking the unwritten policy about sex without being married.

"What should we do?"

"What do you mean?" Corey asked.

"About the baby."

"Charisma. We not kids anymore. If we having a baby, we having a baby. Lots of people have babies in college."

I was so happy he would stand by me. Of course I had seen and heard stories that ended differently for other girls.

"We should get married," I told Corey. "So that when the baby comes, we'll already be man and wife." My eyes were wide with excitement about our future, until his next words.

"We too young for marriage."

Corey didn't even hesitate before he said it, and he didn't seem to notice how he had hurt my feelings.

That was the beginning of the heartbreak. Corey thought we were too young for marriage, but not too young to have a baby.

Three months into the pregnancy, Corey lost the starting spot on the football team. I wasn't showing too much just yet.

Even though I was pregnant and overly emotional, he was downright depressed. Soon, I had to deal with my emotions and his too. He stopped going to classes in summer and nearly flunked out.

By the time our sophomore year came around, Corey was on academic probation and suspended from the team. I had no choice but to do his school work and mine. I thought we'd be free as long as we both got a good education.

We had a new apartment off campus and a new baby. I was happy about the baby, but so tired from doing Corey's schoolwork and mine, my own grades started to suffer.

I was anxious about another football season rolling around because Corey's status on the team never improved. He stopped working out with the team and started gaining weight.

By then, I had dropped out of school too. I was taking care of Corey and the baby. One day I left him at home with our son so I could go to a job interview. Hours later, I got back to our apartment and found an ambulance, a fire truck, and news reporters.

Our baby had died in his sleep.

Corey was so high, he couldn't tell me anything about what had happened. More heartbreak was right around the corner for us, and I should have seen some of the mess coming our way, but I was too much in love to see or even think clearly.

"Charisma!"

The sound of Tiny's voice brought me back from the past.

"You in here daydreaming? I said something to you a few times and you ain't even answer!"

"My bad, girl; sorry, I was thinking about something."

I got up from the chair. "What's up? Somebody looking for me?"

"No, nothing like that." She looked toward the doorway. Tiny lowered her voice. "You hear about C.O. Sanchez?"

"Nooo!" I whispered and rushed to the doorway. I stuck my head out and glanced up, then down the hall. When the coast was clear, I looked at Tiny and asked, "What happened?"

"He got busted." Tiny mouthed, "Con-tra-band!" Her eyes nearly popped from their sockets. If she was stunned by that, I could only imagine how she'd react if she knew I dealt in contraband too.

I swallowed nervously. My stomach felt like it was being twisted in a vise, and my body stiffened. Hours earlier, I had brought in another shipment of pills, so the news that someone got caught petrified me.

The heat that crawled up my back felt like it was gonna take me out. A worrying thought entered my head. What would that do to business?

I needed to talk to DaQuan or even R.J. I wasn't sure how much Tiny knew about the business, but I did know she wasn't part of the team, so I didn't say much to her. But I wanted more details about Sanchez.

I mulled it over for a few seconds, and then asked anxiously, "How you know for sure?"

Tiny shifted her gaze from the door, then back to me.

"It's all everybody is talking about."

That explained why I was clueless. I didn't talk to, or socialize with any of those heifers. Dunbar, Edwards, and Bishop were nothing but trouble waiting to happen, so I did my best to avoid them. Besides, Dunbar ran those two, and since she didn't like me, that meant the other two stayed away from me.

The only time I communicated with Dunbar was when I needed to make a drop or get my money, and even those times were too much for me. Since she was the sergeant on our shift, it was hard to move around like that, but that was what worked best for me.

"So, what happened? How'd he get caught?"

Tiny's eyes were still touched with alarm as she told me what she had learned.

"From what I heard, his backpack was left near the front gate and Richards walked up on it. Come to find out when Richards and a guard opened it, they found two switchblades, a smartphone, two electric razors, a lighter, a set of portable radios, two cartons of cigarettes, and two packs of cigars."

"Wait. What?" I pulled in a deep breath and prayed for restraint. "How the hell was that him getting busted?" I thought she meant he was caught as he walked into the building or something.

"Girl, the backpack had his wallet in it too," Tiny said.

That was it?

I shook my head. "Oh hell, no! I'd fight that."

Tiny looked at me like I had suddenly developed a third eyeball.

Little did I know then, a real fight of my own was in my near future.

CHAPTER TWENTY-SEVEN
KENYA TAYE

"I only wanted you to have better and more than I had. It's why I started with your name. I'm Mary. That's plain and boring. I knew what my life would be like, but with you, I had a chance to do it all different and better. I started with your unique name."

After talking to my mom, I started to think back to my failed relationships. She may have wanted more and better for me, but the fact that I didn't want more for myself led me to DaQuan. How was it possible that I had made the same kind of mistakes with men that she had made with my father?

The thought messed me up in the head. Being attracted to unavailable men had somehow become hereditary in our family. My sick day turned into three. That was the most I could take before I'd have to get a doctor's note.

During those three days, I didn't take a single call from anybody associated with Jester. DaQuan called like crazy, and so did Edwards and Bishop. But I never answered. I wanted to give him a taste of what it would be like without me. When I turned the phone back on, it went crazy with text and voicemail messages.

I only turned the phone on, when I decided to go back to work. There was something different about the place when I walked in. Maybe it was the fact that I had been gone for three days and didn't want to come back.

"Damn Dunbar, you a sight for sore eyes," Franklin's corny butt said.

"Hey," I said as I dragged myself into the guards' booth. It was crowded in there.

Edwards and Bishop greeted me, with wide grins. When that trick Jones turned to look at me, I caught a glimpse of her wrinkled forehead, and the smirk on her face. I wanted to do an about-face, and then leave.

But I wouldn't give her the pleasure. My days off had done nothing to ease the hate I felt toward her.

"Damn, girl! Where you been?" Edwards asked.

She looked genuinely happy to see me. She and Bishop rushed to my side.

"We gotta get you caught up! Why you ain't answer your phone?" Bishop asked. "We *need* to talk." Bishop's lips didn't move when she said that last part, but her eyes shifted toward Jones. I knew exactly what she was trying to say.

"I needed some time to clear my head."

Jones knew better than to say a single word to me. She sat there and tried to act like she was so focused on a report. But I knew she was taking it all in.

Two other C.O.s talked in hushed voices to my right, but I didn't give a damn what had happened while I was away.

"A lot went down while you was sitting poolside sipping fruity cocktails," Franklin interrupted our reunion to say.

The three of us turned to him, and shot daggers with our eyes.

He threw up his hands in mock defense, and took two steps backward. He was always so extra.

"Okay, okay, I get it. We can get to all that later; you hens obviously got other more important gossip to share."

The other two C.O.s left behind Franklin. When we turned, Jones sat there like she hadn't heard a thing because she was so focused on her own little world.

She disgusted me. I walked over, but Edwards jumped up to block my path.

"This ain't the time. You missed a lot; let's go outside for some air," Edwards said.

"Yeah. All of a sudden, it stinks in here," Bishop said.

I took a deep breath and told myself, taking a flashlight to the back of Jones's head wouldn't solve my problems. Edwards wouldn't move.

"She ain't worth it," Edwards repeated.

Her words made sense to me, and I knew she was right. But I had risked everything only to have a fat bitch come in and take it all without even trying. Jones deserved a cracked skull for that, if not something worse.

Bishop moved toward the door.

"Come on; if we leave now, we might be able to take a twenty instead of fifteen."

My eyes were glued to the side of Jones's head. She didn't look a bit bothered by what had unfolded around her.

"Yeah, we really need to talk; something happened while you was sick. That's more important."

Edwards tugged my arm and nudged me away from Jones.

We were almost out the door, when Jones turned and said, "Whenever you ready, just remember ain't nothing but air and opportunity between us, because I already know who's gonna be left standing."

Unable to control myself, I rushed in her direction, only to have Edwards's grip tighten on my arm.

Bishop flew back in and jumped in front of Jones's seat. "Girl, bye!" she barked in Jones's direction. "Let's go, Dunbar; let's go! This bitch don't want none."

All of a sudden, Jones started to laugh. The kind of laugh the villains did in movies. The three of us stopped, and looked at her.

When my stomach couldn't take anymore, I turned and walked out of the guards' booth. Edwards and Bishop followed me and some inmates stared as we passed. We could hear her stupid laughter all the way to the back of the building.

"That bitch is touched," Edwards said.

I opened the door and we walked out into the searing sunlight.

"Yo, Dunbar!"

Temporarily blinded by the brightness, I pulled my arm up to my forehead. It was R.J.

"DaQuan say meet him in the closet."

I froze.

My girls looked at each other, then at me.

"We can do this later," Edwards said.

"Yeah," Bishop added.

"Nah. It's all good." I looked at R.J. who had caught up to us, and said, "Tell him I'm busy right now; maybe later."

I turned and left only to stop a few steps later. Edwards, Bishop, and R.J. all stood and stared at me. Their mouths hung to the ground.

"C'mon! We only got twenty minutes."

Edwards and Bishop left R.J., and we walked out to the edge of the farm. We saw trustees in the distance and a couple of C.O.s on horseback, watching the trustees work. Besides them, we were the only ones out there.

"Sanchez got caught the other day. The contraband he had was confiscated and he was arrested," Edwards said.

"Wwwhat?"

"I kept trying to call you," Bishop whined.

"You should've left me a message or something."

"Really? Saying what? Should I have left a voicemail saying

Sanchez was just busted and now our smuggling business is on the line, please call me back? We don't know who knows what, whether they tapping our lines or what," Edwards said.

I sighed.

"Tapping cell phones?" I asked like it was the most ridiculous thing I'd heard.

Edwards cut her eyes at me. "I ain't trusting shit. All this new technology that keeps popping up; you can't make me believe they can't listen in on our cell phone conversations if they wanted to."

What she said made complete sense.

"So where is he? Sanchez?"

"He was arrested, right there outside the booth in front of everybody. The shit just got real!" Edwards looked spooked.

My mind couldn't take in what she'd said. Images of Richards and police officers as they came to haul me away entered my mind and it suddenly became real for me too.

I risked everything for someone who'd had the balls to drop me when a new piece of ass came along, and the thought made me feel stupid.

My back was to the yard as I listened to Edwards and Bishop tell the story about what had happened to Sanchez. Mid-sentence, Edwards stopped talking.

When I turned to see what had stolen her attention, DaQuan was steps away from me.

Instinctively, my legs went weak; the air became so thick and so electric. I was mad at my body for the way it reacted to him, despite me being mad.

CHAPTER TWENTY-EIGHT
CHARISMA

"You got two kids with him, so we know you'll say anything to try and protect him. We know you wasn't with him like he's saying."

His thick fist connecting with the desk made me jump like I'd just touched a fence that was electrified.

"Don't lie!"

The light seemed extra hot and I was hungry. The room they had me in was small and I was sweating like I never knew possible. My wrists hurt too; the handcuffs felt like they were cutting into my skin.

But I was too scared to ask them to loosen the cuffs or take them off.

They must've thought I might try to escape because they kept me cuffed to that table for the longest. I was so tired of sitting, it felt like my butt was replaced by only a bone. I was also tired of crying and tired of being questioned.

"We're getting the surveillance video and we're gonna see him on it. So, I'll ask you again. Was Corey McCray with you the night in question?"

Spit gathered at the corners of his mouth as he talked to me.

"You bet' not lie to me again!" He was so angry.

I swallowed what felt like a real big hair ball trapped in my throat.

The detective leaned over me, and got all in my face. His breath smelled like stale coffee and old cigarettes.

"Let me remind you. Perjury is very serious. It's a crime. You could go to jail yourself, lose your kids and he'll become a ward of the state."

His threat made me gasp. Before he made another one, thoughts of my kids being taken away popped into my mind. I hated Corey for getting kicked off the football team, dropping out of school, hanging out, getting caught up with his loser friends, and doing whatever he had done to make the cops question me.

We had stayed in Waco after we both had dropped out. We were there and together for like six years, working and living. Then I got pregnant again.

It wasn't that big of a deal because I was twenty-four. Baby number two came at twenty-five; money got real tight and Corey started selling weed.

"Do you love that crook so much you're willing to go to jail for him?"

I was sick of Corey and sick of the drama he had brought into our lives. When Corey went to jail for two years, I moved back to Houston to be closer to family. By then, family only consisted of Lena and Lance. I was never close with my aunt or our grandmother.

Even back at home, for a long time, I was scared the police would come after me.

"Ms. Jones, you are under arrest!"

When the cold, hard metal touched my wrist again, memories of that long-ago day in the interrogation room came back in a flash.

This time I was the one going to jail. And this time, I couldn't pin it all on Corey. I needed to take the blame myself.

The phone rang, waking me up, and I left the past and that horrible time of my life back there. It was DaQuan.

"Say, ma, what's good?"

He made me so happy. It would've been better if he was free, but outside of that, he was as close to perfect as I could hope for in a man.

"Hey, daddy."

I giggled into the phone. We did lots of little talk before we jumped into business and I liked that about him.

"How the fam doing?"

"Everybody is fine. I'm so glad to have you in my life." The words tumbled out before I could stop them.

He didn't say anything at first and that scared me. But soon he said, "Yeah, I'm glad we met too."

Then, it was time for business.

"So peep this. My people got the address and ya should see a few of them between tonight and tomorrow. With that Sanchez shit, I gotta remind these fools who's running the show. Listen, ya got that number I sent over, right?"

"Yes. I have it right here." I scrambled to find the paper I had jotted the number on.

"Call him on three-way."

I dialed the number for DaQuan.

After a few rings, I was about to give up, but all of a sudden, a deep voice boomed into my ear. I quickly connected the call and the three of us were on.

"E-Dawg!" DaQuan yelled.

"Sup', Dee. Listen, I ain't takin' no charge, so don't try to play me."

"Playboy, my lady is on the line, so I'ma need ya to check yo tone."

The guy let go a nervous-sounding chuckle.

"Okay, bet that," he said.

It made my heart sing to hear DaQuan call me his "lady," until E-Dawg responded.

"Say, what's up, KenyaTaye?"

Horror gripped my heart, and I couldn't speak.

"Nah, Dawg, that's Charisma," DaQuan corrected him and jumped right back into the conversation. "Now that situation with ol' boy."

Yes, E-Dawg had just called me by my nemesis's name. I didn't know what to say, so I held the phone and listened.

"Dee, you ain't gon' put that one on me. Don't try to dirty me; we been making magic for years. I say you check *your* team, especially when you changing players after every inning."

"Dawg, don't start buggin' out. This is my jail. Ya understand that? I'm dead serious. I make the final call in this jail. Ya don't worry about the players on this end. I got this."

I felt odd as I held the phone, while those two went at it. But I knew better than to say a word when DaQuan was handling business.

"I need you back on schedule. That's it."

"I dunno, Dee."

"E-Dawg, the game may be rigged, but ya can't win if ya don't play."

"Yo, you ain't even right, Dee. You ain't gotta threaten your boy. But I hear ya!" E-Dawg said.

"Good. So hit yo people and let them know we good to go. That's where Charisma comes in. I told her to expect a few people to come through. The first should get there in about two hours."

"Got it!"

"Yo, Charisma. Lemme' get ya address," E-Dawg said.

It took a second to realize they were actually talking to me. And when I did, I rattled off my address and DaQuan told me to hang up.

Then he called back and once we were on the phone alone, DaQuan told me I needed to brace myself for the workflow.

"We gotta get shit right again."

"Yeah, but, you not even a little worried about the situation up at Jester?"

"Ma, when ya ride with a boss, ya ain't got time for fear. Let's make this money; ya' feel me?"

Twenty minutes after our call ended, I walked outside to get something out of my car and nearly passed out.

"What the fu—"

All four tires were slashed and the car was carved with every name but one for a child of God. I didn't need security video to tell me who had struck.

CHAPTER TWENTY-NINE
KENYA TAYE

Being inside the building made me feel sick. Everything seemed different now that I wasn't leading DaQuan's team. I hated everything about work: the rank smell, the gloomy walls, and the constant chatter among the inmates. It was never quiet.

Things went from worse to disastrous for me faster than I could understand. One day I was *that* chick right next to the bossman; the next, I was invisible, worse than a bottom bitch. I couldn't figure out what I hated more: everything about the Jester unit, or the fact that there was nothing I could do to change my new reality.

"Yo, Dunbar! What's what wit' you?" C.O. Sheppard shuffled up to the guards' booth. She stopped in the doorway and smacked her fist into her palm.

"You know it's been tight around here since Sanchez got popped, right? But I got three smartphones, with charges, a couple bags of weed and…" She shuffled some more. "Drum roll, please!" Sheppard then wildly waved jazz hands and screamed, "Some Henny Beyotch!"

I couldn't believe her stupid, tacky ass. I turned my back on her antics, and Edwards got up and approached the poor chile. It was a good thing Edwards jumped on it, because I wanted to straight punch Sheppard in the throat. She knew good and well we were all on high alert after Sanchez had gotten caught bringing in contraband.

"And, I ain't have to stuff nothing up my coochie!" Sheppard stopped and stepped closer. "I heard that's the way most of these females roll around here. Putting all kinds of *ish* up their twat! But not me. I know how to use my…" She pointed toward her head.

I was disgusted with her.

"Yeah, and my shit works too! It's like top of the line, so I'ma need top dollar!"

As she went on about how much she'd be willing to accept for the contraband, Edwards took her by the arm and steered her around the corner somewhere. But once I was alone, depression settled in as I thought back to my last conversation with DaQuan.

"Since ya don't come or answer when I call, I wanna let ya know we 'bout to change up some thangs," he'd said.

At first, it felt good knowing he was vexed by the fact that I had ignored him.

"Oh, is that right? Like what kind of *thangs*?"

I had served up much attitude because he needed to know he couldn't treat me any way he wanted.

"Jones is taking over the day-to-day operations. I'ma let ya know what territory ya can handle. But from now on, she and R.J. got it covered."

The smirk probably melted right off my face. My heart had started to thud, and panic had flooded my nervous system. I wasn't ready.

"You ain't shit! You know that, DaQuan? You ain't shit!"

It had taken everything in me to swallow back the tears that threatened to burst through. The idea that he'd replace me never crossed my mind. How could he?

"Maybe that's true, but ya needed to get hipped. Since ya went M-I-A, I made other arrangements. This bitnez, shorty."

His news had hit me like a large bulldozer. But I'd pulled it together, mustered up my straight face and listened while he talked. He'd had my full attention. With a dismissive shrug, he'd added, "I'ma let ya know when somebody's gonna come by to get the car."

That's when my heart had dropped.

"What? Get my car? Why the hell would anybody come get my car?" A few tears had escaped despite how hard I'd tried to keep them in.

He had cut me deep.

My mouth wouldn't work. Shots had been fired, and I couldn't think of the right words to throw back at him for the way he had just hurt me.

DaQuan didn't care that he'd broken my heart into a billion pieces. He was just a low-life, hustling user, who tossed people out when he was done with 'em. And it was my turn to be set out by the curb like used-up trash.

My finger had jabbed my chest harder than I'd wanted. "So, me, your pregnant chick, is supposed to do what; catch the fuckin' bus?"

His eyes had moved down to my stomach. When the radio sounded, I snapped back to my present shitty situation.

"Say, Dunbar!"

I whipped around in my chair. It was an inmate and not a C.O. who called my name. What was he thinking?

He wasn't even someone I recognized. I looked around to make sure no one had sent him just to fuck with me. I approached the doorway and even managed to force a smile to my face. I couldn't believe he was being bold enough to step to me like we were equals.

And while I planned to watch his face melt after I threatened him with a violation, it was my face that dropped when he spoke.

"I see yo name written on the wall in that bathroom. You still giving head for hundred-fifty?"

The punk even grabbed his crotch, and shook his package.

Blood actually flashed before my eyes, as they narrowed to deadly slits.

"Inmate, what did you say to me?" I asked through tight lips.

He eased back a few steps, and the smile melted from his face.

Franklin strode past us, but then he quickly doubled back. Deep frown lines creased his forehead as he took a closer look at us. "Everything okay over here?" He glanced at the inmate, then back at me.

"Dunbar, there a problem over here?"

"Yeah, I think there is. This inmate accosted me."

The inmate's face twisted.

"Fuckin' yo! Ain't nobody accosted you! I was tryna offer you a business proposition. Heard ya pockets might be light these days." His eyes slowly rolled up and down my body, and he licked his lips. "'Sides, all ya had to do was say ya didn't want the job."

"Down on the ground now, inmate!" Franklin yelled.

The whole time, from the second the inmate hit the ground to the second Franklin snatched him back up, the inmate looked at me with so much venom in his eyes a shiver shot up and down my spine.

I didn't feel a single ounce of pity for him as other inmates stood around and watched him being hauled off to solitary.

Maybe that would send a message. I might not be DaQuan's main chick anymore, but I was still a C.O., the sergeant on shift, and I'd be damned if I didn't get respect.

All of that commotion was nothing compared to the sucker punch that ricocheted through the right side of my face. It came out of nowhere. By the time I realized she was on me, my face stung and colorful stars danced in front of my eyes.

I stumbled, but managed to break my fall and caught my balance. Jones stood over me like she was Rocky or something.

"Touch something else that belongs to me," she said.

Edwards and Bishop rushed to the doorway, but Jones shoved her way between them and stormed out.

"What happened in here, and what's with her?" Edwards asked.

Because my hand held my cheek, they knew I had been hit.

Bishop looked around the guards' booth. But while she did her inspection, an image grabbed my attention. From the corner of my eye, I saw a group of inmates who watched as another inmate acted out the sucker punch I had just suffered.

I turned my head and saw him swing; then he moved to the other side, grabbed his jaw and stumbled backward. The other inmates doubled over with laughter. It was clear I had become the bona-fide joke of the prison.

"Did that bitch just hit you?"

Too mad for words, all I could do was think about ways to kill Jones and DaQuan.

"Oh, God, she might have a concussion," Bishop said.

"She can only get a concussion if she hit her head real hard on something," Edwards said.

"*She* is right here; *she* can hear you guys; and *she* ain't got no damn concussion," I snapped.

Even if I wanted to, I wouldn't have been able to hide the sarcasm in my voice. All I wanted to do was—kill. Messing up that car was nothing. By the time I was done with her and DaQuan, they'd both know how much I hated them.

$5,865.54

My eyes focused on the account balance and I wanted to pinch myself all over again. I couldn't remember a time when I'd had that kind of money in a savings account. And it was all mine.

The account was in my mother's name, but I had control over it with online access. My name wasn't attached to that just in case anything happened. The money in that account didn't include what was in my own checking account. It also didn't include the $900 I kept in a cash box in my bedroom, or the few hundred I sent to my mother and asked her to keep in the house.

I logged off of the bank's site, closed the case to my smartphone, and eased back in the recliner. I flicked a button and a warm kneading sensation started to pound my shoulders.

"Aaaah."

But all of a sudden, I thought about the blog. I stopped the chair and reached for my tablet. I typed the name of the blog into a search engine and waited for the connection.

Nelson Barnes's blog *From the Inside* was fourth on a page of five other search results.

It began with a brief bio about Nelson and how he was incarcerated for a crime he didn't commit. I scrolled through some of the posts and read a bit. I scrolled through and read a post from Thanksgiving of last year.

It was Thanksgiving morning and I awoke in time to watch the big parade on TV. Holidays generally do not have any serious news stories but I was surprised when I saw ABC network's ticker tape. It read that Governor Greg Abbott had granted 133 clemency petitions. No other information was given so I figured they were all for people who had minor offenses and had already completed their probation or prison time. A lot of people who had been swept up into the system just wanted their records cleared. For the governor it did not involve any potential controversy or political risk. I left the cell around 9 to get my Thanksgiving Day meal. It was one of the few days in the year that prisoners were fed well. Kitchen workers gave us turkey, pork, macaroni and cheese, and a portion of sweet potatoes and stuffing. At the end of the line I was given yet another tray with salad, cranberry sauce, bread, and a little wedge of cherry pie. Typically prisoners receive visitors from their families on Thanksgiving, but I wasn't expecting anyone.

I glanced through a few more of his posts, but there wasn't really anything that held my attention. Just when I was about to bookmark the blog, another post caught my attention. When the phone rang, I reached for it, but put it right back down when I noticed Lena's number.

She was next to one of the last people I wanted to talk to. I went back to the blog and found a post, not about hooking up with inmates on social media, but something that could've caused problems. Although most of what he talked about was his case, this particular post discussed ways that prison life mirrored life on the streets.

His post wasn't that long or detailed, but it was the comments about the post that caught my attention.

Since when did inmates get to use the Internet? one comment asked.

Anyone who sees those videos, are going to be sickened by them. They're going to be angry. Aren't these like murderers, rapists, and other convicted criminals and they are having a good time in prison? Where are the friggin guards? Asleep?

My eyes searched around for the video in question, but I couldn't find it. I read several more comments.

Did y'all see the one inmate talking about this shit ain't half bad? Where are they locked up, camp Fed?

And these idiots are on Facebook bragging about smoking 'loud' talking about everybody in here on the stupid loud; we all hungry! Who's watching these crooks?

Not only did I think the inmates who posted the pictures and videos were stupid for putting that stuff on the Internet, but I felt like Nelson was dumb for adding it to his blog.

At first I was stunned by what I read and saw, until I realized it was nearly two years old. If no one else was bothered by what they had done, there was no point in me raising my blood pressure.

I logged off and closed my eyes. I tried to get comfortable, and adjusted my body in the leather massage chair determined to enjoy the tapping and kneading sensation that vibrated all over my body.

This was as close as I imagined heaven could be without dying to find out. I felt completely at peace and wished I could stay suspended in that feeling forever.

My kids stayed with my mother so I was used to being home alone. But the doorbell's sudden chime made my eyes snap open.

Rest was something I rarely got anymore since I'd started running DaQuan's business. I pressed a button that ended the chair's vibration and moved me into an upright position.

"Ugh, what now?"

As I got up, the phone rang again. It was Lena, so I ignored her yet again. She was determined to get all up in my business no matter what.

One look out of the peephole took me even farther away from the serenity I'd left only moments prior. The tall, light-skinned man, with colorful tattoos that covered his neck, shoulders, and arms looked around as he waited for me to answer.

"Who is it?" I asked.

He let out a growl before he answered.

"DaQuan sent me."

My hands shook as I unlocked the door and pulled it open. I looked into the eyes of a person I'd sworn had killed before. A chill ran through me when his eyes finally locked with mine.

"Here." He shoved a set of keys into my hands, then tried to look behind me. Instinctively, I pulled the door closer to my body.

Before I could say anything, he pivoted and walked away. When I looked down and saw the BMW emblem on the electronic key in my hand, I released a trapped breath I didn't realize I'd been holding.

DaQuan had obviously sent me a loaner. He thought of everything. He was pissed when I told him what Dunbar had done to my car, but he said he'd take care of it. And the more he took care of me, the better it made me feel about working for him and of course, being with him.

I was about to go check out my loaner when Lena pulled up. I wasn't in the mood for her, but since she'd caught me outside, there was nothing I could do.

"OHMYGOD, Charisma! Is this an even newer car? What happened to your other Beamer?"

She got out of her car and went straight to the BMW before I could say hi. "I knew you was right over here ignoring my calls."

"I didn't have my phone," I lied. "Oh, and my car is in the shop. DaQuan just had one of his boys drop this loaner off to—"

The sparkle in her eyes told me I had just made a huge mistake. My heart sank.

"DaQuan? That's not a name you hear a lot. Reminds me of those ghetto mamas who make up names for their kids. So, your top-secret new man has a name after all."

Victory was all over Lena's face.

I wanted to slap myself. I had run my mouth too much. As Lena inspected the loaner, I could only imagine what must've run through her mind.

"Well, this DaQuan, he sure does have real good taste."

My eyes were on her every move.

"This pearl color looks like a custom job too."

"Mmm, I don't think so."

Lena stopped and looked at me. "Charisma, trust me, the BMW 3 Series does not have a coupe that comes in pearl from the factory."

What the hell?

Lena walked around the car slowly, like she was deep in study in case she might be quizzed later or asked to show it off.

"What did you say he does again? I mean, because you swear he ain't out in these streets selling no drugs, right?"

Lena's expression was one of triumph and gloating. She stopped, put her Gucci bag on the hood of the loaner car, then tossed a hand to her hip.

"Well?"

"Lena, like I told you. We like our privacy, and we wanna keep our personal life private. The minute you start putting people all up in your business, that's when things start getting messed up. Why can't you respect that?"

She pulled her arms up and crossed them at her chest.

"I am your blood relative. I'm not 'people' and I don't get why you won't share with me!"

"He just sent us shopping together. I do share with you. But that doesn't mean I need to give you all the details about our relationship."

"Umph. Well, riddle me this," Lena began. "What kind of big baller, who buys luxury cars, designer clothes, bags and shoes for his woman, don't mind her working in some sleazy prison?"

Her question almost knocked me off my feet. I expected her to go on about me keeping him a secret but never expected her to question my job.

Lena came closer.

"Oh, I see I finally hit a nerve, didn't I?"

I swallowed hard. She had invaded my personal space.

"Wait!" Her eyes lit up. "Don't tell me he doesn't know where you work!" She grinned, then gave me a knowing look.

"I knew it!" Lena snapped her fingers and jumped up with glee. "Now it makes sense. You ain't been on the up and up with this DaQuan!" Her happy expression melted from her face and was quickly replaced by a look of bewilderment.

"Wait." Again, her face lit up. Then she frowned and asked, "Does he know you've been to jail before?"

I rolled my eyes at her theatrics.

"I haven't been to jail, Lena. I was on house arrest and probation and I only pled guilty to the fraud charge because I couldn't afford a good lawyer."

She didn't seem interested in her incorrect facts.

"Ah, has he seen you in person yet?"

Her question was loaded.

CHAPTER THIRTY-ONE
KENYA TAYE

This time, I didn't share the plan with either of those two backstabbing bitches. They'd find out soon enough what I planned to do. The more I thought about everything DaQuan had done, the better I felt about what I was about to do.

He had taken everything away from me, then helped a fat, ugly bitch flaunt it all in my face. I wasn't gonna take any more of his shit or hers, either.

I got out of the rental car and walked into the small building.

"Howdy," the man behind the counter greeted me. "You doin' okay?" He was a massive man. He wore large denim overalls and a colorful striped shirt.

"Yeah. I'm good."

My eyes took in all the things he had on display. Two other people stood at the counter and the man looked back at me and said, "I'll be with you in a few minutes, ma'am."

I walked around and looked at a few things I thought I might want.

A few minutes later, the man walked up behind me.

"Are you looking for an automatic or a small pistol?"

"I think something small."

Part of me couldn't believe I was there.

"I might have something of interest behind the counter; c'mon, let me show you what I've got."

He took off and went behind the counter. I watched as he reached down and pulled out a small box.

When he opened the box, there were three smaller boxes inside. "This here is a .22 caliber mini-revolver."

The gun was pretty. It was small and looked like it would be perfect for what I planned to do.

"It's a five-shot, about four inches. It's real popular with my female customers." He placed it in my hand. "Go ahead, see how it feels?"

"Yes; it's nice."

"You have your documents already or you gotta wait for them to come in?"

"No, I've got everything. I'm a correctional officer."

His eyebrows went up.

"So you already licensed to carry?"

"Yup. I don't need it for my job, but I want it for safety."

"Yeah, that's smart. Lots of wild, wacky things going on these days; it's good to have your own protection."

"You ever shot a gun before?"

"Oh, yes. I know how to use them. I really like this one; it's cute."

As he took my driver's license and my other paperwork, I inspected the gun. It would be perfect. Images of the horror on DaQuan's face when I pointed the gun at him nearly made me cream myself. First, I'd put a bullet between his eyes, then I'd go after his fat, ugly bitch.

I might do her right in front of everyone. Maybe I'd get her in the guards' booth. The only part I hadn't worked out was whether I'd do myself afterward. There was no doubt I had already lost everything, and in Texas, after I took those two out, I'd get the death penalty anyway.

The entire transaction took less than an hour. I walked out of the gun shop with my new gun, and for the first time in a very long time, I felt good.

Nearly an hour later, I called my job. "This is C.O. Dunbar. Is Edwards available?"

"Yeah, hold on, please."

The next voice I heard was Edwards's.

"Hey, I think I left my wallet there; can you check the desk for me?"

"Your wallet? How you gonna leave your wallet up in here?"

I rolled my eyes and listened as she shuffled some things around.

"You sure it was in the booth, because I'm here and I don't see anything."

"Maybe I should come up there and look around a bit myself. I don't know what I did with it."

"Well, I don't see it anywhere around here; maybe you can try to trace your last steps."

"Okay; well, thanks for looking."

My mother was in the living room watching her soaps. I took the plastic wrap, a large zipper sandwich bag and a tube of lube into the bathroom.

I grabbed the hand mirror and locked the bathroom door. I pulled up my skirt, took off my panties and eased onto the floor.

I put the gun inside the sandwich bag. After that, I wrapped it in plastic wrap and used duct tape to secure the bag around the gun.

On the floor, with the wrapped gun, and the hand mirror, I spread my legs wide and squeezed some lube into my hand. I lathered the plastic wrapped gun; then I eased it into my opening and slowly shoved it as far as it could go.

The gun went in with no problem. I exhaled and slowly closed my legs. It felt like I had something stashed up inside my twat, but that was what it was supposed to feel like. Instead of putting my panties back on, I put on a leotard shirt that snapped between my legs.

After that, I put my panties back on. I had to make sure I'd be able to walk normally. The biggest challenge would be getting through security and into the prison without being detected.

Once I felt comfortable and ready, I left and drove up to my job.

People looked surprised to see me, but not like they didn't expect me back.

"Hey, Dunbar, you doin' okay?" one of the security officers asked.

"It's all good."

"You working today?" Franklin asked.

"Nah, I think I left my wallet here. I just need to look around a bit."

"Oh, yeah, Edwards said you called."

I walked into the work area, but went straight to the bathroom. Bishop came in from the other direction.

"Hey, Dunbar, I didn't know you was working today."

"I'm not; here looking for something." I needed her to mind her own damn business.

"Oh. Okay."

She eased into the bathroom, and walked to the sink. I went into the last stall and waited as I heard the water run. I undressed so that I could do what I had come to do.

"You okay in there?" Bishop asked.

"Yeah. I'm good."

I was irritated by her and wanted her to leave. Now she wanted to be a bathroom guard.

When I finally heard the bathroom door open and close, I unbuttoned the shirt between my legs and pushed the gun out of my coochie.

"Later," Bishop said.

I grabbed a wad of tissue and wiped off the gun.

If I knew Bishop, I knew she'd go run her mouth to Edwards and they'd be back soon. I didn't need them all up in my business. Once the gun was out, I stood on top of the toilet and reached up to see if the panel on the ceiling still moved. It did.

I slid the large square to the side and placed the gun in the space before I covered it back up again. I got off the toilet, walked out of the stall and washed my hands.

My timing was perfect. As I pulled the door and walked out, Edwards and Bishop were on their way in.

"Hey, I still haven't found it; you sure you left it here?" Edwards asked.

"I'm not sure of anything anymore. I could've left it at the store for all I know."

The way they looked at me made me feel some kind of odd way. But I didn't say anything about it. I knew they were just trying to figure out whether I was up to something, and I was, but I knew I couldn't confide in them.

When Bishop's radio went off, I was relieved. It couldn't have happened at a better time. Two correctional officers rushed past us.

"We'd better go," Bishop said.

Edwards rolled her eyes. "I'll catch up with you."

Bishop left and rushed toward the chaos. "It ain't nothing but another gassing incident," Edwards said. "Not sure what's going on, but these damn inmates been throwing piss and shit in every damn direction lately."

CHAPTER THIRTY-TWO
CHARISMA

If I didn't know what a panic attack was like, I'd swear I was on the verge of one. Everything made me nervous and my mind raced more than ever before.

Being arrested haunted my dreams to the point where I never wanted to sleep. Then the lack of sleep made me feel tired. I started to down those energy drinks like they were water and that didn't help.

There was too much going on and it happened too fast for me to keep up. Paranoia made me feel like the world was about to close in on me.

At work, I expected the worst around every corner, even when things were settled and calm among the inmates. If I didn't see DaQuan, I wondered whether he was doing something that would get us all busted.

For the first time, I actually considered whether I should pop some of the pills I'd smuggled in for the inmates.

Things seemed normal with Edwards, Bishop, and Franklin. But that wasn't a surprise because when things got quiet with the inmates, the C.O.s relaxed and behaved like the job was laid-back. It seemed like as long as they got their money, they were good. It was obvious I was the only person on edge.

"Hey, you got a sec?" R.J.'s question caught me off guard. I hoped he didn't notice how jittery I had become. The last thing I wanted was for DaQuan to decide he didn't need me anymore.

I stepped all the way out of the booth and walked with R.J.

"Yeah, what's up? DaQuan looking for me?"

R.J. looked around. "Nah, nothing like that. Just wondering; we need a specific order filled."

His request sounded odd, but I figured it was something DaQuan needed me to do, so I was okay with it. I usually only brought in the pills and R.J. knew that.

"Man, we really need two cells with chargers, like yesterday."

I wasn't sure how to react. I coordinated everything, but I had never smuggled anything other than the pills. R.J. and I had talked in the past about how I wouldn't be comfortable smuggling anything up in my coochie or my ass. I would need to talk with DaQuan himself because that's when I'd have to draw the line.

I stopped myself. Maybe it was a test to see how I'd handle a specific order? I wasn't sure.

"Hmmm. I could check with Sheppard; she's usually good for those. Is that it?"

"Yeah, yeah. Uh, when is your next pill shipment coming in?"

"Next week; on Thursday."

"Okay, cool. That's what's up." R.J. nodded. He glanced around again. "Let me know when you got a line on the cellies and I'ma holla at you later."

R.J. took off in the opposite direction after I nodded. I watched as he left, then turned and prepared to go back to the booth. There was still no sign of Sheppard, of course.

It was just my luck that when I needed her, she was nowhere to be found. Most days, she bopped around the halls like she had nothing better to do.

I knew for sure it would cause too much confusion to ask where she was, so I decided I'd focus on something else. The more I looked for her, the harder she'd be to find.

My energy level was so off the charts there was no way I could go and sit back in the booth, so I decided to do some rounds. As I walked the halls and checked things out, thoughts of my simple cousin Lena flowed into my mind.

She was determined to find the source of my money. The problem was, what would she do with the information once she found out? If I wasn't careful, she could blow us all up and get everyone caught.

"Charisma!"

I turned to see C.O. Scott jogging to catch up with me. She looked over her shoulder, back in the direction she came from.

"Hey, I meant to ask you. What's up with you and Dunbar?"

Her question seemed odd. Scott didn't work on our shift and although she knew all the players, she wasn't privy to the game.

Her demeanor made it clear that she knew the question was a sensitive subject. When she asked, she lowered her voice, and her eyes darted around. "I don't know all the details, but you're right to stay away from them. I'm gonna tell you something, but you didn't hear it from me. Word around here is that she and DaQuan are having some issues. If I was you, I'd stay clear of them all. You might even consider putting in for a transfer."

"A transfer?"

"Yeah. I don't trust anyone around here. Ain't no telling what they're up to. When they ask me to work this shift, I always wanna say no, but I only do it because I want to be a team player."

"I think you're right. I already don't get along with Dunbar so I'm gonna make sure I stay the hell away from her."

Scott nodded. Her expression changed to satisfaction at my answer.

A couple of trustees walked in our direction and Scott went into super C.O. mode.

"Inmates, are you guys cleared to be walking the halls over here?"

Her voice was firm and boomed as it left her tiny body.

"They're trustees," I tried to whisper to her.

"Oh. Okay, as you were then." She eyed me, then settled down a bit.

When the inmates turned the corner away from us, Scott leaned closer to me and said, "Just be careful around here. I know I don't have to tell you 'cause from what I hear, you're a loner, and I think you should keep it that way, but I just thought I'd let you know for sure; nothing good can come from hanging with those three."

By those three, she meant Dunbar, Edwards, and Bishop. I never wondered how other correctional officers felt about them. I assumed that most, if not all, were part of the smuggling team, but I was wrong.

We arrived at the guards' booth and it was time to end the conversation. My mind was still stuck on Sheppard and the only woman I could say I hated.

CHAPTER THIRTY-THREE
KENYA TAYE

"So, you asking for three thousand, five-hundred dollars for this?" I looked at the gold-colored 1995 Honda Accord and tried to find anything that was wrong with it. He must've bumped his head trying to charge that much for an old used car. It was clean, but wasn't worth his asking price.

"It's in good condition," the man, who wore a turban, said.

I pulled the door open, looked inside and it was clean enough. It smelled fresh too. But that was nothing but well-placed Febreeze air fresheners; it didn't justify his outrageous price tag. There were a few stains on the seats, but the seatbelts worked and I noticed brand-new mats on the floor. I couldn't find anything wrong with the inside, either.

When I eased out of the car, I stood back and looked at the hood of the car. There were a couple of small dings in it, but you had to focus hard to notice them.

"For a twenty-year-old car it's nice, but the *Blue Book* value puts it at one-thousand dollars. That's two less than what you're asking."

His bushy eyebrows turned into a unibrow. "It's in very good condition."

"Yeah, I heard you, but I'm not about to pay two-thousand dollars above the market price, just because you're proud that you've kept it clean."

He had me messed up.

The fact that I had to be haggling with a man about an old used car only made me more pissed. DaQuan was out of order for taking back my car. By the time I'd finished with him, he'd be sorry for sure. I had to push thoughts of the hidden gun out of my mind.

"Well, make me an offer."

The car was nice, but it already had close to two-hundred-thousand miles on it.

"One thousand." I opened the gas tank and looked at it like something might be wrong there.

"You wanna pay one-thousand dollars?" The man released a chuckle and looked at me like he was ready for the next buyer to step up.

"I told you what the *Blue Book* says."

"Before I let it go for that, I'll keep it as an extra vehicle."

He didn't know, I wasn't pressed. After a brief shrug, I turned and took a few steps away from him and the car, before he yelled, "Ma'am! Wait."

I stopped, but I didn't face him right away. I took a deep breath and cheered a little to myself. I knew he'd come to his senses.

When I turned, he stepped closer.

But I noticed, his expression hadn't softened at all. That really pissed me off because here I was all but haggling with this dude over an old bucket, and he still had a smug look on his face.

"Two thousand."

Instead of responding to his counteroffer, I shook my head, turned back toward the rental and kept it moving. I needed a car because the bill on my rental was running like a broken meter.

"Well, you tell me. How much you willing to pay?"

Men made me sick.

"Look, I got three other cars to look at today. I don't have time to play *The Price is Right* with you."

"It's worth more than what that *Blue Book* says."

"Yeah, well, that's not my problem. Either you take that up with the folks over at *Blue Book* or you keep the car for yourself. Nobody in their right mind is gonna pay more than the market value for this car. I'm out!"

Almost thirty minutes after I'd left the man who'd tried to sell me the Accord, I felt more disgusted and dejected than before. There were no other cars to see. I didn't feel like haggling with anyone else over used cars. All I wanted was to shoot DaQuan right between his eyes for doing me so dirty.

Since money didn't roll in for me like it used to when I was with DaQuan, I knew I needed to watch what I spent. I needed a car because using a rental to get back and forth to work had gotten very expensive. I had another stop I needed to make. I exited Gessner off I-10 and pulled into Memorial City Mall.

For a change, parking wasn't bad. I rushed into the mall, found the store, and got in line.

The chick behind the counter looked at me like I had warm shit smeared all over my face. Before I made it up there, I could tell there was about to be a problem. But it wouldn't be mine, because I was on a mission and I needed cash like nobody's business.

She had been all sweet and friendly with the person in front of me, but that didn't stop her from mean-mugging me at the same time. So, the minute she finished with that customer, I walked up, brought an attitude of my own.

"I need to bring these back," I said, and placed the old, crinkled bag on the counter.

She looked down at it, then back up at me, her face twisted like she was too disgusted for words. She'd better be glad the store was packed, and I needed my money. I knew my stuff was in a Ross bag, but what difference did that make?

"These are some of those panties I bought when they was on sale. Y'all said they wouldn't show lines, but they do, so I don't want 'em no more, and I'm gonna need my money back."

She looked around, picked up a pen that she used to pry the bag open and peeked inside. Suddenly, she gasped. "Have these panties been worn?"

Her worried expression didn't bother me one bit. But what did was her tone. Why did she have to loud-talk me like that?

"Uh, how the hell else would I know you could see the panty lines?" I gave her much attitude because I didn't appreciate the way she treated me.

"But, ma'am, you've worn these, and now you're bringing them back?" she balked.

Was she for real?

My hand flew to my hip and my neck elevated. I know she wasn't trying to front on me while all people stood around.

"Yes. Like I said, I bought them because the commercials, the ads, and the picture right above them claim they won't show your panty lines, but they do. That's false advertising, ain't it? Either way, I just want my damn money back. They cost thirty dollars for three, so I spent sixty plus taxes. I want all my money back," I said.

"So, you wore all of these?"

I wanted to say, *no bitch, I only wore one pair, and guessed about the others.* She must've gotten the hint from my expression because she stopped with the questions and started hitting buttons on the register. I couldn't care less about her damn attitude. To me, she needed to find a better job if she didn't want to deal with customers.

"Now that's just downright nasty!" I heard someone behind me say. I turned and shot the lady the look of death. But she ignored me and kept talking.

"Eewww. I wouldn't take 'em back. That's so nasty!"

"Just look at her; you surprised?" someone else tossed in.

I didn't trip off any of their comments at first. My focus was on the woman behind the counter, who acted like she didn't remember how to work the cash register. But I didn't care how long it took, she was gonna give me back my damn money. As I waited, I listened to the lady bump her gums about me and how disgusting it was for me to bring worn panties back to the store for a refund.

Victoria's Secret was my last stop and once I got that money back, I'd get my mind right and prepare to go back to that horrible job.

"Here you are," the woman said. Her wrinkled white hands trembled as she counted out the cash she placed in my hand.

When I turned to leave, the nosy chick had the nerve to mutter, "Just nasty," as I passed her.

Her words stopped me in my tracks. I looked at her and squinted.

"What did you just say?"

"You heard me." Her neck swiveled as she spoke.

I looked at her real good, then tucked my money away and walked out of the store. Instead of leaving like I needed to, I went across the way and slipped into Bath & Body Works, where I could look into Victoria's Secret from a distance. A few minutes later, the chatterbox who had been behind me, walked out of the store and made a quick right.

I rushed to catch up to her and followed as she walked through a department store as she left the mall. I was right on her heels.

Her stupid behind even held the door for me as she left and headed toward her car.

"Hey, remember me?" I asked, right as she stopped and dug for her keys.

"Uh—" She looked up, but by the time recognition settled onto her face, it was too late.

I swung and clocked her at the right side of her jaw and head. Her eyes grew wide as she stumbled back and fell to the ground.

"Next time, learn to mind your own damn business!"

I glanced around the parking lot, then dashed back into the store. I was late because I'd stalked her and smacked her, but it was well worth it. Maybe next time, she'd think twice before she butted into other people's business.

As I drove around with no real destination in mind, I thought about some of the people I had helped out when I was rolling in cash. But I couldn't come up with a single one who would be able to help me out. It didn't take long for me to realize that without DaQuan, I had no one and nothing to lean on.

For the first time since I'd found out I was pregnant, I started to think about whether having a baby was smart. DaQuan knew I was pregnant, but still, that didn't stop him from doing me dirty.

He was clear that I and his unborn could suffer, and it was no biggie for him. I took the scenic route and passed by Jones's place. Even though I had no business being near her place, I couldn't ignore what I saw.

I brought my car to an abrupt stop and jumped out. I walked up to her door and banged on it like I would break it down if she didn't answer.

"Who is it!"

She didn't ask; she yelled. I was so desperate for her to open the door, I didn't give it a second thought. If I had my gun, she'd be dead even if it meant a shot through the damn front door.

"Your coworker!"

When she opened the door, I went ballistic.

"What kind of filthy trick are you? It's not bad enough you screw my man right underneath my nose, but he takes my car from me and gives it to you and you actually drive it? I sure as hell hope you enjoy all my sloppy seconds!"

Her rough-looking face was twisted like she didn't know what was up. I may not have been Ms. America quality, but Jones looked like a man. There was nothing soft about her. I still didn't get how DaQuan could look at her and call her anything but butt-ass ugly.

"How you know where I live?"

Her beady eyes looked around like my backup might jump from the bushes.

"Yous a dumb bitch." I shook my head. "If it's the last thing I do, you gon' pay for this shit."

I made a gun figure with my hand, and pulled the trigger.

"Yeah, yeah, yeah," she mocked me.

"Get yo life, bitch! This shit ain't over!"

She finally slammed her door in my face. That was probably best because several porch lights came on. Because they did, I didn't get a chance to fuck up that car like I had done with hers before.

Tears barely waited for me to strap on the seatbelt, before they busted through. DaQuan was such a dirty dog. Who does that? He actually had taken my car and given it to her. I couldn't believe it. It only drove home the feeling of total and complete betrayal and isolation. I had no one and absolutely nothing left.

The thought scared me even more when I pulled up at home and was still no closer to a solution to my transportation situation.

When I walked into the apartment, my mother looked like she had been spooked. I glanced around and looked over my shoulders dramatically. The doors were locked, so I didn't know what had her so bothered. But I wasn't in the mood to play whose problem was worse. I was sure I'd win for sure.

"What's wrong with you?" I didn't really want to know because my cup already overflowed, but her expression couldn't be ignored.

"Somebody came by here and left a package for you." My mother motioned with her hand.

That confused me, because I hadn't ordered anything.

"I'm just glad the kids wasn't here."

When she said that, I turned to look at her.

"Well, where is it? Did you open it?"

"No, it's got your name on it. None of my business to go opening your stuff." She mumbled some more under her breath, but I
didn't hear it.

"Well, what's the problem? The stank look on your face tells
me something ain't right."

"It was the guy who dropped it off. He looked like a slimy gangster, and for a minute there, I was scared he was about to push his
way up in here, and tear up some stuff. I didn't like it at all."

The sound of her voice told me to expect a whole lot more.

"I ain't got no idea what you out there doing, or how you making
all this money, and I really don't need to know, but if you selling
drugs, Kenya Taye, I can tell you how this is gonna end and it ain't
gonna be good for you."

While I heard what my mother said, I didn't have the patience
to really listen. Especially since if she only knew I was selling a
whole helluva lot more than drugs, she'd croak. I was so curious
about the package and who had delivered it, she might as well
have been talking in a foreign language.

As she went on about doing right, and the risks involved in
messing with thugs, I focused on the package. It was in a little
black duffle bag and it had a lock on the end of the zipper. I had
never seen such a small combination lock.

There was a note attached to it.

I picked up the bag and walked back to my bedroom. My mother
only stopped talking when I closed the door. The combination to
the lock wasn't on the note, so I dialed the phone number that
was there and waited.

CHAPTER THIRTY-FOUR
CHARISMA

I wasn't ready. My stomach was in my throat when I saw Kenya-Taye. In daylight, she looked pregnant as she strolled into the guards' booth at work. Is that supposed to be DaQuan's baby? I felt sick to my gut and I wanted so badly to ask her, but I knew I couldn't.

When she showed up at my place the night before, I didn't notice anything but hate and jealousy. I tried to talk to DaQuan about it, but he wasn't pressed.

"KenyaTaye showed up at my house raising cane, saying you gave me her car," I had said to DaQuan about the incident.

"That wasn't her car; she knows that. And she'll be ai'ght," was all DaQuan had said.

He'd jumped right into business, so I didn't mention it again.

He may not have wanted to go on and on about it, but I knew me having her car, even just temporarily, would only make things more drama-filled on the job.

That meant work would become more of a headache than I needed. On my way in, I thought about talking to DaQuan about something I'd been considering, but seeing KenyaTaye with child made me want to rethink all of this.

We went out of our way to avoid talking to each other and that was exactly how I liked it. She couldn't hate me any more than I hated her. If our eyes connected, it turned into a race to see who could roll them first. Several times I caught her as she gave me the look of death, but she never said anything.

I finished my paperwork, placed it in the outgoing tray, then got up to leave. Anytime Dunbar and the rest of her followers crowded the space, I knew it was time for me to move around. I hated being in their presence.

"You making rounds?" Edwards asked me.

"Yeah, I'm out," I lied.

"Umph."

That was Dunbar, but I ignored her.

Once I rounded the corner, I rushed down the hall before my legs made good on their threat to give out on me. I couldn't believe that bitch was pregnant.

"Yo, Jones. I was just coming for ya. DaQuan is in the closet."

Even though it shouldn't have been, that was music to my ears. Maybe a really good and strong orgasm would help me think more clearly. If I asked for a transfer, would I have to deal with a whole new group of attitudes?

Women outnumbered men on the job, so a transfer to get away from KenyaTaye didn't mean I'd avoid drama. Everyone knew a job that was filled with females, meant there would be lots of drama.

I almost skipped into the closet. I nearly forgot that I had serious issues to discuss with DaQuan. Two of DaQuan's workers were at their usual posts, which allowed me to slip right into the closet with no worries about getting caught.

Once inside, DaQuan was naked and ready for me. I wanted to talk, but his mind was on nonverbal communication.

"Hey, ma."

"Hey. You haven't been waiting long, have you?"

DaQuan stroked himself and beckoned me closer. He pulled my hand and eased it down to his crotch as he kissed my neck. I rubbed him rough and hard, the way I knew he liked it.

"Take off ya clothes."

I pulled back and took off my top, then my pants. DaQuan lay on his back and swiped his hand between my thighs.

"Ya good and wet; come ride me."

I straddled him and eased onto his stiffness. He felt so good as my body opened wide to accept him. DaQuan grabbed my hips and pulled me down.

"Do ya thang, ma. Do that shit!"

If I thought I was going to lay on top to make our chests meet each other, I was wrong. DaQuan pushed me upright and grabbed my nipples. He squeezed them so hard, I nearly released a yelp. Sex with him was everything. He was rock-hard and I couldn't help but move in sync with his thrusts.

"Oh Jesus, DaQuan."

"You like that?"

"Em-hmm."

"Tell me. Tell daddy what ya like."

He clutched my hips and rolled his midsection up into mine. In the darkness, I couldn't make out his expression, but everything felt so intense.

DaQuan smacked my ass and pulled me closer. Our breathing was fast, hot and hard.

Suddenly, he grabbed me, then swung his body to an upright sitting position. I clung to him and wrapped my legs around him as tight as I could.

"I'ma 'bout to get this nut!"

"Take it, daddy! Take it!"

When he moaned hard and loud, I felt so incredibly good. In the aftermath of another intense lovemaking session, I just wanted to cuddle and have him hold me for as long as possible.

"Ya good?"

"Yes, daddy; I'm always good with you."

"Okay, bet that."

He eased away from me, got up and started to get dressed.

"Hey, you gotta go already?"

"Yeah, ma. Gotta meet with the workers. Things ain't been right since Sanchez. Gotta go make it do what it do."

I hoped my face didn't reveal how disappointed I was because I didn't want DaQuan to think I was being too emotional.

"But I wanted to talk to you."

"Okay, ma; what's up?"

Dressed now, with his chin lowered and one eyebrow raised, DaQuan looked at me, like he really needed to go. I felt so cheated. How could I say, I'm thinking about putting in a transfer request, and oh, by the way is KenyaTaye pregnant with your child?

"You know what, never mind."

"Ya sure?"

"Yeah, babe. I'm good. We can talk about it later. It's no biggie."

"See, that's why ya cool with me. Ya know how to handle yours and then some. No time for all that bullshit."

The weak smile on my face must've told him I agreed with his assessment because I didn't have anything else to say. I felt like such a punk. The issues I needed to discuss with him were piling up and I didn't want to bother him.

Before I could say anything else, he was out the door and I was naked and alone. My body felt good, but everything else was jacked up.

When I opened the door to the closet and looked down in each direction before stepping out, I thought the coast was clear. A few steps down the hall and KenyaTaye appeared out of nowhere.

"We've been looking for you."

I didn't respond. What the hell was she looking for me for? I walked and turned the corner to get to the guards' booth. I purposely sped up my steps to try and shake her.

C.O. Scott rounded the corner and looked back toward Dunbar. "Hey, what's going on?"

"Nothing, just finished my rounds; headed back to the booth."

"I was just heading there to look something up," Scott said.

As I walked with Scott, all I could think was, when had Dunbar ever personally come and look for someone, especially me? What she meant to say was, she was looking for DaQuan and knew what was up since I was near the closet.

The booth was crowded and that sent my heartbeat into overdrive. What was really going on? Scott stepped in first.

From behind, KenyaTaye spoke up as she stepped inside after me.

"Jones, there was an error on your paperwork and I need to understand if you need additional training."

All eyes were glued on me. I couldn't believe she had called me out in front of everyone the way she did. I frowned, but told myself to check it.

"What kind of error?"

C.O. Franklin spoke up next.

"Actually, Jones, I caught it; it wasn't Dunbar." I looked at him like, who told you to chime in?

"I didn't ask who found it; I asked what the error was," I repeated with lots of attitude.

"You approved an inmate for meds and we don't have a prescription on file for him. That's a dangerous rookie move, but you need to fix it."

I rolled my eyes. She had just called me out in front of just about every C.O. on staff for something like that? I pulled my arms up and crossed them at my chest.

"If you can't handle the job, maybe this isn't the career for you," Dunbar said.

When I realized she was serious about that last comment, I wanted to tell her this wasn't a damn career, but I wasn't about to ruin her moment.

"Now, in the future if you're unsure about something, I want you to ask instead of guessing and putting us all at risk."

The nerve of her; she loved to show off in front of a crowd and it made me sick. I chuckled. Once our eyes connected, I said, "Well, I want all your confidence gone by the morning shift."

Eyes grew wide.

Dunbar's mouth dropped and the room went still.

"Can we go now?" another C.O. asked.

The question seemed to shock her back to the present. She shook her head and stammered a bit before she said, "Um, yeah. I just wanted to use this as a teaching moment. We gotta stay on our toes around here or these inmates will take advantage."

The more she talked, the more I prayed she had seen me as I walked out of the closet. She hated me because I had taken her man and there was nothing she could do about it. Since Kenya-Taye was powerless regarding DaQuan, I knew she'd try to make the job miserable for me.

As the other C.O.s filed out of the guards' booth, I could feel some of their frustration. Everyone knew she was being petty.

Left alone with her and her two flunkies, I turned and said, "You know, KenyaTaye, maybe if you begged DaQuan to meet you in the closet, he might. Although I can't imagine why he would need to, considering just how good I am at fucking him."

Edwards's eyes grew to the size of saucers. Bishop stepped to block Dunbar's path to me, but I didn't flinch. She needed to know I could be petty too.

As I walked out of the booth, I heard Edwards ask, "Is that true?"

There was no need to hear Dunbar's response. Every woman in that booth was aware that the only way I knew about the closet, was because I was fucking DaQuan. The only people privy to knowledge about that closet, were DaQuan, his top workers, and the female C.O.s they were fucking.

I didn't get far before Scott caught up with me.

She glanced around in both directions. "Look, I don't know what's going on around here, but you need to watch yourself around Dunbar and her little crew. I have a feeling she's out to get you. I don't trust her."

Scott had no idea just how right she was.

CHAPTER THIRTY-FIVE
KENYA TAYE

Tuesday afternoon, I talked to R.J., but I kept my eyes on the halls and scanned all of the inmates who passed us. We were in a spot where we had a little privacy, but could see everyone who passed.

"I'm warning you, R.J., I need to holla' at DaQuan and I need to talk to his ass inside the closet."

It wasn't that I wanted to sex DaQuan, but there was still that tiny part of me that felt like maybe if we could be alone, and really got the chance to talk, things would be different.

"Yo. I can't make bossman do anything he don't wanna do. 'Sides, you putting me in a bind."

"Nah. That's not what's happening here at all. Things are getting out of hand real fast and I need to look into his eyes and talk to him."

"KenyaTaye, I don't wanna get in the middle of what's going on with y'all."

I used my hand to count down the infractions. "Okay, okay. Well, listen to what I'm telling you. First, he doesn't secure a delivery truck, and we almost got our shit checked; second, Sheppard's crazy ass is trying to unload contraband all out in the open, even after Sanchez was busted; three, he fucking Jones and she bragging about being in the closet in front of others. Now, this stuff may not be a big deal to you, but I ain't tryna go down because the bossman got his head so far up Charisma's fat ass that he can't see how he's putting us all in jeopardy."

"Damn! Like that?" R.J. asked.

His features twisted as I presented my evidence. R.J. wasn't a fool and he knew and understood all that was at stake.

"Listen, I get it. He don't want me no more, and it is what it is. I'm having his fucking baby, but he still kicks me to the curb. Okay, whatever. But should we all be okay with his sloppy mistakes?"

R.J.'s silence told me he thought about what I told him.

"Yo, so, what happened with the delivery truck?"

"It was crazy! As soon as the K-9 unit came through, the officer wanted to know why I had gone to the back of the truck before them."

"Word?" R.J.'s eyes got big.

"Yeah. The question threw me so off guard, I didn't know what to say."

"Daaayum, so what happened?"

I felt like I had finally reached R.J.

"Thank God, Franklin is fast on his feet. He quickly said I needed to go organize the trustees in the back."

"Aw, damn! Good looking out!"

"Look, you need to convince DaQuan that he needs to talk to me. I ain't going down with the ship and I mean that!"

"Yo, what that mean?"

Instead of answering, I walked away and left R.J. there to figure it out. I knew for sure that message would get back to DaQuan if nothing else did.

For weeks, I'd thought about how to make them pay. When I decided to get the gun, I knew it would be easy to sneak it into to the jail, but the opportunity to go get it, then get next to DaQuan would take some time.

My goal was to get him and Charisma, and I couldn't wait to fix their asses. I gave the message I sent through R.J. two days for results. If I didn't hear back from DaQuan; I was gonna do what I needed to do.

By Thursday, when Jones slipped me an envelope, she acted like she barely wanted to look at me. That was just fine by me because I had to struggle to avoid spitting in her damn dog-like face.

But the insults kept rolling in. When I ripped the envelope open and five measly twenty-dollar bills fell out, I wanted to toss that shit back at her. I didn't risk my freedom for one-hundred damn dollars! They both had me messed up.

DaQuan must've thought he was being funny by paying me one-hundred dollars. I couldn't remember the last time I'd ever made such little money. He really had lost it. Dumb ass. How could he think he could repo my beamer, give it to his new trick, stop paying my bills, and cut my money and I'd just sit back and take it? Every little thing made me want to go get the gun.

Edwards walked by and glanced at me.

"What we gon' do about that bitch?"

She motioned in Jones's direction.

Her question pulled me away from my traitorous thoughts. I wanted to kill them both, but I knew that would take some time.

"I'ma try to talk some sense into DaQuan. If he won't budge, I might put in for a transfer."

Edwards whipped her head in my direction.

"A transfer? You gonna let that bitch take what's yours, and chase you away?"

I stopped and turned to her. She looked at me like I had gone and lost it all.

"Nobody is chasing me away, and if she took DaQuan, that means the punk-bitch was never mine. I ain't got time to be stressing over his simple, careless mistakes."

"Well, everybody is talking about how they never took you for no punk. You the damn sergeant around here and you letting them do all this shit to you and all you doing is taking it! I don't know what happen to you, but the KenyaTaye I know wouldn't take this shit!"

Edwards did something she had never done before. She said what she wanted, then turned and left. The look she tossed over her shoulder and back at me was worse than disgust.

It was all too damn much. No one respected me anymore. Before Charisma's trampy ass, the other females and some of the male C.O.s looked up to me. But now, DaQuan had made me the running joke of the Jester unit, and Edwards was right. There was no way I was about to take that shit.

After that exchange with Edwards, I was ready to spit fire when someone tapped me on the shoulder. It was R.J.

"Yo. Bossman will be in the closet in ten."

I was so nervous, I wasn't sure what to do. I needed to let go of all the anger and pull myself together. I never expected him to agree to meet. I figured his stubbornness wouldn't let him give in to common sense. My mind was set that I'd have to go through and do what I needed to do.

"Okay, in ten."

R.J. walked away and I wanted to find a bathroom. I had ten minutes to pull myself together. I needed to make sure my hair was on point, and I even considered borrowing some lipstick from Edwards.

That thought didn't last long after I remembered her last words to me. So, I didn't have any makeup, but I'd do the best with what I had. My reflection looked average at best. In the mirror, I adjusted my breasts in my bra and unbuttoned several buttons.

I turned my hips and looked at my ass in my work pants. I wished my stomach wasn't protruding, but there was nothing

I could do about that. I took a deep breath and left the bathroom.

As I made my way down the hall, I couldn't calm the butterflies that had come to life in the pit of my belly. I might have hated him for all the things he had done recently, but the thought of getting some private alone time with DaQuan still brought me joy.

So much was possible. If I could get him to see how crazy and sloppy things had become, he'd understand how important I was to the business and maybe we could go back to the way things used to be.

When I approached the closet, one of his guys nodded, letting me know it was good to enter.

It had been so long since I was inside the small space, it took my eyes some time to adjust.

"Yo, ma, whassup?"

Being in his presence did something to me. I felt so at ease. For the first time in a very long while, happiness started to creep through my entire nervous system.

"DaQuan, I'm so glad we could have this time together. Baby, we needed to do this a long time ago."

What happened next made me throw up a little in my mouth.

"See, I told you this was just some bull for her to try and get next to you again," a female voice said.

My heart threatened to stop.

Suddenly, my eyes adjusted to that bitch, standing in the corner. She looked like she was fixing her clothes and that was when the stench hit me.

The scent of musty sex filled the air, and I felt like I was gonna upchuck. Had that heartless bastard brought me in there after he'd finished screwing his tramp?

I kicked myself because that would've been the perfect moment. I could've clipped both of them, easy peasy.

"Charisma, I told ya, ma. Lemme handle this," DaQuan said.

I frowned. Deep down, I knew, I might have missed the only real opportunity I had to put a bullet into both of them within seconds of pulling the trigger.

Damn!

"You seen Dunbar?" Edwards asked as I rounded the corner and stepped into the guards' booth. I wasn't in the mood to talk to her or anyone else.

I wanted to say, "yeah, inside the sex closet, throwing herself at a man who doesn't want her." But instead, I shook my head and said, "No." I didn't get why she had even asked me, but then it made sense. They must've known about her plan to try and get her man back.

On the inside, I couldn't stop laughing at Dunbar and her thirsty behind. The sheer desperation was so obvious I felt embarrassed for her. She had sashayed into the closet with her titties all but hanging out, and tried to talk all sweet and sensual.

All of that was until she realized DaQuan wasn't alone. The way her face melted when she realized I was in there must've been priceless. I couldn't really make it out, because it was kind of dark in there, but I could well imagine.

"What the fuck is she doing here?" she had asked.

Her sweet voice vanished so fast, it was hard to believe she could ever muster it up again. I had to stop myself from laughing at her cheap and desperate move.

"She just leaving; we just finishing up a meeting," DaQuan had said.

I had stepped out of the dark corner, still adjusting my clothes. Then I'd planted a wet kiss on DaQuan's lips and strutted out the door.

The look on her face was a mixture of tears and rage. She should've known her plan wasn't gonna work and she didn't have a plan-B, dumb bitch.

I should've stayed in the shadows until she made her move. She would've slithered up close to my man and smelled me all over him. But knowing her thirsty behind, she would've probably overlooked the strong scent of sex all over him if she thought she'd be able to get him back.

The shit was so pathetic, it was funny.

"So, you with DaQuan now?" Edwards looked me in the eyes and boldly asked. Her question took my mind off the drama that had unfolded inside the sex closet.

I wasn't sure what Edwards was up to with her bold question, but I didn't trust none of 'em. I allowed my gaze to travel up and down her body, then stop at her face. She seemed like she was being real with me, so I reluctantly answered with a question of my own.

"Who wants to know?"

"I'm just trying to understand the chain of command around here now. I really don't give a damn who he's screwing. As long as I'm getting my money and nobody is making a bunch of careless mistakes, I'm straight."

"Is that so?"

Edwards threw her hands up in mock surrender. "Listen, I'm always on my grind. If my paper keeps flowing, then I ain't got beef with nobody."

"So your girl know you over here making nice with me?"

"I'm my own damn woman. KenyaTaye is all up in her feelings, talking about putting in for a transfer, so to me that says she's looking out for herself. I just wanna be part of a winning team."

I nodded.

Edwards popped her collar that was already upright. "So, if you the hot chick in charge now, I just need to know. I'ma keep working my jelly, no doubt, and as long as I keep getting paid, it's all good. I just like to know all the players on the team and everybody's position. I'ma play mine."

"Hmm. Well, that's good to know, Edwards. I never took you for the logical type. I guess I had you wrong."

"Well, whatever you took me as, you need to know, I'm always rolling with *she* who keeps my paper flowing."

There was no way for me to tell if she had told the truth.

She could've been trying to play me, but something told me I needed to keep her close. Having someone who could give insight to KenyaTaye and the way she worked couldn't hurt.

"So, how much you willing to do for that paper you want to keep flowing?"

An eyebrow went up.

"You tryna say I can do more?" Edwards moved closer to me. She looked around. "I mean, KenyaTaye never let us do anything more than bring in the goods. You sayin' you're willing to let us, um, I mean, me, do more?"

"Listen, things are kind of strained with what happened to Sanchez, and it's hard trying to figure out who's doing what. It would be nice if I had someone to kinda help me out; things might run more smoothly, you know, to get us back on track."

"KenyaTaye didn't trust nobody. She was the only connection to DaQuan, R.J. and his inner circle and she wanted to keep it that way."

Instantly, that told me that KenyaTaye was truly out for herself. The more Edwards talked, the more I realized things might work out better for us all if I opened up a bit.

The only reason I didn't ask her about Sheppard was because I still needed to feel her out, but I wanted to.

CHAPTER THIRTY-SEVEN
KENYA TAYE

When DaQuan's baby mama got pregnant again, the same time as me, I was devastated. But I looked past it. When he replaced me with Charisma, repossessed my car and gave it to Charisma, I didn't want to get out of bed for days, but I pulled myself up anyway. When he stopped paying my bills without any warning, I cursed myself for putting all of my trust in one man.

But when he invited me to meet him in the closet, only minutes after he screwed her and all but laughed in my face, that was it.

I thought about all of that as I sat outside in the yard and waited on her. To some, it might have seemed desperate, but I had finally had enough. I was about to show him and his fat bitch that I was not to be fucked with.

After a wait that was too long under the Texas sun, C.O. Clarkson waddled in my direction and I immediately felt like this would be another waste of time. But I told myself this was all part of the process.

"What now?"

She seemed miserable. She rubbed her big belly and breathed hard like everything was a struggle.

"You talked to DaQuan lately?" I asked.

"Why?"

"You know he's screwing C.O. Jones, right?" Her expression didn't change and she never flinched. Again, she rubbed her belly.

"Don't you get sick of him doing this? It's like he's gonna knock up every willing chick in TDCJ."

Clarkson seemed as if she couldn't care less about what I had said. I needed her to get angry.

"Listen, I wanted to talk to you to see if you wanted in on a plan to get back at him."

"Get back at him?" She looked at me like I was crazy. "Girl, DaQuan takes real good care of me and our kids. Why would I help you do anything to hurt him just because you mad?"

I couldn't believe my ears. Her question made me feel more stupid than smart.

"You come to me like we're sorority sisters, or even friends." She laughed a little. I wasn't sure whether she was laughing at me, or because she thought she had said something funny.

"You're real special. I can't believe you came to *me* thinking I'd help you get back at *my* kids' father. You hurt him, you hurting my family! It's not fun when you're the one being replaced, huh?"

I had no words.

It didn't really matter because C.O. Clarkson said what she had to say; then she turned and waddled back in the direction she came.

Once back inside the building, I had to look around to make sure I was on the right shift. From where I stood, I watched, damn near speechless, as I saw Bishop and Edwards chatting it up with Jones inside the guards' booth. They were the ones who looked like they were part of a sorority.

Had those bitches gone and lost their ever-loving minds? Didn't they remember *we* didn't like Jones? I couldn't believe what I saw. How had everything fallen apart right before my eyes?

It was hard to tell whether they had seen me as I walked up to the booth. If they didn't see me coming, it was because they didn't want to. The booth was made mostly of glass.

"What the hell is going on in here?"

They got quiet and turned their focus on me, but no one said anything.

"Since when did y'all become besties?" I said to no one in particular.

Jones moved in her chair, and kept her eyes on me. I was still pissed about that stunt she had pulled inside the closet, and I was sure she had probably put all my business out in the streets since now all of a sudden, she had friends on the job. I wish she knew how close she had come to a bullet.

"If you wasn't all caught up in your own feelings and thinking the world fell off its axis because you was having a bad day, you might've noticed," Edwards said. She shrugged as if it was no big deal.

"I thought we was better than this," I said.

"KenyaTaye, go on with that bullshit. You ain't cared about nobody but your damn self for a very long time. The minute DaQuan dropped your ass, all you've been obsessed with was how to get back at him. I don't wanna be part of that petty bull!"

I couldn't believe she had put me out there like that, and in front of Jones too. I didn't expect much from Bishop because she had been a follower from day one. I knew that if Edwards switched teams, Bishop's weak ass would follow.

The way Jones sat there with that smirk on her face made me want to go over there and slap it off of her, but it was clear that I was now outnumbered, so there was little I could do.

It was now official. Jones had taken everything from me. It was crazy that they thought I would just fall back and leave the game without a fight.

"So you've taken sides; is what you're telling me?" I said to Edwards.

"You knew what I was doing since I told you earlier; don't try and play that loyalty bull with me. KenyaTaye, you only look out for you. I gotta look out for me."

I was itching for Jones to say something, but she sat quietly and watched Edwards and me go back and forth like she was at the French Open.

There was only one thing left to do and I needed to do it fast. These bitches and DaQuan would be the death of me if I allowed it to go down that way.

I stepped into the booth, opened the drawer, removed what I needed and left. As I walked out, they carried on like friends who chatted over drinks. Where did they even get common topics to talk about?

It was hard not to think about whether Edwards and Bishop had told Jones all of my business. But then, after a while, I didn't care anymore. I knew that once I left there, I needed to get a transfer.

DaQuan didn't give a damn about me or my baby. He acted like he didn't care what I had to say about the business, so that told me I needed to get ahead of what was to come. I walked over to the bathroom and waited for the three people to leave.

Once they were gone, I walked into the last stall and stood on top of the toilet.

"Fuck this, and fuck them all! I'm tired."

I moved the ceiling panel and felt around for the gun.

It was gone!

Panic flushed through my entire body. I felt around some more. It had to be Bishop or Edwards. Who else would take something from the spot? Just to be sure, I pulled out my flashlight and felt around again.

The gun was gone! I hopped down and leaned against the stall's door. Now what?

"Fuck it!"

I made up my mind. Going out in a hail of gunfire wasn't gonna happen, but I knew what would be just as effective.

CHAPTER THIRTY-EIGHT
CHARISMA

My eyes barely wanted to stay open, I was so tired. But I double-checked my paperwork and made sure it was error-free. Edwards had told me about some drama that had broken out between inmates over those Green Dot cards. I hardly listened, as I tried to focus on my paperwork. When I was wrapping up, a loud voice boomed through the air and disrupted our conversation.

"Yo! Where Dunbar at?"

Edwards and I stopped talking and looked toward the doorway where C.O. Sheppard stood loud-talking as usual. I simply rolled my eyes. I was in no mood for her antics. I had been looking for her ass for more than a minute. There was something about her that I didn't like nor trust. I needed to talk to DaQuan about her.

"She's making her rounds," I said. It would've caused too much confusion to tell her simple butt the truth. Knowing her, she'd sound the alarm by shouting information like she was on a megaphone.

Edwards got up and started to move toward the door.

"What's up? You got something for us?" she asked as she approached Sheppard. It was funny how everyone who talked to Sheppard tried to speak in a low tone. Everyone wanted it to rub off on her, but it never did.

"I got some good stuff, but I need to give it to Dunbar. She hooks me up all the time. I ain't got time for nobody tryna low-ball me!" Sheppard yelled.

Edwards looked around, and I did too. That chick was crazy. Why would she talk so loud about doing illegal shit? It was like she wanted to get busted.

Having Edwards on the team was cool. She acted as a buffer and intercepted lots of bullshit. When I told DaQuan about how she had stepped up, he told me that if I trusted her, we could give her a few extra dollars for her efforts.

Things had been going smoothly for the past week. The only thing was that KenyaTaye was MIA and I didn't have a good feeling about that. She didn't strike me as the type who would calmly accept defeat and go away.

"Maybe she got that transfer after all," Edwards said when we had talked about it earlier.

"Would it happen that fast? I thought it would take weeks for a transfer to go through."

Edwards shrugged. And we probably would've talked about it some more if Sheppard hadn't come up with her foolishness. My shift was coming to an end and I was ready to get off. So much had happened lately that the job had become more stressful, without the extra pressure of smuggling in pills.

To help alleviate some of the stress, DaQuan would send flowers and he'd even sent a masseuse to the house for me. He was so thoughtful.

As I walked out to my car, I thought about how great things had gone with DaQuan since KenyaTaye had disappeared.

"Hey, Cuzzo!"

"Whoa, girl!" I had to clutch my chest to calm my heart. "What the hell are you doing here?" I looked around, spooked.

Lena nearly scared me into an early grave.

"My friend told me about this Facebook page and I met a friend. Girl, he works here, so I'm here for a visit."

I was too tired to grill Lena on her story. I couldn't imagine Lena going for a man who worked as a correctional officer, considering the low pay, but whomever she was visiting would find out soon enough that her bourgeois ass wasn't worth the headache she'd cause.

"So, this is where you work, huh?"

Lena looked around like she was waiting for me to offer her a tour.

"Look, I'm tired and I need to get home. Good luck with your friend, and I'll talk to you later."

"Charisma, what's up with you? Where's your manners? You're not gonna tell me anything about this place and all the hot men that are probably locked up?"

Her mouth hung open like a trap door.

"Lena, why you worrying about inmates. I thought you said your new dude worked here."

She blinked fast.

"Um, he does. But I'm just saying, I'll bet there are a bunch of hot, horny men in here, huh?"

I wondered whether she knew what was up with DaQuan and me; then I told myself, she couldn't.

"Look, girl, I'm tired. I had to pull a double when someone called out, so I'm sorry, you caught me on a bad day."

Lena looked like she wasn't sure she believed my explanation, but I didn't care. I was literally running on my last bit of energy and I didn't feel like wasting any of it on my nosy-ass cousin.

I got into my car and pulled out of the parking lot. From the rearview mirror, I waited as she stood there looking lost, but that was her problem, not mine.

It must've been family night because seconds after I pulled into my driveway, Lance jumped from the bushes. I nearly peed myself.

"Damn! What's with the people in this family?!"

"Hey, Charisma. What's going on? I know you not expecting me 'til tomorrow, but I'm going out of town to the casino, so I thought we could settle up tonight."

Again, my energy level was near the bottom. I looked at him and asked, "Okay, how much I owe you?"

My pulse returned to its normal rate of speed.

"Three bricks."

"Okay, hold up. Let me go inside and get your money. I'll be right back."

I unlocked the door, dropped my things on the sofa and went to the safe. I plucked three stacks and rushed back outside.

"Damn! You couldn't grab a bag for a brother?" Lance said.

He was right. I was so tired, and I knew he was waiting, so I figured the faster I got him his money, the faster he'd leave. I gave him the cash, he gave me the pills and I turned to go back inside, until he stopped me with a question.

"Lena catch you up at the prison today?"

My ears started to burn. I turned to Lance and thought back to what Lena had told me.

"What do you mean? She was at my job, but I thought she said she was there to meet someone she's dating or something like that. I was tired and ready to come home."

"That girl," Lance said. "She's always up to something. She's been riding me for more than a minute about some mystery dude. She claims you won't tell her who he is."

Lance gave me a knowing look, but I ignored it and what he tried to imply about my and Lena's troubled past when it came to men—my men.

Lance and I stopped talking when a floral truck pulled up. Another car pulled in front of us and stopped. We both looked on with puzzled expressions.

A white guy jumped out of the truck with a clipboard. He

walked to the back of the truck and emerged with twenty-four long-stemmed roses. I was instantly excited.

"Delivery for Charisma Jones."

"Oh, wow!" I said.

When I finished signing for that, a woman who wore yoga pants and carried a large black contraption under her arm, walked up and asked, "Are you Ms. Jones?"

"Yeah," I said and looked at Lance.

"Oh, I'm here for a sixty-minute full body massage," she said.

"Daaayum!" Lance covered his mouth and chuckled.

I moved closer to Lance.

Despite all that was going on, my mind was still on what we'd discussed before the flowers and masseuse had arrived. What he had told me didn't make sense. Why would Lena be at my job looking for anyone?

"Ma'am, can I have a few minutes?" I asked the masseuse.

"Sure. I need to grab some stuff from my car."

When she was out of earshot, I leaned over to Lance. "Lena ain't got no business up at that prison."

Lance shrugged. "She said you're the one who told her about the dude. It didn't sound right. I couldn't believe you'd try to hook her up with somebody who's in jail. You know how Lena is with her highfalutin' self."

"So, she told you that I was trying to hook her up with a mystery man?"

"I think that's what she said. It all sounded kind of off to me, but when she told me about your new car and the shopping spree, I told her that had to be the 'ol boy we work for."

And here I thought KenyaTaye was the only threat to my relationship with DaQuan. Now, my jealous-ass cousin was snooping around too?

My stomach dropped.

CHAPTER THIRTY-NINE
KENYA TAYE

I went straight to the administration building and asked if I could see Mr. Richards. I planned to take my shit straight to the top.

"Is he expecting you?" the meek, pudgy receptionist asked.

"No. But I think he would want to talk to me."

She looked at me, then picked up the phone. I stood there and waited.

"Yes, Mr. Richards. There's a correctional officer here to see you."

She covered the phone's mouthpiece with her hand, and asked for my name again.

"Yes, Sir. Ms. KenyaTaye Dunbar." I watched as she shook her head. "Yes, Sir. I'll let her know."

Once off the phone, she looked at me and said, "Mr. Richards is in a meeting right now. We're not sure how long it will take, but he'd like you to wait."

Ten minutes into my wait, I asked myself whether I was really about to do what I had come to do. Frustrated with the wait, the missing gun and all the stuff on my mind, I got up and left.

Hours later, I decided to take a different approach. It was easy to walk up on them without being spotted. But the minute I stepped into view, the look on their faces told me those bitches thought I was gone and forgotten. They should've known better. Just as I suspected, Edwards and Bishop were inside the hole in the wall they liked to go to on the north side.

When I strolled up on them, Edwards nearly dropped the beer bottle she was sucking on. Bishop looked nervous as usual. Those were clear signs that both of them had betrayed me.

"So that's how we doing it now?"

Edwards shrugged like she wasn't fazed by my question. She knew I had so much dirt on her, I couldn't believe she had been so reckless.

"KenyaTaye, what's up with you? You come sneaking up in here like a hurricane trying to do as much damage as possible. I don't get why you trippin'," Edwards said, then pulled the bottle to her lips and took a healthy swig.

"You don't get why I'm trippin'?" I looked at her, then at Bishop. Her eyes quickly looked away when I focused my stare in her direction.

"What do you want us to do?" That was Bishop.

At the sound of her question, Edwards and I both whipped our heads in her direction.

"How about being loyal? Y'all see what I'm going through and neither one of you stepped up to help. Y'all supposed to be my girls, and what y'all do the moment I'm down? Y'all ready to get in line and kick me right along with DaQuan and that bitch Jones."

I choked back tears, not over them, but more so over the messed-up situation I was now in.

"It's like y'all ain't even trippin' over me. You see him dog me out over her and next thing I know, y'all sniffin' right behind her just like him. That shit is foul."

Edwards stepped closer to me. She lowered the bottle from her lips and looked me square in my eyes.

"See, that's where you got this all wrong. The shit ain't foul; the shit is called survival. Do you know how much money I've made working for DaQuan? I may not have had the luxury car or him paying my rent, because you thanked him on your back before either of us could, but I live real good because of him. Now why would I go and mess that up just because you're all caught up in your feelings?"

My eyes filled with tears. I felt like a real big boulder was caught in my throat.

"I get it. You're pregnant, so you're real emotional, but be honest with yourself for a sec. If the tables were turned, you know damn well you wouldn't give either of us a second thought. If you was faced with losing everything you worked for, or guarding our friendship, what would you do?"

Edwards pulled a finger up to her pursed lips and hushed me. "Nah, you ain't even gotta answer that. You've threatened to blow everybody's spot up so many times, I already know the answer."

When I realized that most eyes in the little pool hall/bar were fixed on me, Edwards, and Bishop, and the girl fight bystanders probably hoped they'd see, I stepped off. She had made her position real clear and that was good for me.

As I rushed out of the place, a question made me stop. "Say, I thought you was tight with those females back there."

I barely looked at the dude, when I said, "I thought I was too."

"Well, if you ever need help getting rid of your problems, I may know someone who can get that done for you."

That was when I turned to face him and realized exactly who he was. At the sight of him, memories of the cryptic phone call we shared flooded my mind.

"Hey, this is KenyaTaye. I'm calling about this package that was dropped off at my house."

"Yeah, what about it?"

"Well, I need to know why it was dropped off and what's inside."

"You'll find out soon enough. Don't worry; someone will come talk to you all about it. Just chill."

"Someone? Who is this? And when? What if I get rid of it?"

"You don't wanna do that, ma. We still working out the details, but like I said, someone will reach out to you and let you know what's what."

Seeing E-Dawg face to face made me wonder whether I was being set up. I didn't know what to make of the offer he'd just proposed. But I did know, I didn't need to be seen out in the open talking to him.

My nerves were bad. What was he even doing checking for me?

"Who sent you? DaQuan? Why he got you checking for me?"

E-Dawg slowed his roll and looked at me closer. With his head slightly tilted, he said, "Wait up, I thought ol' boy dumped you, and word on the block is you circling the drain."

My blood boiled at his comment. Did every fucking body in Texas know DaQuan had left me for that mud-dog Jones? And why did I have to be circling the drain? I threw a hand to my hip and prepared to serve up much attitude, until he stepped closer.

"Wait; no disrespect, ma. I'm just saying I wouldn't even be stepping to you right now if I knew y'all was still good. I just thought that since he was kicking it with Charisma, that y'all was through."

Even his tone softened.

I scaled it back once I realized he wasn't the enemy.

"Actually, we are. I mean, he's with her now, but you just threw me off the way you came at me, that's all."

His nervous smile made me calm down a bit. I still glanced around the parking lot just to be sure nobody was paying attention to what was going on with us.

"Okay, so am I wrong to think that you might wanna see them all pay for the way you've been treated?"

I cocked an eye in his direction and pursed my lips. This was all too much, too soon, and too convenient. I didn't know him like that.

"Okay, peep this. I know you probably real jittery right about now, not sure who to trust, and I get that, but I think we can help each other out."

"I'm not interested in talking right here, all out in the open like this."

E-Dawg looked around.

"Okay, I feel you. So, how about this: can I meet you over at your place? I just holla at you and run a few ideas by you. I don't have to come inside or anything. We can sit in the car and talk."

"Can I call you? I mean, let me get to the house, get things settled and maybe we can meet around the corner or something like that."

"Okay, however you wanna do it. Just make sure you call me, bet?"

I nodded. I looked around again.

The entire drive home, I looked in my rearview mirror every few seconds. If E-Dawg had followed me, who else might be on my tail? Then I told myself to calm down.

When I made it, I checked with my mom and made sure everything was okay. When I was convinced nothing was out of the ordinary, I called E-Dawg and told him I'd meet him at a neighborhood park in an hour.

Before I forgot, I walked outside to put the little duffle bag in the car. As I closed the trunk and turned to walk back in, I flinched because a white man walked up on me.

"What the fu—"

"Aww, shoot! Ma'am," he cut me off. "My mistake. I'm so sorry. I must be lost, looking for an address and I think I got all turned around." He jumped back like he was scared he was about to get hit. And he probably was.

Once the threat seemed to be gone, I looked at him and he seemed harmless enough. He was middle-aged, wore khakis, a button-down Polo shirt, and a pair of loafers.

I inched close and motioned for the paper he held.

"So, what address are you looking for?"

He cautiously stepped closer and showed me.

"Oh, you're one street over," I said.

"Whew! Okay. Again, I'm sorry I startled you. But thanks. Thank you!"

I told him a shortcut and sent him on his way.

CHAPTER FORTY
CHARISMA

"Look, ma. I don't want ya splitting ya focus."

I looked into DaQuan's eyes and tried to be the type of confident woman he obviously thought I was. But inside, things had fallen apart for me. First, I still wasn't sure what Dunbar was doing, and why she had gone missing, and that was a major reason for concern. After I learned that Lena was snooping around the prison, it all made me feel uncomfortable and off my game.

"Ya know I run thangs in here, and er'body knows what's up with us, so I need ya to chill and be the female boss we know ya are."

DaQuan wouldn't win any awards for his pep talk, but I knew he was right. And it made me smile when I realized, he was actually trying to lighten things up to help me feel better, but it didn't work. Although the roses and the massage were thoughtful, my mind was stuck on all that might be around the corner.

"Besides, if ya that high-strung, call Lena and work that shit out."

Before he suggested it, I never even thought about checking Lena out myself. He was right, my focus was split and we couldn't afford for me to be off.

I took a deep breath and tried to formulate a plan to figure out what Lena might've been up to. She pressed me about my new man and whether he had any friends, but I ignored her. I mostly ignored her because it felt good to finally turn things around on Lena.

All our lives, she had been on top, got the best of everything, and in the rare moments when there was something I had and she wanted it, she'd simply take it.

Steven, George, and Craig were all so irresistible that Lena couldn't help but throw herself on them. She didn't give a damn that I was in love with each of them throughout the years.

After Steven, she cried and claimed she had gotten drunk and slipped up. I forgave her and we moved on.

Then with George, she said he confessed it was her he really wanted in the first place, but because she was taken, he had settled for me. Still, I forgave her, because she was family.

But by the time I found out about her and Craig, she lied and said he had come on to her and she only gave in to show me how "no good" he was. The only problem with her story was, Craig recorded it all on his tape deck and gladly played it for me to hear how it really went down.

In the end, Craig said we were the most fucked-up women he had ever encountered and he didn't want anything to do with either one of us.

Yeah, Lena and I had a troubled past, but when she pointed out to me that I had been just as lowdown for getting with Craig's brother, Corey, I kinda had to let go of the bitterness. I guess that's why Corey turned out to be such a loser.

DaQuan kissed my lips before he eased out of the closet. I was physically spent and emotionally empty. I didn't feel like dealing with any of the mess.

As I slowly dressed, I thought about what I would need to do to get the real information on Dunbar. It wasn't that I didn't trust Edwards, but I still couldn't be sure that she'd choose me over Dunbar if or when it came down to it.

The more I thought about it, the less likely it seemed that a transfer would have gone through that fast. I didn't need any more surprises, so I left the closet determined to get some solid information on Dunbar.

When I approached the guards' booth, Edwards, Bishop, and Franklin were in there chilling. I strolled in and instantly commanded attention.

"What's up, Jones?" Edwards greeted me. "Everything all right on the cell-block?"

"It's all good. For now, the inmates are all on their best behavior."

"That's what's up!" Bishop said and slapped a low high-five with Franklin.

The festive atmosphere continued and I busied myself with nothing in particular on a nearby chart.

I waited for what I thought was a lull in the conversation, then I asked, "So, anybody seen or heard from Dunbar?"

Bishop suddenly found something on the floor to focus on. We were all screwed if Bishop was ever questioned about anything illegal. She didn't have a poker face.

Edwards's expression changed, but it was Franklin who spoke up first.

"I heard she put in for a transfer, but when they told her it would take a few days or at least a week, I heard her doctor ordered her to take a few weeks off because of stress and the baby."

I hoped they didn't notice the twitch in my eye when he mentioned the baby. The fact that her pregnancy was common knowledge gave me more than a twinge of jealousy, but I quickly reminded myself I had no desire for any more kids and that feeling quickly passed.

These correctional officers were just as dirty as ever. Less than a month ago, all three of them probably smiled all up in Dunbar's face; now they treated me like I was the queen bee and no one wanted to get on my bad side.

I didn't trust any of 'em.

"So, are we getting a replacement or are we supposed to keep pulling overtime to cover her shifts?" Edwards asked.

All I thought was, damn, that was your girl and you worried about her shifts?

"I kinda like the way things are without her," Franklin said.

That was followed by another high-five with Bishop.

"I know what you mean, Franklin; it's like a whole new day around here without her. She didn't know how to lead—plain and simple," Edwards said.

When the radio went off about a problem on the yard, that broke up our impromptu meeting and we all rushed out of the booth and left Bishop behind. Safety procedures called for at least one C.O. to be in the booth at all times.

Because we didn't know what to expect out on the yard, I wasn't in a hurry to get there. We were a minimum security facility, so we didn't have a lot of the problems that probably happened at other lock-ups.

And DaQuan wasn't exaggerating when he said he ran things. Most times, when there was beef between two groups, he could calm things down before the C.O.s and the administration.

Once outside, we saw some C.O.s as they tried to keep a group of inmates back.

"What the hell is going on?" I said.

"I'ma 'bout to go find out." Franklin left Edwards and me and headed toward the group.

We stood off and waited.

Nearly thirty minutes later, Franklin returned.

"It was a drone."

"A what?" I asked.

I knew drones were used to take pictures and Amazon planned

to use them to deliver packages, but I couldn't imagine them being used to smuggle contraband into a prison.

"Don't tell me someone tried to get a drone up in here," Edwards said.

"Yeah, and get this. The drone was carrying a cell phone and charger along with some tobacco." He looked around, and lowered his voice. "You know that wasn't ours, right."

I paid attention to the conversation, but I couldn't help but focus on the two people near the far end of the gate.

DaQuan was chatting with a visibly pregnant correctional officer. And from his body language, I could tell, the conversation wasn't going his way.

There was no way I was about to blow up his spot. The rumors had been flying around for months. I had heard all about C.O. Clarkson and the fact that she was pregnant for him again, but that was none of my business.

Once I got the all clear that it was good on the yard, I turned around and went back inside the building. I decided there was no point in me even mentioning what I had seen to DaQuan. What would be the purpose? It wasn't like I was about to leave him and give up my spot. Dunbar showed me what life was like on the other side and the last time I saw her, she pushed a bucket, and her weave looked real loose. She looked broken down and broke.

I was the first one back at the guards' booth and I was happy to tell Bishop it was a false alarm.

There was no question about it; I knew how to play my position because I loved being on the team.

CHAPTER FORTY-ONE
KENYA TAYE

Could it be that DaQuan made so much money that he didn't even miss the few thousand E-Dawg had locked up in that duffle bag? And why did E-Dawg bring the money to me in the first place?

True enough, I needed that money worse than I needed the air I had to breathe. But I also didn't want to start a war when I didn't have the soldiers to back me up. The truth was, even though DaQuan was locked up, he was powerful, both in jail and on the streets.

Ever since I'd met with E-Dawg, I thought that maybe I deserved the money for all I'd been through. After all, my bills had piled up. But I still wasn't completely sure E wasn't trying to use me.

My mother walked into the kitchen after dropping off the kids. At first she didn't say anything to me. But she didn't have to speak for me to know there was something on her mind.

When I got up from the table, she started in on me.

"You're grown and I get that. But I'm still your mother and when you're wrong, it's still my right to tell you that you're wrong."

The problem with Mary was she couldn't get straight to the point. Although she didn't talk a lot, when she spoke, for some reason, she acted like a lecture would help drive her point home.

I wasn't in the mood for a lecture.

But since she followed behind me as I walked down the hallway, I knew I wouldn't be able to avoid her until she said whatever was on her mind.

"I told you that sleazy gangster was nothing but trouble, and it seems like since then, you've been drawn to him even more." Her eyes zeroed in on mine. "I don't know what's going on with your job, but he's been over here twice this week and you still not back at work. All of this, but you say you not selling no drugs."

"Mom, work is complicated right now. I'm trying not to get stressed out," I touched my stomach, "with the baby and all."

If I thought if I threw the baby in there, it would help her back up off me, I was wrong. She came even harder.

"Yes, the baby," she began. "Are things complicated with the baby's father too?"

That wasn't what I expected when I mentioned the baby.

"I don't know what's going on with you, KenyaTaye. You're here more, but totally detached from the kids and me. Either you stay locked up in that room, or you're zoning out so bad that it's almost like you not here."

How could I get her to understand that this wasn't the time for her to analyze my life? Everything was fucked up. If I had answers, things wouldn't be complicated.

"Then that nasty-looking new friend of yours, where'd he come from all of a sudden?" She twisted up her face. "I've made my mistakes in my day, but even at my lowest, a man like that? Umph, he couldn't do nothing for me."

It was hard for me to really be mad at my mother, because she had been my true ride-and-die. Long before I made money with DaQuan, she helped me make ends meet no matter what she had to do.

"All I know is things are changing around here, and I know for sure nothing good is going to come from it."

"I get it. I know how you feeling right now, but I'm trying to make some moves and figure a few things out."

"You know I don't usually get all up in your business, but I have a feeling things might get the best of you and I don't want to see that happen to you. I've been there and back and it's not fun."

Whenever problems came knocking, my mother would talk about her relationship with my father. I knew the reason she worked so hard to help me was because he left us, but what happened with my father was nothing compared to what I was going through with DaQuan.

When I didn't say anything else, my mother's eyes moved down to my stomach. She swallowed, then looked back up at me. The look on her face reminded me of the look she had when she'd first met E-Dawg.

Since I knew my mother was strong, there was no use in trying to prepare her for what was ahead. She'd be able to handle whatever would go down.

"I have a real important meeting at my job, so I gotta get ready."

She stared at me like she didn't believe a word I said.

I shrugged, but she didn't move.

"So you're going back to work?"

"Kinda, I think. It's complicated all around."

"Well, I'm not trying to slow you down anymore, but thought I'd try to get through to you."

I didn't move an inch as I waited for my mother to turn and walk back toward the living room. I stood for a few minutes after she had left to think about whether I should try to warn her or move on as planned.

There was no point in backpedaling so I went to my room to get dressed.

Two hours later, as I sat across from Mr. Richards, things got real. His secretary had called me to say I needed to bring in my doctor's note so we could talk more about my transfer request.

That worked for me because I'd planned to share a few things with him anyway.

But as I looked into Mr. Richards's hazel-green eyes, I realized my transfer was not the only topic he had on his mind. He never got off that conference call the first time I stopped by, so this would be my first chance to offer him the solution to his contraband problem. As he wrapped up another call, I thought about how hard it was to get to him.

First, I had to wait nearly an hour-and-a-half to get into his office, and he was the one who had summoned me. But after I got over that, I tried to pull myself together because if I got that transfer, I'd be far enough away from the drama at the Jester unit.

"What do you mean, why do I want to leave Jester?"

I repeated his question, because I needed to remember what I had written. I thought the transfer was already done, or close to being done.

"If you leave Jester, what's gonna happen with the people you leave behind?"

Frowning, I played like I didn't know what he was talking about.

Instead of saying another word, Mr. Richards pressed a button on his phone. "Send them in," he said.

Moments later, two of my coworkers walked into the office. Both of them looked different than I'd ever seen them before.

Suddenly, the collar around my neck felt like it was too tight.

CHAPTER FORTY-TWO
CHARISMA

A blank stare focused in on me.

"The gig is up! What the fuck are you up to?"

DaQuan told me to be straight with her, and that was exactly what I planned to do when I called and invited her over. She rushed over, like she might have already been trolling the neighborhood. I watched as she skipped herself in, like we were about to have a sleepover. I ushered Lena straight to the kitchen and that's where we'd been for the last twenty minutes.

We had no idea what all she knew and we didn't know what she would do with whatever information she had. But I'd be damned if I didn't find out.

Lena blinked a few times and gave me that prim-and-proper expression she liked to pull on people who didn't know any better. But I wasn't about to fall for any of her shit. My time was too precious to play a guessing game with her.

"What are you talking about?"

It was obvious she was gonna make things difficult, as usual.

"Lena, you've been following me around, snooping around my job, asking a million questions and you've been hassling Lance. Now what the fuck is going on? What are you looking for?"

She had pissed me off and I didn't have time to play her game.

"I just wanna know more about your mystery man." She giggled like she was nervous. But Lena was so used to playing the innocent role, she couldn't even tell it wouldn't work with me.

The batting lashes, the lost and confused expression.

This time, that shit was not gonna cut it.

"Who you working with? KenyaTaye? Did she get to you and put you up to this?"

Lena's perfect, pretty face contorted. "Kenya who?" She tilted her head slightly, her shoulders shifted, and she crossed and uncrossed her legs. I wasn't sure whether she was telling the truth. But because she couldn't keep still, all the fidgeting made me feel like she was lying.

All of a sudden, Lena jumped up from her chair and threw her hands up. "I swearforGod, I don't know nobody named Kentaye, Kenta, Brumquisha, or whatever the hell you said. I really only wanted to find out who your mystery man was because you wouldn't tell me more about him."

She paced the area between the table and the couch. Silence hung between us for what felt like a really long time.

After a few minutes, she looked up, pulled in a deep breath, then exhaled. "I know you're gonna be pissed, but honestly, Charisma, I'm the one who deserves to be pushing a Beamer that *my* man bought. *I* should be taking *you* on shopping sprees for designer bags and shoes. I get up every day and go to that stupid job at the insurance office and I hate it." She started to fidget with the button on her shirt. "I know you don't trust me, and I've given you lots of reason not to. But I really just want to know about your dude, so I can help you figure out how to keep him." Her eyes fell to the floor. "And, we need a man like him in the family. Well, I thought, if he had a brother, or even some close friends, then maybe I could find someone like him too."

Translation, I'd find him, then convince him that it was me he really wanted and screw him into believing that.

Her little performance told me that she really was trying to figure out how it was possible that I could be on top while she still lurked on the bottom.

Lance had told me everything. And from what he'd said, Lena worked overtime to figure out how my money flowed the way it did. There was no way she'd consider helping me keep anything she wanted.

But after almost two hours of grilling her, I was exhausted. I felt like Lena had at least told the truth about one thing. She didn't know KenyaTaye. In the end, it seemed like she really was just trying to get next to my man, as usual.

"So, you finally believe me?"

Before I let her completely off the hook, I stared her down real cold and hard. If looks could say anything, I hoped my mean mug told her that blood or not, she shouldn't try to fuck with me.

"Yeah, Lena," I finally said. "It's just all this shit's got me paranoid and messed up in the head."

Lena moved closer to me.

"See, that's what I was trying to tell you. You can't be the best you if you all stressed out and shit." Her eyes lit up. "I know." She rushed to her bag and pulled out a large bottle of Coconut Ciroc. "Here, let's get white-girl wasted and you can tell me all about it, Cuzzo."

I looked at Lena, and busted out laughing.

She wasn't slick. Everything else she had tried didn't work, so she figured my lips might loosen up a little if she got me drunk. With all the mess I was dealing with, her idea and her drink didn't seem like a bad idea.

So, we drank.

Sometime after we started, I glanced over and noticed the massive liquor bottle was empty. Had we drank all of that liquor? My eyes suddenly struggled to focus, and I felt sick. The bottle looked bigger than I remembered.

When I got up slowly and cautiously, I looked around the room and noticed Lena stretched out on the couch. Her face was frozen in a frown, and she had one shoe off and her legs cocked wide open. We had no business drinking that entire bottle of vodka. When my stomach rumbled, I actually begged God to help me throw up, but when that didn't work fast enough, I stumbled toward my bedroom and collapsed onto my bed.

Either I passed out, or slept fast and hard.

When the shit started to fly, there was no place for cover. Before daybreak, a loud, booming noise disrupted my sleep and I was completely discombobulated. It must've been before dawn, because it was still dark outside. Or were my eyes still closed?

Was I dreaming? Was this my life?

"Charisma Jones!" a loud, angry voice yelled. I bolted upright, or tried to, but was shoved back down in a forceful way.

What the hell? How did someone get into my room?

The last thing I remembered was being in the kitchen, or was it the living room? DaQuan and I had talked last night about some changes we needed to make, or me dealing with Lena, but what was this?

The fucking pills, the cash?! Was somebody trying to hit us for our stash? Jesus! What if that was Lena's game all along? What if she had been working with or for somebody who wanted to hit DaQuan?

My heart was about to explode, or was that my head? Oh shit, the liquor. Was I still drunk? When did I go to bed? Had Lena left? All of a sudden, I was wrestled to my stomach, in the dark, with green and red lights dancing all around the darkened room.

I heard scuffling down the hall, and noises from the front room. One of the kids screamed, or was that a kid? My kids weren't here, were they? It was chaos, and it was in my house. I needed to call DaQuan. Yeah, he'd help me figure the shit out for sure.

But I couldn't move. There was a sharp pain in the middle of my back, like an elephant squatted on me. The angry voice jerked my arms, one at a time, to my back.

"Stop resisting!"

"I'm not! What the fuck is going on? Who are you?"

When I tried to turn my head to see, he yanked it back and shoved it into the mattress. I couldn't breathe. I wanted to tell them where to find the money. They could have it all. I knew DaQuan wouldn't want me hurt over money and pills.

Suddenly, cold, hard steel connected with my wrists, and that's when I realized, it wasn't a robbery. I was being arrested!

CHAPTER FORTY-THREE
KENYA TAYE

The wooden chair felt hard and cold as my ass pressed down on it. I tried to adjust my butt in the seat, but it didn't work. Suddenly, the temperature in the room seemed to drop from comfortable to freezing within seconds. Mr. Richards cleared his throat, and was cooler than a cucumber. It was clear he felt good about something.

He walked around me and moved behind his desk. He had the nerve to whistle a song I couldn't place.

"Dunbar, you should know by now, that this is not going to end well for you. Right now, you're probably trying to consider your options, but let me warn you, they are few, and limited."

As I looked into Mr. Richards's eyes, I knew he meant every word. He was calm and straight to the point. When Sanchez and Sheppard stood by on either side of me, I swallowed hard. It was clear, the gig was up.

I wondered if they had ratted me out; everyone knew, the first one to get the deal usually sealed his or her fate. I hadn't moved fast enough. Neither of them looked pressed or worried.

Mr. Richards opened a folder and slid two sheets of paper toward me. My eyes glanced down at it, and he said, "Go on, pick it up, read it; it's quite amusing."

With shaky hands, I reached for it. But he snatched it back before I touched it.

He held it up like those reporters do when they're showing something on TV.

"It's okay; allow me to give you the *Cliff Notes'* version. This is a how-to-guide, confiscated from inmate DaQuan Cooper's cell. You've probably never seen it before, and I won't bore you with all the details, but I'll let you know this. The kind of tips include, dropping a 'kite,' or love note, confessing to your C.O. target that you 'felt a connection to her, and that she was beautiful.'"

He looked up at me, and raised his eyebrows. "But, Dunbar, my favorite part in here…" He shook the papers. "My favorite and the most creative part is the tip that tells the inmate soldiers they should only target women who have low self-esteem, insecurities, and certain physical attributes."

It was clear to me that he ended with that for the most impact, and he was right to do that because I was pissed beyond words. But mostly, I was hurt.

I didn't want to believe my ears. DaQuan had a how-to guide like that?

There was no way I could hide the way I felt. So that bastard thought I was insecure? He thought I had low self-esteem? And what were the certain physical attributes? Jones was fat, but I was *phat*, wasn't I?

After the assistant warden dropped the bomb and watched it explode, I looked on with hatred as Mr. Richards leaned back in his large leather chair. He exhaled. Again he chilled, while I choked back tears and struggled to keep the bile down.

After a few minutes, that felt like hours to me, Mr. Richards leaned forward, but this time he looked at Sheppard instead of me. "So what can you tell us?"

She spoke on cue, "All of the contraband I delivered is properly marked and tagged. Obviously, the cell phones and batteries as well as some of the pre-paid cards are all we will have left," C.O. Sheppard said.

In all the time I had dealt with her, I never once heard her speak like she had sense. As she delivered her report, she wasn't fidgety and she sounded real believable, even smart. I was sure about one thing—she was one helluva actress.

I was dumbfounded; all this time, that bitch was a plant, a fucking informant? How could I not have realized she was playing us all?

"I made sure to speak loud and clear so that the wire could pick up conversations I had with C.O.s Dunbar, Edwards, Franklin, Jones, Bishop, and inmates DaQuan and R.J."

My mind raced with memories of her crazy behavior. I thought she was a crackhead. Who knew she was undercover all that time?

"Good work. How would you say things changed after Sanchez was busted?" Mr. Richards asked.

My head started to spin again. Sanchez was a snitch, too? What the hell was I doing?

"We thought for sure after we set it up for Sanchez to get busted and spread the word, that things would've slowed down. At first they did, but as you will see in my report, the flow of pills never slowed. Also, when inmate Cooper started to show a romantic interest in C.O. Jones, a power struggle began between her and Dunbar. Again, all of this is detailed in my report."

After she spoke, C.O. Sheppard stepped back to my side. It was obvious, I was fucked.

Mr. Richards looked me in the eyes, but he spoke to C.O. Sanchez.

"C.O. Sanchez, to whom did you report regarding your contraband, before the well-publicized bust?"

"Sir, I reported directly to C.O. Sergeant Dunbar here, and she acted as a go-between by delivering my items to DaQuan or his minister of finance, R.J." He quickly added, "All of those items are properly detailed in my report, and items are tagged and marked as well, Sir."

Mr. Richards's unibrow elevated slightly.

"Oh, and as the sergeant on duty, did all of her subordinates take part in the illegal smuggling business? What about C.O. Scott?"

"Sir, Scott was not in on the business. She was an outsider. Everyone who had a role has been properly identified and his or her role is clearly detailed in the reports."

Without another word, Mr. Richards opened his drawer and pulled out a large plastic bag. He put it down on his desk, in front of me. I wanted to die right there.

It was my gun.

I swallowed hard and dry. How the hell had they gotten my damn gun?

Our eyes met, but only mine started to fill with tears.

The only time Mr. Richards's focus left me was when his phone rang. He looked down, pressed a button on it, then spoke. "Yes?"

"Mr. Richards, Special Agent Anderson on line one," the secretary's voice said.

Mr. Richards pressed another button and a different voice rang out through the speakerphone.

"We have three females in custody, and two minors in state care."

"Great. When will you pick up the others?"

"We're headed to your unit now."

"Roger that!"

Mr. Richards ended the call, then returned his focus to me. A single tear ran down my face like it wanted to escape too. I was speechless and helpless. My heart had gone through so many emotional highs and lows, I felt empty. I had no one to turn to.

Were those my kids in state custody? What must Mary have thought when they came to the door?

What about E-Dawg? What about the plans we'd talked about?

"I ne-need to make a phone call," I said.

My voice acted like it didn't want to work.

Mr. Richards stood and pressed another button on his phone.

"She's ready to go," was all he said.

I couldn't wrap my mind around what was going to happen next. Was he going to let me walk out? My answer came the moment his office door swung open and two uniformed police officers stormed in.

"On your feet," one commanded. Sheppard and Sanchez shuffled out of their way.

It took a moment for me to react because I couldn't believe this was happening to me, and that they were talking to me.

"Now," he repeated.

I eased up out of the chair, and a female officer approached me. "C.O. Kenya Taye Dunbar, you are under arrest, for plotting to smuggle drugs, cell phones, and other contraband into the Texas Department of Criminal Justice facilities, criminal conspiracy…"

Everything else was a blur until my hands were yanked behind my back, handcuffed, and I was led out of the office like one of the criminals I used to guard.

CHAPTER FORTY-FOUR
CHARISMA

Being on the other side was nothing I could've ever imagined. I knew my mind should have considered the possibility since what we did was illegal, but if the thought of getting caught had crossed my mind, I'd told myself I'd have a way out.

As I sat inside a cell, it was hard to formulate any kind of plan. One of the main reasons was my lack of focus.

"Jesus! Can you stop with all the damn crying?!" I shrieked. It didn't matter that I was frustrated, and pissed off; Lena wouldn't let up.

She had been going ape-shit crazy since we were booked, processed, and thrown into a holding cell at the Harris County Jail.

"Why don't you tell them, I didn't do nothing wrong? I was at the wrong place at the wrong time!"

"Shiit, me too," a woman whom I thought was sleeping suddenly bolted upright and said, from a bench in the corner of the large holding cell.

I rolled my eyes at her and Lena's whiny behind.

"Can't you call your baller boyfriend to bail us out? I can't be in jail. I'm too cute to be in this nasty cage! Can't your baller boyfriend hire Dick DeGuerin to defend us? He's got the money to do it. Don't he?"

I wanted to bitch-slap my cousin, but figured jail wasn't the place to be beating up on anybody. Unfortunately, the cell wasn't big enough for me to put any real distance between us, so I had to sit there and take it.

She wanted me to call my *baller* boyfriend; if only she knew. There wasn't anyone for me to call. DaQuan was already behind bars, so what the hell would he be able to do? Inmates weren't allowed to call jails. I was now an inmate. I felt so down and desperate, I couldn't think straight.

The moment I tried to formulate any kind of plan, Lena started to cry and threw my thinking all off. I knew for certain that KenyaTaye was behind this. That low-down bitch went and sang for sure.

I had to find a way to get the word to DaQuan. She had thrown us all under the bus. He'd be next if they hadn't gotten him already. I was anxious and nervous at the same time.

"When are we going home?" Lena howled again.

Her nonstop crying and nagging hadn't helped in any way. I got that she was scared and she was right; she was caught up in the wrong place, but I needed her to chill.

"We will go before the judge; then we go from there," I said.

"A judge?" She looked down at herself. "You mean I have to go to court looking like this?"

I shouldn't have, but I did. I turned to look at my cousin. I couldn't believe she was worried about what she looked like and we were sitting up in jail. She needed to be worried about whether she'd make it to see the judge the way she had worked the last of my nerves.

"God, Charisma, don't you watch any TV court shows? People who look dirty and tacky are assumed guilty. We need to shower and put on a change of clothes before we go to court. What's the jury going to think? They're gonna send us away to prison. OhmyGod! What to do? What to do?"

Her lips quivered, she grabbed the sides of her head and started to bawl again.

That was when the lady must've taken pity on her. She looked at me, then she looked at Lena.

"Jury?" she asked.

I tried to ignore them both.

"Nah, honey, you got it all wrong. You see the judge first; he's gonna say whether there's enough evidence for the charges to stick. Hell, who knows? He might even let you go."

Lena's bawl subsided a bit and she sniffled.

"I didn't do nothing. If I wasn't at her house, I wouldn't even be in here right now. I've always been the responsible one. I should've known she was doing something illegal."

Even being in jail didn't stop me from wanting to kill her with my bare hands.

My mind raced. While the woman talked to Lena, I started to try and figure things out. All of a sudden, a voice called my name. I looked up to see C.O. Scott.

My eyes grew wide, but I wasn't sure whether I should respond. We had always been friends, but the more I moved up in the ranks, the wider the gap spread between us.

I rushed closer to talk to her.

"Girl, how you holding up?"

"This is a mess; my cousin is having a fit."

She looked past me. "Damn, I did hear that Lena got caught up too."

Was she here to gawk or did she have helpful information? I tried to check myself; there was nothing I could do.

"How'd you know I was here?"

"It's all everybody is talking about. They got Dunbar inside the warden's office. I heard they set her up, but Clarkson, Franklin, Edwards, and Bishop were all picked up right inside Jester."

"Whhhaaaat?" My eyes grew with every word she said.

How could Dunbar be in jail too? She was behind this, I knew for sure.

"Yes, girl. DaQuan is in solitary, along with R.J. and all of his top guys."

"What the hell?"

"Girl, this is huge. It's all over the news too."

"The news?"

"Yes, girl. You'd better get a real good attorney when you get out of here."

C.O. Scott looked at me. "I just wanted to come check on you. I don't know what I can do to help, but I didn't know if you knew what was going on with everybody else." She looked around, and said, "I need to get back to my post."

"Okay. Well, thanks for the info."

As she turned to leave, I called out to her again.

"Can you call my mom for me?"

"I did already. They're working on getting you guys out."

When Scott left, I was more confused than before. If KenyaTaye was arrested too, then how did this happen? Could it be that she was blindsided too? Maybe they only arrested her so it could look good in front of everyone else. That thought died when I remembered where Dunbar was arrested.

There was no use in me sharing any information with Lena. She and her new friend were talking and I wanted to leave them alone.

So, we all got busted.

CHAPTER FORTY-FIVE
KENYA TAYE

So many crazy thoughts swam around in my head that I didn't know what was what.

I couldn't believe what I'd heard. I needed a moment; the only plan I came up with wasn't going to work. Someone took the gun and it had been connected to me. Then, someone else had gotten my deal before me. I was pregnant and couldn't get any sympathy.

"We don't need you," the detective said. "We've got this on lock." His smug attitude made me sick. I should have gone to the warden when I first thought about it—back when I talked to Edwards about it and she made it seem like ratting everyone out was a bad thing. I should've followed my mind way back then. I had waited too damn late.

"I sure hope he was worth it, because you're about to go to prison for a real long time. And that baby you're carrying, get ready to kiss it goodbye. You betrayed a lot of good, hardworking correctional officers, who are proud to wear the uniform, for your own selfish greed and gratification."

Who did he think he was talking to? I didn't know a single correctional officer who could be described as proud. We were overworked, underpaid, and considered the laughingstock of the justice system. The higher-ups expected us to be a barrier between the bad guys and the rest of society, with nothing but a radio on our hips. You pay us peanuts, then you're surprised when we try to make a little extra on the side?

"Is there a reason you brought me out of my cell? I'm done talking. I need to make a phone call."

"Oh really? Who you gonna call? Your mother is in the city jail; your kids are in state custody; and your ex, well, he's in solitary. So, tell me, Dunbar, who you gonna call?"

I bit down on my lip so I wouldn't haul off and say anything they might be able to use against me.

"I'm gonna take you back to your cell, but I want you to try and think about whether you have any information you think might be useful. The problem is, we've said the same thing to all your partners in crime, so you know how that goes. I'm sure Edwards, Bishop, and Jones are probably scrambling to knock down the door to get to us first."

I tossed and turned, and finally sat up. That conversation had taken place while I was being processed, but it still felt like it was just a few seconds ago. I looked around, to confirm I was still in jail. I hoped I was dreaming, but no such luck. This nightmare was real for me and obviously for a lot of others too.

Cradling my head in my hands, I struggled to think about any kind of information that might be able to help my situation. My mother and kids had nothing to do with this. I needed them released.

DaQuan is the one who'd fucked things up for everyone. He just couldn't stop thinking with his dick! He had messed everything up and now I had to figure a way out.

Nearly a week after being released from jail, I was still saying sorry to my mother. She was released on her own recognizance, but I had to be bailed out.

"We need to figure out how to get the kids back. This is a royal mess for sure," she said as we walked into the apartment.

I wasn't ready for what we saw.

The couches were turned over, with cushions and pillows slashed; magazines, books and papers were strewn all over. Plants were dug up and potted dirt was left all over the floors. The TVs were smashed, dishes were piled on the table, and all of the doors to the cabinets and drawers were wide open.

My mother stepped cautiously toward the kitchen.

"They left the refrigerator open like this?"

Food, from the freezer and elsewhere, was deliberately pulled out. I didn't want to see what the other rooms looked like.

"What were they looking for like this?"

Too mad for words, I walked around and took in all of the damage. If I had anything left, I couldn't see it; everything my eyes saw was destroyed.

The scene was even worse in my bedroom. The mattress, dresser drawers, clothes were all mixed with liquids. They ransacked the closets, and the stench of all kinds of stuff mixed together was enough to make me upchuck.

"What have you done to make the law come down on us like this?"

My mother leaned against the doorway as I stepped over the trash that had become my room.

"I warned you about drug dealing. I told you that trash of a man who came by here, who you couldn't stay away from, wasn't gonna be no good for you. I ain't never in my life broke a single law and now, I'm looking at a record, and my grandkids are caught up in the system."

She sighed hard and I felt like shit.

I couldn't even tell her I'd fix it, because it was a lot to fix. She'd be right not to trust anything I said.

Later, I took a call from E-Dawg and we agreed to meet. Of course I couldn't tell my mother and I was okay with that. I needed to figure out what to do about this mess.

E-Dawg agreed to meet anywhere I wanted. That was easy. I told him we would meet inside a movie theater. I picked a movie, a showtime and texted him with the information.

The next morning, I left around eleven for the 11:50 showing. I arrived and found a seat in the last row of the dark theater. A few minutes after the previews started, a tall, dark silhouette strolled into the near-empty theater and looked toward the back.

I waved him up and he came and eased into the seat next to me. He smelled good, like he had just walked out of a weed dispensary.

"Thanks," I said.

E-Dawg had bailed me out. A bust like ours traveled fast through the criminal world.

"It's all good. How you holding up?"

"Not good. My kids got taken away; Moms is pissed and worried."

Usually I was a real good judge of character, but I couldn't call it anymore. I felt lost because when I rode high with DaQuan, I couldn't imagine I'd be on the outside looking in at what the good life used to be like.

"Ma, we can do this. I tried to tell you we needed to move fast."

E-Dawg wanted me to help him take over DaQuan's business, but that was before the arrests. Now, I didn't think there was anything left to take over.

"What are we gonna do? I'm facing an indictment. As far as I know, so is everybody else who was working on the inside. I heard DaQuan is in the hole. What's there to take over?"

"With ya' boy out of the game, these cats gonna go bananas trying to jockey for position."

I wondered whether E-Dawg had been dropped on his head as a baby or maybe he didn't want to get the message; the business was dead.

"For a long time, I couldn't figure out how ol' boy was able to hold it down the way he did from the inside. But the more I peeped the way he moved around, I realized he really was only good because of the females who had his back."

"Too bad he didn't realize that."

"Bae, don't get mad. Get better and beat him at what used to be his game; that's the way you get revenge. Let 'em see you doing good despite everything."

E-Dawg's pep talk sounded good, but unlike him, I couldn't ignore what loomed. I was looking at doing time myself, and although I believed he really wanted me as a partner, I didn't think he was being realistic about the fact that my days of freedom might be numbered.

"So, what you say, ma?"

CHAPTER FORTY-SIX
CHARISMA

The stash account was my lifesaver and I was glad DaQuan had insisted that I set it up. Unfortunately, I didn't do it as soon as he told me, so there wasn't a whole lot of money in there.

Once out of jail, I tried to figure out what my next move should be. I had no way to reach DaQuan and I sure as hell couldn't go up to Jester.

Worse than being in jail, I had to hide out at Lena's house. The only reason I had a reprieve was because she'd been taking two-and-a-half-hour baths. We'd been out for nearly a week and she complained that jail stench still came out of her pores.

Her irritating voice announced her arrival before I ever saw her. I rolled my eyes as she approached.

"Eeww, I can't believe you were hooking up with some nasty inmate." She scrunched up her nose as she flopped onto the sofa. "I mean, who does that?"

She was so flippant when she talked about my relationship with DaQuan, and she didn't understand.

The last thing I wanted to do was talk about him with Lena. She didn't get what that man had done for me. I knew from the outside, most people would say I was a fool, but I had never had a man tell me I was beautiful. He took care of me better than anyone else ever had.

Lena got up and pranced down the hall. I knew she wouldn't be gone for long, but I was upset when she returned too fast.

She hadn't sat for five minutes before there was a knock at her door. Lena jumped up and screamed, "I'll get it!"

Not in the mood for any company, I figured I could ease my way into the background as soon as she and her company walked back into the living room.

"Now, Charisma, I knew you wouldn't agree, so I made an executive decision. I think you need someone who can relate to you and what you're going through."

Confusion settled on my features because I had no clue what she was talking about. No one I knew would be coming for me at Lena's house.

As I tried to make sense of what Lena had said, Corey came around the corner and looked at me with pity on his face.

"Man, what the fuck you been doing?"

He frowned, hard and intense.

I looked at Lena, then back at Corey.

"I knew something wasn't right! I knew it, man, like I felt it, but ain't no way I woulda' took you for one of them thirsty broads trolling jailhouse sites for dudes."

Lena stood off to the side like she was an adult chaperone.

"That's like one of the oldest hustles around, them dudes just looking for a female to help do time with them." He shook his head and Lena shook hers, too.

"Ah, and don't even tell me, he probably had you putting money on his books too, huh?"

"If you must know, he has been giving me money and lots of it. It's not what you think and I don't really wanna talk about this. I don't even know why you're here."

With his hands extended in my direction, he moved toward me.

"Corey, I got this. I don't know why crazy over here called you. But DaQuan took better care of me and your kids than you ever did. We didn't want for nothing while I was with him."

"That fool bought you that whip?"

"And he bought us designer purses. He had lots of money, but if I knew he was in jail, running a gang and all of that hood stuff, ain't no way I would've condoned that relationship," Lena said.

"Newsflash!" I jumped up. "I'm a grown-ass, educated woman. Whatever I did, I did because I wanted to do it. I don't need you," I pointed at Corey, "or you," I pointed at Lena, "all in my damn business."

"I told you this intervention was not gonna be easy. She's deep in this," Lena tried to whisper.

As I got up, I caught a glimpse of the news from the corner of my eye. That made the intervention party's focus turn to the TV too.

Lena brought a hand up to cup her gaping mouth.

"Jesus! You've made the news!" She rushed and grabbed the remote with her other hand and turned up the TV.

Corey stood as if he was stunned silent.

The newslady said, "Shocking, stunning! And downright unbelievable! Those are just a few of the words being used to describe what lawmakers are calling one of the worst cases of corrupt correctional officers gone wild. They say control of Texas Department of Criminal Justice's Jester unit in Richmond, Texas, just south of Houston, was effectively handed over to a group of gang member inmates who seduced and bribed the female guards. Federal prosecutors say twelve female correctional officers, seven inmates and five others with gang ties have been charged with plotting to smuggle drugs, cell phones and other contraband into the Jester unit. An indictment unsealed earlier today said the ring also involved sex between inmate and guards that led to four of the officers becoming pregnant by DaQuan Cooper, leader of the jailhouse gang."

At that announcement, two sets of eyes turned and locked on me. Their stares dropped to my stomach.

"I am not pregnant!" I snapped.

I quickly turned my focus back to the lady on the screen.

A man's talking head popped up on the screen, and he said, "The inmates literally took over 'the asylum,' and the jail, along with the processing center, and it became a safe haven for the gang members and their workers. The correctional officers are now out of a job and may face up to twenty years in prison themselves. Gina, we just got our hands on this indictment, and it reads like a steamy, but raunchy, romance novel, with a storyline that includes sex, luxury cars, and a cash-flow that would rival any legitimate small business."

"Damn, Charisma. I didn't think you had it in you," Corey said as he looked at the screen. "I mean, if it didn't mean you was headed to the big house yourself, that would've been real gangster."

It was easy to ignore Corey, but Lena was so overdramatic that ignoring her was that much harder.

"All this time I was jealous thinking you had yourself a real good man and you out here running behind some nasty-ass jail inmate?"

There were no words to describe the sheer disgust in Lena's eyes when she looked at me.

Lena shook her head. "Now I finally know why people call some women desperate and thirsty."

Despite all of the insults, something in me was satisfied because she had finally admitted, she had been jealous of me.

CHAPTER FORTY-SEVEN
KENYA TAYE

anic flooded my system as I watched the news with my mom. She handled the whole mess a lot better than me. I couldn't believe all that had happened, even though that didn't stop it from happening.

"So you been indicted."

It didn't matter that I knew it was coming, I still didn't want to think about what was going to happen. As the news people rattled off all the raunchy stuff we did on the job, my mother shook her head and frowned.

"You got that man's name tattooed on your body?"

There was no point, so I ignored her question. All I could do was stand, watch, and listen. I didn't remember twelve or thirteen C.O.s being on payroll. And who ate salmon and drank Belvedere Vodka in Jester? I missed out on that party. It was catfish, tilapia, and Skyy Vodka.

"They don't even know what the hell they talking about."

That comment made my mother look at me like I was crazy.

I grabbed the remote and changed the channel. That was a huge mistake because on the other channel they had actual pictures of us all. Most of the pictures were from our work badges, but the inmates pictures were mugshots.

"Girl, this is going to be a mess!"

Just when I thought nothing could be worse, a somewhat familiar woman popped up on the screen. I didn't remember her.

"I knew KenyaTaye Dunbar was dangerous after our first encounter." The woman's eyes grew wide. "It was so scary."

Now I was curious. I knew people came out the woodwork for their fifteen minutes, but this was absurd. I had no clue whom the woman was, but she claimed she'd had an encounter with me.

"So you say she assaulted you in a parking lot?"

"Yes, ma'am. And a friend of mine recorded the entire thing on her cell phone. She was so scared, she stayed away and recorded the entire incident from a safe distance. Ms. Dunbar was angry, and she was on a rampage."

I studied the woman's face, but still, it didn't register. That was until she told her story.

"So what happened in the lingerie store?" the interviewer asked.

"I'll admit, I might have overreacted when she confirmed that she was trying to get her money back for some panties she had already worn, but who does that?"

"She did what?" The interviewer's reaction said it all. That was another ding against me.

My mouth fell. Oh shit! That was the nosy customer I had smacked in the parking lot. I was embarrassed. On top of everything else, the image that had been painted about me looked very bad.

I couldn't remember a time when my mother had looked at me with an expression that said she was too disgusted for words.

The news was still on when my phone rang. Without a thought, and probably because I wanted to escape all the crap they talked about on TV, and my mother's little comments, I just answered.

"Hello?"

"KenyaTaye? Is that you?"

The voice wasn't familiar, despite the way she sounded.

"Um, yeah, who is this?"

"Are you pregnant by DaQuan?"

I pulled the phone from my ear and looked at it. I didn't recognize the number and I sure didn't catch the name.

"Who is this again?"

"Are you the correctional officer from the Jester unit? Is your name on the bathroom walls advertising that you'd have sex with inmates for the right price?"

My temper threatened to burst.

"Who the hell is this again?"

"How much money did you make working with inmates you were supposed to be guarding?"

Part of me wanted to listen to the other questions, but I ended the call.

It seemed like the phone rang as soon as I ended the last call.

"Hello?"

"Hi. Ms. Dunbar, I'm a reporter with *The Houston Chronicle* and I wanted to know if we could conduct a quick interview about the charges you're facing."

"How'd you get this number?"

There was a knock at the door. My mother's eyes were stuck to the TV so I figured I'd answer. I moved away from her because I thought that would give me a chance to curse the *Chronicle* reporter out while Mary was occupied.

"Ma'am, did you know inmate DaQuan Cooper has fathered children with two other correctional officers?"

Her tone said it all: *Bitch, what's wrong with you?*

"Don't call this fucki—"

Doing too much at the same time, I was still on the phone when I pulled the door open and was instantly blinded by a bright light.

A microphone was shoved in my face.

"Who is the father of your child and were you aware that it is illegal to have a relationship with an inmate confined to the custody of the Texas Department of Criminal Justice system?"

My reflexes made me slam the door shut. My heart was beating faster than I could handle. I ended the call and leaned up against the wall because my legs felt weak.

"What the hell is going on?"

"Everybody does stupid things, but this has got to be the dumbest shit you've ever done! What the hell was you thinking? How did you think this was gonna end for you?"

I couldn't remember the last time my mother cursed at me.

There was another knock at the door, and the phone rang at the same time. My head started to spin. My mother stood over me and went in on me about my stupidity; and I wasn't sure what to do.

When the phone in my hand rang again, I was tempted to throw it across the room, but it was finally a number I recognized.

"Edwards, Jesus, is the media calling you?" That was the way I answered the call.

"Bitch, you did this shit to us! Just because you couldn't take being replaced, yo monkey ass went and threw every damn body under the bus! And don't even try to lie and say it wasn't you because I remember when your dumb ass told me you wanted to do it."

"What the hell are you talking about?"

Now my heart raced for another reason. I should've ignored her call too.

"Don't play dumb with me! I don't care what anybody says, I know it was you! You couldn't handle it when your boy moved on. I can't stand insecure bitches like you."

It was hard to believe that Edwards was going off on me like that.

"You need to check your facts! Sanchez and Sheppard are both plants! They was working undercover all this damn time! So, bitch, don't come for me."

Silence.

"Sheppard's simple ass?" Edwards asked. Her tone had changed quickly.

"Yes, both of them. That whole thing about Sanchez getting busted, it was all a setup. And you think Sheppard is strung out, always talking loud and acting crazy? Well, all of that was just a front! Both of them been spying on us all along. Matter-of-fact, the reason the bitch was always loud was so the wire she wore would pick up every word being said."

"What the fuck?"

"Yeah, so get yo life, bitch. They got all kinds of shit on all of us. I'm in the same boat as everybody else."

All of a sudden, another voice rang through the phone.

"I knew I didn't trust Sheppard," the other person said.

"Who's that?"

My heart threatened to stop.

"Oh, um, that's Jones; she's on the line too," Edwards said meekly.

Edwards better be glad it was a phone call because I'd be on her ass for trying to set me up. Those simple bitches were just stupid.

"So you lurking in the background on a secret three-way call for what? What kind of middle-school bullshit y'all into?"

"Look, we didn't know what was going on," Jones said.

"But I see y'all quick to try and blame me for this shit."

"What would you have thought? You're the one who asked me about blowing up everybody's spot. Why wouldn't I have thought you made good on that?"

"Well, I didn't and like I said, they've got everything they need. Both Sanchez and Sheppard had detailed reports, logging all the contraband they smuggled in. Oh, and everybody's phones were tapped."

"Girl, no!" That was Edwards. She acted like we were suddenly cool again.

"They know it all. So whatever we did in the Jester unit, I didn't have to rat anybody out. They've been watching it all from the beginning. Shit, for all I know, they probably listening to this call too."

Instead of giving the bitches a chance to act like we were all friends who were gonna come up with a plan, I ended the call. Hell, I had already said enough!

CHAPTER FORTY-EIGHT
CHARISMA

I wasn't ready when Edwards called gassing me up and talking about she could prove KenyaTaye was behind everything. I was out for blood too, but we were both stunned speechless when KenyaTaye broke it down and blamed everything on Sheppard and Sanchez.

"Watch, I'm about to get her backstabbing ass on the phone," Edwards had bragged before the call.

"You ain't gotta prove nothing to me. I know for a fact it was her."

"I'm calling her ass. Hold on; put your phone on mute."

I couldn't prepare myself for what KenyaTaye had to say. And it was obvious Edwards wasn't ready, either.

The more I thought about Sheppard, I couldn't imagine her holding it together long enough to tell on anybody. But maybe that was the whole point. She had been one helluva actress if what KenyaTaye said was true.

Being up under Lena wasn't good for my thought process. I needed to figure out a defense or something because the shit just got real, now that I knew what all they had on us.

I grabbed my bag and left. I needed to go home and get away from Lena and her constant negativity.

As I pulled up, I thought it felt good to be back at my own place. It was a mess. Obviously the officers hadn't left a single thing untouched. Despite the chaotic state of my place, it still beat being at Lena's.

"Who is it?!" I yelled as I walked to answer the door.

When no one answered, I didn't think twice about pulling the door open, even though I should have.

Camera flashes and bright lights flooded the doorway.

"Is it true that you guys made more than sixteen thousand dollars a month selling cell phones, prescription pills, and other contraband behind bars?"

My eyes were frozen wide.

"Are you one of the correctional officers who got pregnant by inmate DaQuan Cooper?"

Eyebrows went up.

"What can you tell us about the sex closet?"

Was this legal? The way they stood at my front door, and threw questions at me in rapid-fire style.

"Did you smuggle pills and contraband into the prison in your underwear and your hair? Is that a weave or a wig?"

Something in me finally woke up and I slammed the door shut.

Alone and away from the media that acted like paparazzi, I leaned against the door and for the first time since it all went down, I allowed myself to cry.

It was clearer than ever before, I had really, really fucked up.

E mpty, or just plain tired, as I stood in front of the judge, my heart didn't feel a damn thing. I actually wanted her to hurry and do whatever the hell she was gonna do. The anticipation made me more scared than what was to come.

If things had gone the way I'd planned, people would've been at my funeral a while back, so as far as I was concerned, I had died a long time ago. Nothing she'd say could hurt me.

My court-appointed lawyer seemed like she was just as ready to get things over with as me.

I remembered the first time I'd met her. That was nearly an entire month after she was appointed as my damn lawyer. If she was going to really work for me, that first meeting wouldn't have taken an entire month. Since I didn't have any money to pay for a decent attorney, and E-Dawg was arrested too, I was really screwed. The money in the duffle bag was gone.

"You need to prepare yourself for a rough ride," the lawyer had said.

When she had first said that, I thought she had lost her mind. She had finished going through a thick folder that had my name on it, and shook her head often.

I knew she was right, but her audacity stunned me. What happened to the lawyers who tried to at least act like they'd fight to the very end?

It would've been better if she had just said there was nothing she could do for me. I was far from stupid and I knew my shit looked hopeless. Hell, it was. But I expected a little bit of a fight from the person who was supposed to be looking out for my interests.

"Just throw yourself on the mercy of the court." That was her game plan and conclusion.

"Damn, so that's the defense? None?"

She looked up from the folder and frowned.

"KenyaTaye, they've got you on tape discussing illegal contraband you obviously knew was illegally brought into a TDCJ prison. In addition to that, there are countless wiretaps on various phone calls with you and your gang-member boyfriend conspiring to sell the illegal drugs, cell phones, and other contraband."

I swallowed back the sharp words that sat on the tip of my tongue. There was no point in going off on her. She was basically correct.

"You've got DaQuan's name tattooed on your body; you're carrying his child. It is illegal to carry on any kind of relationship with an inmate confined to the TDCJ system. Not only did you have sex with this inmate, you also became impregnated by him."

I followed her wide eyes down to my large belly.

"I get it. I'm going to jail. But damn. For you to sit there and act like you couldn't be bothered with me, and this is a slam dunk for the prosecution makes me sick."

She sighed.

She placed her hand on a massive stack of folders and drummed her fingers.

When I looked at it, she began.

"This is my caseload." She tapped the stack again. "There are tons of cases in here. Some of these people are probably innocent; a few are probably questionable at best. But you, KenyaTaye, when they tested the DNA from the plastic sandwich bag that held the gun that you'd illegally bought and snuck into the prison—"

I raised a hand and stopped her rant. She had said enough. And everything she said was on point, but that didn't mean I had to sit and listen. As it turned out, DaQuan was nothing but a bitch-made man. He quickly accepted a plea deal. He agreed to testify against the other members on his team, and us, so his time remained the same.

He was already serving a twelve-year prison sentence, and after the deal, he still had a twelve-year sentence, with time served from before. That told me that he could actually be out on the streets before I would be free.

Years ago, if someone would've told me that things would end with DaQuan taking a deal, I would've put all my money on the opposite; then I would've doubled it.

When it came time to step up, his punk ass took the easy way out. So after all he did, ran the yard, taught inmates how to pick just the right, desperate, vulnerable female C.O.s, when it was over, he caved like a little bitch and sang. Bitch-made.

The judge's gavel brought me back to the situation I found myself in.

"KenyaTaye Dunbar, you have pled guilty to racketeering…"

My head felt light as she read off the list of charges against me. The rest of the words went soft because my ears had started to ring. Suddenly, I tasted saltwater as it rushed through in my mouth, and I felt weak. As I tried to focus on the fact that I wanted to throw up, I heard a sound that made me look down between my legs.

"Oh shit!" That was the lawyer. She looked down too.

"My freakin' water broke." I wanted to die—literally.

Bang! Bang! Bang! "Order in the court!" the judge yelled.

But the opposite happened. Pure chaos broke out. The next thing I knew, I was on the floor, spread eagle and a group of people surrounded me. How could this be my life? How had things led to this?

"We need a doctor in here!" my lawyer yelled.

I closed my eyes because I couldn't believe it. When would the test be over for me? Hadn't I been through enough?

The next thing I remembered was being coached to push. Right there on the courtroom floor.

I pushed, and pushed, and pushed. It felt like I had lost all strength, but still, I pushed some more. I was tired, not just physically, but emotionally, mentally and in every other way possible.

Nearly an hour later, I was carried out of court on a stretcher, with my new baby daughter. As we were wheeled past people, I saw some of the usual suspects in the hall.

Edwards and Jones stood off to the side and watched the commotion that surrounded us. But it wasn't until I got outside that I came face-to-face with Bishop.

She rushed up to the crowd as they prepared us for the ambulance.

"Oh, wow! Dunbar, you had your baby?"

She tried to act like we were long lost coworkers who had been kept apart. Bitch, we weren't friends.

It was hard for me to even fake the funk with her. I couldn't stand any of those bitches, and even after being away from them for six months, time hadn't eased the hatred I felt. I got that it was Sheppard who threw us all under the bus, but Edwards, Bishop, and even Jones had twisted that knife in my back way before then.

As they loaded me into the back of the ambulance, I pretended like I didn't see or hear that bitch as she tried to act all goo-goo, gah-gah over my baby.

CHARISMA

When I saw my former coworkers at the courthouse, it felt like déjà vu all over again. I hadn't been under any kind of false sense of hope over the last few months. I was all alone. Being away from them, the drama, and the jail made me push it all to the back of my mind.

There was no doubt that we'd all get jailtime. I hadn't heard from DaQuan since the last time we talked that night he told me to confront Lena, and unlike some other people, no one escorted me to court.

I had no family, no friends, no character letters for the judge and I had already accepted my fate. I realized that there was no way to save myself after all the salacious details poured out. It didn't matter that most was exaggerated; the media and the people who watched them couldn't get enough of our story.

After all the commotion of Kenya Taye giving birth inside the damn courtroom, it took an hour or two for things to get back to normal.

Edwards was surrounded by a posse and Bishop rushed in to join the crowd.

It wasn't like I was mad at them; I just had nothing more to add to our pathetic situation. I didn't see how being in a huddle with them now would help.

Even though I hoped she wouldn't, I looked up and saw Edwards headed in my direction. I didn't want to talk to her or anyone else. I needed to prepare my mind for what was about to happen.

"Did you ever get a private attorney?" Edwards walked over and asked.

"I talked with one, but honestly, after he told me the evidence was completely stacked against me, I didn't waste any more money." Edwards's eyebrows went up.

Her expression went from hard to bewilderment, but it made her back off of me.

We were all in the same situation. By the time the media was done with all of the stories about the harem DaQuan and his fellow gang members ran behind bars, all of our names were done anyway.

And the reporters didn't care when we didn't want to talk. They'd find someone else who would, and the rest, they just made up.

Months passed before reporters stopped following me around. And it seemed like the minute I thought my life was about to return to normal, something else kicked the drama back up again.

Edwards sensed my sour mood, so she walked back to her part of the hallway and rejoined her crowd.

There was a small part of me that felt a little jealous about the fact that she at least had a support team, but that didn't last long.

Unfortunately, it also made me think back to the other case I nearly caught. I was ready to kill my damn cousin with my bare hands.

"You are running around town talking on TV and radio to anybody who will listen? What the hell is wrong with you?"

She batted her lashes and licked her lips. But I could tell that Lena was trying her best to think of something she thought would be an acceptable answer.

"Charisma, I couldn't help the fact that I got caught up in what you did, but if you're mad at me because I did what I had to do to clear my name, I don't know what to tell you!"

I had stormed into her living room to confront her for the way she'd been bumping her gums on the five, six, and ten-o-clock news, but she tried to defend her recent actions.

"Think about what you did, Charisma. You dragged our good family name through the mud. I don't think my brother would've been stealing from his job if you hadn't forced him to doing that!"

As she spoke, her eyes darted behind me. At first, I thought she was trying to keep an eye on the TV. What good family name?

"What? You don't even get along with Lance." I frowned.

"Charisma, you have always been the outcast of this family. We have done nothing but tried to embrace you since your mother couldn't take care of you. I personally have tried my best as we were growing up to get you to learn to love yourself, but obviously it didn't work. Now, not only have you ruined your own life, but you also messed up my brother's life!"

Again, her eyes darted behind me.

"You know what, Lena, you're on to something else. I'd better get out of here before I hurt you."

"Haven't you caused enough pain and misery? You betrayed the oath you took to serve and protect." She used her hands to emphasize her words. "And now you're threatening me?"

Her comments made no sense, but I didn't feel right about being in her space. Before I reached out and slapped the shit out of her, I turned and left. I needed to get away from her because being in her presence meant I was too close to committing another crime.

It wasn't until later that night while I got ready for bed that I realized what my scandalous cousin was doing. The bitch had recorded everything. Apparently she thought she might be able to get her own reality TV show.

She sold or gave the video of our earlier confrontation to the local news stations and I was fit to be tied. After the newslady shared the raw, uncut video of me and Lena's exchange, the story took another turn. That's when details of the reality TV show came up. I clicked the TV off. I had heard enough.

When the bailiff walked out of the courtroom, I pushed thoughts of my cousin and the woman out of my mind.

"Okay, we're ready for you guys to come in. I need you all to take your cell phones out." He waited. "Okay, now turn that cell phone completely off! I don't want to hear it vibrate. I want it off. If it vibrates and I hear it, I will confiscate it."

After he discussed some additional courtroom rules, he allowed us to enter.

In the end, I was sentenced to two-and-a-half years in prison and three years of probation upon my release. Edwards and Bishop both got seven-and-a-half years; they'd been working at TDCJ longer than me.

Since we didn't have private attorneys and none of us was rich, sentencing moved quickly.

It was hard to believe the kind of money they said DaQuan had made over the years. I kicked myself often because I didn't set up the accounts when he told me to. But I tried to take it easy on myself because when the feds moved in, they snatched every dime connected to any of us.

In addition to the money, DaQuan had multiple luxury cars, bank accounts all over. He bought designer clothes, shoes, and purses for his women, and a house that Clarkson tried to say had been in her family for years. Everything was gone.

The one thing they didn't seize was the bank account attached to my mother's name. It wasn't much money, but since she had my kids, I thought it was best that she kept it.

"Charisma Jones, you are hereby remanded to the custody of the Texas Department of Criminal Justice immediately." And with the bang of her gavel, two officers moved in, cuffed me, and took me into custody.

There was no one in court for me, so there was no need for me to look toward the gallery. I followed the deputy to the cage and joined the group of other inmates who had been sentenced to jail.

It was hard to believe this was my life. I was now an inmate. And I sure as hell couldn't believe who my cellmate was. Kenya Taye joined me as soon as she got out of the hospital. And her baby came with her until she was done nursing. I couldn't see my own kids, but had to put up with hers. The only satisfaction I got was in knowing she'd be there for five years after I'd gone home.

ABOUT THE AUTHOR

By day, Pat Tucker works as a radio news director in Houston, Texas. By night, she is a talented writer with a knack for telling page-turning stories. A former TV news reporter, she draws on her background to craft stories readers will love. She is the author of seven novels and has participated in three anthologies, including *New York Times* bestselling author Zane's *Caramel Flava*. A graduate of San Jose State University, Pat is a member of the National and Houston Association of Black Journalists and Sigma Gamma Rho Sorority, Inc. She is married with two children.

If you enjoyed "Guarding Secrets," be sure to check out

FREE FRIDAYS

BY PAT TUCKER

AVAILABLE FROM STREBOR BOOKS

PROLOGUE

"What the hell?!" a stunned voice exclaimed.

Expensive champagne sprayed from Leela Franklin's perfectly painted lips as her eyes widened in stunned disbelief. Her mouth fell open and she struggled to believe what she saw.

"Jeeee-sus!" someone shrieked.

The Waterford crystal flute slipped from Leela's fingers and broke into pieces as it hit the marble floor. Two people jumped out of the way; droplets flew in every direction.

"OhMyGod!"

Leela's heart pounded against her chest. She looked around anxiously. Where was her best friend, Samantha Thomas? Better yet, where was her husband, Riley?

Every eye in the room was glued to the screen; the mouths of many people hung to the floor.

"Umph, umph, umph. Ain't that Samantha's husband, Bill?" Linda, Leela's mother, leaned closer and asked. "Chile, what kind of Mickey Fickey foolishness are these folks into?"

The dimmed lights that blanketed the room made it nearly impossible for Leela to make out where Samantha stood.

Had she planned this?

Why do it in front of an entire house full of friends, family, and co-workers?

Leela was embarrassed for her friend.

Minutes earlier, Samantha said she needed go get something from her bedroom and vanished. That was when the *anniversary video* started. Leela never thought much of Samantha's abrupt disappearance at such a crucial time. She figured Samantha had gone to find her husband. Wouldn't the happy couple want to be near each other while the video played?

But Bill had been across the room talking to Leela's husband, Riley, and a few of their colleagues.

Bill and Samantha Thomas were Leela and Riley's closest friends. Plans for their tenth anniversary party had been in the works for the past two months. Leela and Samantha had painstakingly gone over every detail. The video was supposed to set the tone for the evening and put everyone in a festive, celebratory mood. It was supposed to be a compilation of pictures that chronicled Bill and Samantha's life together.

Instead, it looked more like a raunchy, homemade, sex tape. The couple on it seemed to hump each other vigorously, on furniture, on the floor, and several times, in various showers. Their different outfits indicated that all the screwing had occurred over a period of time.

It was obvious that the video was recorded in secret, because it looked grainy, and from an angle that implied the camera was too far away to get the clear, crisp images most could appreciate.

Unfortunately for Bill, even with it being shot from a distance, the image of him and the woman who was not his wife was clear.

This was despite the fact that some shots looked like they were blocked by furniture and even curtains.

Soon, gasps and whispers rose from the crowd gathered in the room. Noises and chatter grew louder as the shocking images continued to play out on the seventy-inch flat-screen. The size of the screen made their explicit acts appear larger than life.

"I need to find Sam!" exclaimed Leela.

She looked around, and cautiously stepped over the liquid and shattered glass at her feet, and went in search of Samantha. But a sudden rush of brightness stopped Leela cold. She looked up and saw Samantha perched on the second-floor landing, looking down at the crowd.

The expression on her face was not one of horror or devastation like Leela expected to see.

How could she appear so calm and collected while all of this was going on? People in the room were seconds away from flying into a frenzy, and Samantha was upstairs, seemingly coasting above it all.

"That's just a glimpse of the steamy love affair that's been going on between my husband and his tramp at the office," Samantha said. Her voice was just as calm as her demeanor.

Samantha wore her fancy sequined dress, but was barefoot, and her hair looked like she'd been on the losing end of a tussle. Leela struggled to get a handle on the situation. When had things spiraled so out of control? Earlier, Samantha seemed fine, didn't she?

"You nasty, cheating bastard!" Samantha finally screamed. She pointed a crooked finger in Bill's direction.

All eyes found, and zeroed in on Bill.

Bill appeared nervous under the glare of the sudden attention. The color seemed to seep from his face and perspiration settled on his forehead. He was fidgety and he wore a guilty expression.

"Samantha! Stop this shit right the hell now!"

"You don't tell me what the hell to do! I'm not Kelly! Go tell Kelly what to do! All of the lies and deception. You are one sick, cheating, low-life bastard!"

Riley looked back and forth between the two, as did almost everyone in the room.

Bill made a move toward the staircase, but Riley stepped in and blocked his path.

"Not a good move, Dawg. You're too mad right now," Riley said.

Bill's nostrils flared; rage flashed in his eyes. He looked at his friend, then up at his wife, as he balled and unballed his fists. "Samantha, this is completely uncalled for!"

"Oh, I'm just getting started!" Samantha spat. "You wait 'til I'm done with your no-good ass!"

The video still played while they fussed at each other.

Leela's body stiffened. Her eyes were touched with alarm as she glanced around the crowded room. She wasn't sure what she should do.

All of a sudden, a loud clapping noise sounded, and Linda's voice rang out. That seemed to pull people's attention away from the video and the argument.

"Okay, folks, this party is over! Please, start making your way to the front door." Linda walked toward the TV, and snatched a plug from the outlet. Her knack for taking control came in handy because Leela had been frozen into inaction by the series of events and how everything had played out.

The screen finally went black.

Leela looked at her mother and mouthed the words, "Thank you," as she moved toward the stairs. She needed to talk some sense into Samantha.

People seemed reluctant to leave at first. But Linda walked around, removed glasses from hands, and reiterated that it was time to go.

"C'mon, please, see yourselves out," she said, as she motioned toward the front door. "C'mon, right this way; let's keep it moving."

Soon, Riley followed her lead, and urged the remaining guests to leave. Once the room was finally cleared, Bill seemed to get lost in the shuffle, because he was nowhere to be found.

The Monday afternoon following the anniversary party fiasco, things had gone from bad to worse quickly.

"Don't do nothing stupid, Dawg," Riley warned Bill over the phone. "She ain't worth a second in jail. Believe that, Man!" He sighed. "I know you pissed, and you have every right to be, but try to calm down, Dawg."

This was the kind of shit Riley himself would never put up with. He wore the pants in his house and not a day went by that he didn't let it be known. His buddy Bill was cut from a completely different cloth. Riley felt that Bill allowed his wife to do as she pleased; she dressed any kind of way, and she was far too loud and too damn outspoken. It was no wonder they were in the mess they were in.

But as a good friend, Riley knew he couldn't point those short-comings out at that moment. His goal now was to try and keep his friend and co-worker out of jail.

"I could kill her, Man," Bill said. His hands gripped the steering wheel so tightly, his knuckles changed colors. "I could lose it all. Everything, Man," he said. Spittle gathered at the corners of Bill's mouth as he pushed the words out angrily.

Riley could feel his pain, but still, he would never be caught up in anything like this. It wasn't just that Bill was a Beta Male; of course that played a role, but Riley felt Bill was just too soft when it came to managing his household.

Riley knew women behaved like they wanted equality, but when it came down to it, all women wanted a man who could put them in their place. They'd never widely admit it because they didn't want to be attacked by feminists, but Riley knew deep down, that was just about every woman's true desire. Riley was the epitome of an Alpha Male.

And Leela was perfect for him because she didn't make much of a fuss about anything. Even when she had her moments, she knew better than to act out the way Samantha had at that party. Oh no, that would never happen under Riley's watch.

"Aey, Bill?" Riley called into the phone again.

Bill's Hummer screeched to a stop in the circular driveway as he pulled up in front of the house.

"Look, I just made it here, Man. I'ma holler at you later," Bill huffed. Adrenaline raced through his veins like a NASCAR competitor.

"Bill. Remember what I said, Dawg. Just chill. Don't do nothing stupid."

If he were in Bill's shoes, this might be the one time he broke his own cardinal rule: never lay hands on a female. Riley didn't want to see his boy go to jail for domestic violence, but this time, Samantha had it coming after all she had done.

"I hear you, Bruh. I hear ya'," Bill said.

He ended the call, barely cut off the ignition, threw his Hummer into park, and hopped out. His heart raced at an uncontrollable rate as he rushed up the three steps in one leap and pulled open the massive, cast-iron and smoked glass double doors. Bill was breathing like a bull when he stormed through the front door and stopped at the foyer.

"Samantha! What the hell? You put that crap on Facebook?!" he yelled as he stepped inside.

His thunderous baritone was filled with rage as it echoed and bounced off the vaulted ceiling and brightly colored walls. With wild, desperate eyes, he searched the room for his wife, then headed to the spiral staircase when he didn't see her.

"Samantha! I know you're here! What the hell were you think-ing?!" he yelled up toward the second level of their lavish home. Spittle fanned out in every direction as he fired off his words.

Moments later, Samantha strutted into view. Satisfaction was written all over her face. "I told you Saturday night that I was just getting started. I guess you thought sneaking outta here, like the true punk you are, was gonna somehow make this all go away. Umph! I knew you was screwing that tramp! I just knew it; I felt it in my gut! Can't deny it now, can you?!" she yelled back from upstairs.

The smirk on her face was unapologetic. With her arms spread on both sides, she swiveled her neck as she leaned over the banister and taunted Bill even more.

"You nasty, cheating dog! Now the whole world knows what a sleaze you are!" Samantha's voice was thick with hatred. She twisted her face and looked down at him with a menacing glare.

Rage tore through every fiber in Bill's body as he looked up at her. He was ready to kill.

His cell phone rang and he considered ignoring the call, but figured he couldn't. Clients had been calling nonstop since the posts went live. With his eyes still glued to his wife, he snatched the phone from his waist, then pulled it up to focus on the screen. It was his boss, Gary Watson. He had to decompress and pull him-self together—quickly.

Gary Watson was a grumpy old man who ruled his family-owned finance firm with a hawk-like eye that rarely missed a thing.

"Hello?" Bill struggled to calm himself. He had to handle Gary just right.

"Bill. We're all very concerned about these social media postings," Gary said.

"Yes, Mister Watson. This is all just a big misunderstanding. Kelly and I are—"

"The board has decided to launch an investigation," Gary said firmly, cutting Bill off. "We're placing you on leave pending the outcome."

"Yes, Sir," Bill said.

Bill's heart thudded so loudly, he feared his boss would hear it through the phone. It had been bad enough that a house full of people saw the video, but now, with everything prominently on display for the world to see on social media, Bill felt he had no leg to stand on. He'd have to get an attorney to help clean up this mess and hopefully save his job.

"We're in the business of protecting our clients' assets. How does it look to have your inappropriate personal business spread across social media for everyone to see? It's very unprofessional, not to mention irresponsible. We've talked with Ms. Anderson as well. There is a morality clause in your contracts," he said.

Ms. Anderson was Kelly Anderson, Bill's coworker, and mistress. Bill palmed his forehead as he listened to his boss. But his mind raced with the many ways he could possibly kill his wife with his bare hands.

She had gone too far this time. Seven-figure jobs didn't come along often.

With his eyes closed, he was instantly transported to that moment, nearly two hours earlier, when he was in his office at work. Riley had called and dropped the bombshell.

"Dude. I see you and Sam still at it. I know she's pissed, but damn, Dawg, why she call you out like that, and on Facebook too?"

"What you talking about, Playboy?" Bill had asked coolly. He didn't like the sound of Riley's question. He hated social media sites and used them only for business and networking purposes.

"Oh, snap! You ain't seen that shit yet?!" Riley yelled. "See, this is why you need to have more control over your woman and what she does."